CRYING OUT LOUD

'Jean is a social worker, unmarried, in her forties, who has gained the confidence of her client Steven; Steven has had sex with his small daughter . . . Steven kills his son, kidnaps his daughter from a foster home and takes off – pursued by Jean. A moving and courageous book – for it takes courage to tackle this subject – and sometimes bitterly funny' *DAILY TELEGRAPH*

'There is no writer today who transmits as well as he does the frustrations and anger of the inarticulate . . . Cook's other gift, lies in creating comedy in scenes which are essentially tragic' *TIMES LITERARY SUPPLEMENT*

An unusually disturbing and powerful piece of writing . . . once read it will not be quickly forgotten' *SCOTSMAN*

'It requires writing of the most careful intensity to establish all the emotions involved . . . The picture of departmental panic and blame-shifting is all too topical, the achievement is in the pity and the sense that, against every righteous instinct, we are all members of one another' *GUARDIAN*

'Beautifully written and potentially prize-winning material . . . David Cook has imparted an immediacy and poignancy to his story, which carry the reader along to the shattering final scene. A very good novel indeed. Read it, please' *BOOKSELLER*

David Cook

CRYING OUT LOUD

ARENA

An Arena Book
Published by Arrow Books Limited
20 Vauxhall Bridge Road, London SW1V 2SA

An imprint of Random Century Group

London Melbourne Sydney Auckland
Johannesburg and agencies throughout
the world

First published by The Alison Press/Martin Secker
& Warburg Ltd 1988

Arena edition 1990

© David Cook, 1988

Printed and bound in Great Britain by
The Guernsey Press Co. Ltd., Guernsey. C.I.

ISBN 0 09 966370 8

For Daphne and Derek Holbrook

PART ONE

Present Continuous

The Police Constable in the front room stood almost to attention as he waited for her to get ready. He looked like a child who has outgrown his strength, prepared for a party he was determined to hate, and not at all sure that the over-large fancy-dress in which he had been costumed would respond to his movements. Michael's movements were repetitive and predictable, as he paced backwards and forwards from the door of the kitchen to that of the room which contained the immobile policeman. Michael's accelerated discourse to himself, together with the wringing of his hands and shaking of his head, would prevent the Police Constable from becoming bored while Jean found some wearable tights and a skirt suitable for country walking.

It was not yet clear how the police had discovered her connection with the Gaines family so quickly, or whose body she was being taken to identify. All the Constable seemed prepared to divulge was that it was the body of a boy, and that if she owned a pair of wellington boots she should bring them.

She found a pair of short rubber boots, bought cheaply against the snow, and presented herself at the door of the living-room, where the Constable asked a question about Michael's state of health. Jean answered by suggesting that the Constable should put the question to Michael himself, since, whatever his disabilities, they did not include deafness. She then turned, and kissed Michael as he reached her, causing his non-stop commentary to become even quicker and more incoherent. He hugged her briefly and without warmth, then turned on the spot and continued his ritual pacing.

A police car was waiting for them outside the house, its

blue light flashing. The driver threw the tabloid newspaper he had been reading onto the rear seat beside Jean, and pulled away from the pavement, missing a milk-float by what could only have been centimetres. Jean had often wondered whether the noise made by the siren of a police car was as unpleasant for the occupants of the vehicle as for passers-by, and now discovered that it was.

The ride was at high speed, jerky and noisy, ending in suburban countryside. The two policemen indicated a field across which she was to walk, and she did so. At first she could see nobody ahead of her, but then the field sloped downwards, the ground underfoot became muddier, and she saw at the bottom of the slope a clump of trees, a few bushes and a fluttering band of orange plastic tape, which, she assumed, would mark off the area of the incident. There were people by the tape, who had their backs to her, police personnel in plain clothes and in uniform, and all wearing wellingtons except for a WPC who moved around the men in what had once been sensible brogues and now looked like the oversized shoes of a clown in a circus. Jean marvelled at the contradictions of the body-language of this WPC, whose head and upper body struggled to maintain a posture of efficiency, while her legs and knees were those of a cart-horse forced to practise dressage.

Someone noticed Jean approaching with her escort, and the line of backs turned into fronts with faces which considered her approach with interest. The uniform with the most silver trimmings came forward to greet her with hand outstretched to be shaken, and Jean wondered if perhaps she had won some prize, and if so what it might be. For a few moments the person inside the silver-trimmed uniform found nothing to say to her, and then (as if she had been given a choice in the matter) said, 'Good of you to come! We think we know who it is, and that you'll be able to confirm it.'

Jean looked at the mud-covered black lace-up shoes, which she knew to have cost over twelve pounds. She looked at the darned grey socks with red trim, the short trousers and jacket which had once been his brother's, at the blue V-necked pullover and the white shirt. Only then did she look at the face, clear-skinned, well fed, now smeared with dried clay, and the violent purple and mauve bruises surrounding the neck. Then

the silver-trimmed uniform said, 'If you c̶
name? A simple identification,' and Jean rep̶
ordering a drink in a pub, 'Adam Gaines, aged n̶
croft Close, SE 23,' and turned away, blinking to re̶
image of the boy's cheek pressed against the spikes of haw̶
and a spotless white trumpet of convolvulus.

'We can't be sure yet, but there's usually sex when it's a
boy that sort of age. The split lip and the knot-marks on the
back of the neck would tie in with the assailant's panicking
after having indulged in a bit of how's-your-father.'

There was a man in a tweed suit and a pork-pie hat leaning
over the body, who shouted something about the rigor's not
being right to fit with the boy's having been killed where he
lay.

'Thought not. Get him blooded and bagged up and back to
the mortuary. A fiver says there'll be you-know-what on the
back of his underpants.' Silver Trimmings scratched some
dried mud from the front of his tunic, and muttered to his
sergeant, 'That daft sod could confirm buggery for us right
now if he wasn't such an old woman.' Then, turning again to
the tweed suit, he shouted, 'You're an old woman, Geoff. What
are you?'

'Careful is what I am, and so I should be. There is something
there which might be seminal staining, but we'd look a pair of
wallies if it turned out to be sap from one of those bog-plants.'

'See what I mean? Surprised he didn't bring his binoculars
and a butterfly net.'

Jean was handed over to a man in a raincoat, a Detective
Inspector, who walked back with her across the field towards
the police car, where the driver had reached page four of his
tabloid; he read with his lips moving. The Detective Inspector
said, 'Well, Miss Davis, that's one client past needing help,
one less to weigh down your heavy case-load. I am right, aren't
I? It is still "Miss"?'

'How did you know who the boy was, and that I'm the
family's Social Worker?'

'A large bit of luck and little bit of police work. I may be
able to tell you about it later.'

*   *   *

...rniture had been left behind. Since ...-piece suite and dining chairs had ...someone would presumably come to ...lice had finished.

...ree floors with an attic, divided by its ...one-room flats for families and single ...ts. The one-room flats were bed-sitters ...sink; the single rooms were bedrooms, ...ting about. There were two shared bath-...the house, one on the ground floor and one on the ... ...anding. The Gaines family of five members had occupied a ...ne-room flat on the third floor, where the parents slept and the television was kept and the family ate, and a single room above it in the attic, where the three children slept.

On entering the house, the Inspector had covered the lower half of his face with a handkerchief in a not very convincing pretence of blowing his nose, and Jean had remembered her own first response to the mingled stenches of urine, damp, rotting vegetables and highly spiced food. They had mounted the uncarpeted stairs, crunching fallen plaster into a white dust beneath their feet. On the wall of the stair, a child had executed drawings in red and green crayon, using what plaster was still intact and incorporating the many patches of exposed brickwork. The drawings were of trees, flowers, a rocket-ship and a fairground with roundabout. There was even, Jean noticed, a convolvulus.

The two boys had slept on single beds on one side of the attic room, Marianne Gaines on a mattress laid out on the floor at the other side. In between was a cheap melamine bedside table with a plastic table-lamp. The bedclothes had been taken from the beds, and of course the children's clothing had gone, but the mattresses, table and table-lamp had been left. Jean was glad to see that there were mattresses on both the single beds, since that indicated to her that Adam Gaines' brother, James, had been alive when the family left, and might still be alive.

Someone was asking if she could help them. A large number of people seemed to have crammed themselves in to so small a room. 'This was his bed, wasn't it?' She nodded. 'I'd say he was definitely killed in this room, and not where he was found.' She nodded again, hoping that the Inspector would not go into details of how he knew. A young Police Constable walked over Marianne's mattress, and was rebuked by his superior. Yes, that was the mattress on which Jean Davis, Social Worker, had first interviewed the possibly abused child, Marianne Gaines.

'Varnish gone from here.' The Inspector pointed to one of the legs of the nearer bed. 'Under the boy's fingernails, I expect. We reckon these scratches are fresh. Probably clung to that during the struggle when he was being buggered. It all helps with the jigsaw.' He moved round the bed on which Adam Gaines had until recently slept, his right hand close to the edge of the mattress but careful not to touch it. The mattress was old, its colour, once pale grey with black stripes, now brown with the stains of urine, with a pattern of rust-marks imprinted on it by the springs of the bed. There were lumps in the mattress where the stuffing had gathered, and a hollow made by the boy's body; it was a miniature version of the field across which Jean had walked to identify him.

'What a cess-pit!' The Inspector stared down at the indentation in the mattress, as if something about its shape might explain to him what had happened and why.

'Do you mean the bed or the flat?' The Gaines family had called their two rooms, one above the other, a flat, and a good Social Worker must move on her clients' wavelengths. She could feel anger mounting inside her, knew she must be careful. If allowed free rein, the anger would do damage, show as weakness. She would not give him that pleasure.

'Flat? Is that what they called it?'

'Two rooms. They were on Social Security, and the Council didn't want to know. If you feel like mounting a crusade, I'd be more than happy to give you the phone-number of the landlord's agent. Perhaps your bedside manner may be more effective than mine.'

The policeman turned to look through the room's one window, first down into the back-yard, then at the buildings opposite, and finally sideways in the direction of the main road, where half a bus could be seen disgorging its passengers. Then he said, 'I'd rather you gave me the phone-number of wherever Adam Gaines' father could be found right now.' He paused before adding, 'And for the moment I have to assume that you would if you could.'

The urge to turn and walk out of the room lasted no more than a moment. He was playing a game with her, and he wasn't very bright. He was clueless and desperate, and needed results quickly. She could almost feel sorry for him.

'He was reported, wasn't he, for having unlawful sex with his daughter?'

'Sex with any six-year-old would be unlawful, Inspector.'

'And you blew the whistle on him?' Jean nodded. 'But it never came to court. Lack of evidence?' No reply. 'Yet you continued working with the family, and he didn't object?' So he had done some homework. Jean wondered when he had found the time.

'He said he was pleased to have been found out. Glad to have been stopped.'

'Said to whom?'

'To me. It still wasn't hard evidence. There were no witnesses. He never confessed to the police.'

'So you must have had a whatsit with him . . . a thingummy . . . a doodah . . .?' She waited for him to find the word, and when he did it was not one with which he was comfortable, since he pronounced the final 't'. 'You must have had a rapport.'

'He talked to me, and I listened, yes.'

'So you got to know him quite well?'

Jean explained that 'quite well' was a relative term, and that she had no idea where the Gaines family might have gone. She told him some of what she remembered of her conversations with Steven Gaines, the dead boy's father, and promised that if she remembered more she would inform him straight away. With a policeman's talent for stating the obvious, he reminded her that the last remaining Gaines' child was now seriously at risk, and Jean politely countered by reminding him that there were in fact two children remaining, the youngest, Marianne, being with foster-parents. Having done so, she instantly wished that she had held her tongue, imagining some heavy-handed Constable Plod trying to elicit from Marianne information about where her father might have gone, and in doing so, letting slip the fact that her brother Adam had been murdered.

'I suppose she's too young to know anything?'

'Much too young, and anyway she doesn't speak, not even to her foster-parents. She hasn't spoken since she was taken from here. That was where she slept.' Jean pointed to the mattress on the floor, now marked with the muddy footprints of the young Constable. 'I hope you won't find it necessary to –'

'What do you take us for?' She had been gabbling in her alarm, and he had cut her off. Someone had come upstairs with a message, and the Inspector moved away to the door, sidestepping his Detective Sergeant, who was on all fours, and appeared to be testing the smoothness of the linoleum.

'More bad news. Marianne Gaines was lifted from the garden of her foster-parents' home at approximately five pm yesterday. Why didn't they tell you? Or did they?'

'I was off duty at five thirty, and I haven't, as I think you know, been in to the office this morning.'

'Ah!' Then a pun she had hoped never to hear. 'Yet another little Gaines lost!' The young Constable at the door began to titter, and then thought better of it. Jean discovered that she was kneeling down and using her fingers to brush dried mud from Marianne's mattress. The Inspector had returned to her. 'Where were we?'

Jean shrugged, and got to her feet slowly. She was interfering with evidence, she supposed, though they were police feet which had put the mud there. The Inspector looked down at the mattress, and asked, 'Has that thing been left there on the floor ever since the girl was taken from this house?'

'Where else would they have put it in a room as small as this?'

'They could have thrown it out. Dumped it somewhere.'

'But they thought she'd be coming back.'

The Inspector, not pleased at being put down by a Social Worker, visibly changed gear, and began pacing the room, firing questions and observations at her. 'Jesus Christ, woman! You're the only one who knows him well, the only one he's talked to, the only person he trusted.' Well, that was true enough. Jean remembered long afternoons in the park, walking beneath trees or sitting on a wooden bench, while Steven Gaines talked and she listened. 'You must have some idea of how he thinks, what he feels.' She had indeed had some idea, but that idea had not included the murder of his son. 'Yet you don't seem to know anything, other than where everybody slept. Was that the extent of your job in this house? I mean, a man who doesn't demand a new Social Worker when the old one shopped him must be a fool, wouldn't you say? Either a fool or very shrewd! Was he onto a good thing, perhaps?' What good thing would that be? Steven Gaines had not found himself able to speak to anyone, not to his depressed wife, and he had no friends, and he had spoken to her. At length. Certainly she had thought that a good thing, and could not, even now, believe it to be a bad one. 'How do you feel about men who bugger small children, Miss Davis? What, in your experience, induces a father to drag his nine-year-old son around the room, fracture his arm, split his lip, and then throw him face-down on the floor to fuck the tiny arse off him? Is that how your unemployed clients get their kicks these days?'

Jean did not feel that she could reply in words. If she were to scream, he would not understand, and if to weep, he would think he understood too well.

The Inspector waited through her silence, and then began again more quietly. 'Come on, Miss Davis. You're a qualified Social Worker in your – what? mid-forties? Plenty of experience, then. You talked with your client. He chose to keep you, when he could have changed. He must have bent your ear for hours, talking about his hopes and dreams. All you lot are amateur psychiatrists. Why would your client do what he's done? Why is his son dead, and where has the father gone? You must have a few ideas to offer us.'

'They were all my clients, all the family, the quick and the dead.' She was shouting at him, seemed to have no control, shaking from head to foot with anger and outrage. She had allowed him to get to her, and broken the promise made to herself. The silence pressed in on her, while the faces in the room, now all turned towards her, waited. They had not known Steven Gaines, and neither had she. Her notes about him were filled with questions; no one has answers for something like this. Now she had added hysteria to her charge-sheet and to the mess which these self-satisfied servants of the public were trying with their instruments, plastic bags and guesswork to clean up.

Then she was on the landing, taken there out of that room by the Inspector, who was gripping her arm, and would know that it was trembling. He spoke now in a whisper, as though she were his closest friend, loosening his grip. 'The only important thing at this moment is where he's gone and how fast I can get to him. Nobody's dishing out blame, me least of all. If sometimes what I say and the way I say it don't match with what I feel, please try to accept it as my method of getting through the day.'

She had declined to be driven home by the police driver, who was now halfway through his second newspaper, and had chosen to walk. It was midsummer, 1987, and after seven days of heavy rain the weather had changed. In back-street and in side-street, like the flags of all nations, people of different colours leaned against doorways or sat on doorsteps enjoying the sun. And yesterday, at about five pm during a torrential downpour, Marianne Gaines had been standing in the garden of her foster-parents' home, and had been taken from there, presumably by her father. No one had seen Steven Gaines, but it would have been too much of a coincidence for Marianne to have run away of her own free will on the same day as the rest of her family went missing.

In a small square containing newly bedded-out begonias, a man rose suddenly to his feet from a crowded bench at Jean's approach, startling her. Was it someone she knew, and could not remember? No, the man, without the use of words but by an exaggeratedly gallant gesture of one arm, was offering her his seat. She had not asked for it, nor even appeared to be looking for somewhere to sit, but she accepted with a 'Thank you', and the man made a noise which sounded like the removal of food from his teeth, touched his forehead, and walked away, folding the sliced-bread wrapper which had contained his lunch, and slipping it tidily into his pocket.

She must be looking old for that to have happened. Perhaps the slowness of her approach had prompted the man's concern.

But Jean was in no hurry to return home; she would walk all the way, take her time, and do it in stages. She would get there eventually. What she had to think about wouldn't be rushed, or she would remember nothing.

A female blackbird hopped in and out between the newly planted flowers. People drifted past as if in a heat-haze. Why had the man picked on her, since all the people were moving slowly, some, she supposed, because they were reluctant to return to work, others because they had nothing more pressing to do with their time than to sleep it away on the grass. Nineteen years ago Jean had taken the decision never again to join the ranks of those who slept the days away in parks and squares. Then the ranks had been much shorter, and the opportunities to break them far more frequent.

She began to walk again. How could she have spent so much time listening to Steven Gaines, yet end by knowing so little about him? It was true that there had been long silences, often painfully long, but it was he who had talked. He had told her he was more relaxed out of doors, in the park or by the canal. She had tried not to ask questions, had let him make his own way while she listened and made notes in her head, to be written down later. It was unlikely that these notes would help her now, or the police, for they were mainly questions – questions to herself and to her supervisor on how she should proceed. The notes were in short sentences: '*S. talked about father. Lot of anger. Asked after M. Has she spoken yet?*' '*S. depressed, but promised to return to sex-counsellor. Asked about M. Can't accept she still doesn't speak.*' '*S. great deal about lack of work and human dignity. M. again.*' '*S. hinted had been rejected as mercenary in Angola or Martinique. Fantasy?*' He had described at length the physical exercises which he performed to keep his physique at its peak; the unemployed did not have to pay for entry to the local Leisure Centre. She had never been able to get him to talk about his feelings towards his wife, and as for his children, the sentiments he expressed when speaking of them were stilted and sentimental, as if culled from *The Reader's Digest*.

The Inspector had said that anyone who didn't insist on a new Social Worker after having been shopped by the old one was either a fool or very shrewd. Steven Gaines was not a fool. She remembered their first meeting after she had removed

Marianne from her parents' care. She had been nervous, made more so by his suggestion that they should walk in the park and talk. They had sat on a bench, watching children playing ball. He had asked how Marianne was, what the foster-parents were like, what the man did for a job, and how old the woman was. He had said, 'I'd been for a walk. I do that. Have to get out of the flat sometimes. I must have been out two, maybe two and a half hours. It was the longer walk, down by the canal and towards the Circular Road. When I got back, Marianne wasn't there. The wife was sitting with her face turned away; the boys stood close together, almost to attention, looking up at me. No one said anything. It's hard to describe something snapping in your head, and all the time you're watching it from the outside. I didn't touch the kids or Maureen. Didn't even shout. I just knew. The moment I knew Marianne was taken was the moment I think I returned to being normal. I knew why she'd been taken, and it was like a weight being lifted. I'd always been gentle with her. What happened was done out of love. It wasn't just sex; it was loving her. I wanted to give her affection, and I just went too far, that's all. That's what I want you to realize if you can. What I'm trying to say is, she's a wonderful child. I idolize her. I know she's safer where she is. Although I could trust myself with her at the moment, that might change, mightn't it? And anyway I know we won't always be separated.'

In the hallway, Jean looked into the fly-blown mirror, and knew why the man in the square had given her his seat. It wasn't just the calling cards left by flying insects which made her look a hundred and four. *'Come on, Miss Davis! You're a qualified Social Worker in your – what? mid-forties?'* The house made noises, the creaking as floorboards or stairs expanded, the tapping of a water-pipe, the hum of draughts being forced past ill-fitting window-frames. These sounds reassured her, being marginally more predictable than the noises made by the occupants of the house.

Michael and Joy would be in the kitchen, he slumped over the table, she, just returned from night duty at the Residential Home where she worked, would be cooking herself a meal.

Joy's period of duty officially ended at ten am, but the hand-over was of variable length. Joy would be filling the kitchen with her size and energy, forcing Michael to shrink even smaller. Michael had endured a morning which had already lasted several years, since the arrival of the police, and had a low tolerance for the tuneless, wordless vocalizing with which Joy always accompanied her favourite pastime of cooking food at high speed. Fifteen years of working in Residential Child Care had made its contribution to Joy's figure. Fifteen years of dispensing (and sharing) reassurance in the form of jam butties, crisps, chocolate bars and Coca-Cola had been responsible for a steady over-all expansion. Every emotional crisis had meant a little more work with needle and thread. Joy laughed off this occupational hazard, saying, 'Never mind, chuck. At least when I cuddle you, you stay cuddled.'

It was true that Joy's cuddles left an impression. Jean knew as much, because Joy had cuddled her for a while, shortly after they had first met. This cuddling was not sexual, just the affection of two homely but homeless middle-aged women, clutching at straws and cementing a friendship. Joy either cuddled people or thumped them, which was another consequence of Residential Child Care, and was also to demonstrate affection and trust. The thumping was only marginally less painful than the cuddling.

With Michael, Joy's rough-and-tumble remained verbal, since both knew that any reminder of the physical indignities he had endured during his years of hospitalization would diminish him entirely. 'What's the matter, Mike? Having one of our sad days, are we?' He would be hoping to be cosseted, and offered some of the food she was cooking. The effort required to express the depth of his depression left none over for the preparation of his own meals. 'Why don't you make yourself a spot of brunch like me, since it's now after two, and I bet you haven't eaten yet.' Michael's response to such a lack of sympathy, and indeed to the totality of the world's rejection of him, was to press the side of his face even flatter against the plastic table-covering. 'I'd run around waiting on you hand and foot, Mike, you know I would, if I only had the time.' Cutlery and jars of pickle were slammed onto the table near Michael's head. 'What you going to do with yourself this afternoon, Michael?' No reply was ever expected to a question of this nature. 'Same as always, I expect, bugger-all.' By now Joy's mouth would be full of food. Tasting a meal in preparation was even more pleasurable than the meal itself. 'You are a big girl's blouse, Michael, do you know that?' The head on the table would have become that of a ten-year-old bed-wetter who had been discovered decorating his skin with a rusty razor-blade. 'There's that wonderful world out there, eighty-five in the shade with everyone stripped down to their knickers, and you lie there in your best suit, wanking your life away.'

This was how they lived. There were four of them, each with a separate bedroom, sharing the kitchen, bathroom and the small front room which housed the television set, Joy's record-player, a sofa and armchair and the occasional Police Constable standing almost to attention. The 'arrangement' was that two mature and balanced female members of society with a background in Social Work, sponsored and to a certain extent financially assisted by a charity, should share living accommodation with two men who had spent most of their lives in institutions, Michael, who had been a long-stay psychiatric patient, and Tony, who stole money and food without conscience, whose faulty memory was expressed in such minor ways as forgetting to pull the chain of the water closet after use, and who at this moment would be standing alone in the corner of some Amusement Arcade. When Tony was five, his younger brother had drowned in a canal. His mother had become obsessed with the belief that Tony had caused his brother's death, and she had offered Tony for adoption. Since nobody had wanted him, he had gone into Care at eight years old, and, since leaving Care eight years ago, his accommodation had alternated between hostels for the derelict and short spells in prison for petty theft, vagrancy and (once) soliciting men.

'What's all this drama about?' Jean had entered the kitchen, and consequently was within range of Joy's conversation. 'Chap next door was wetting himself to tell me you'd been whisked away by the filth. Was it about the girl?'

'She's not "the girl". She has a name.'

'Suit yourself.'

'I had to identify a body.' Joy went to the fridge to check

on its contents, some of which she had brought back from the Residential Unit where she worked. Jean said, 'Doesn't it ever turn your stomach, taking food out of the mouths of children?'

'I didn't take; I was given. And it hadn't reached their mouths, thank God; it was presented to me for services rendered. Anyway it's past its expiry date, and would've gone off. So don't go picking on me, Snow White, just because you've been on a tour of the Morgue, and didn't find anything you fancied.' She returned to the table with a generous portion of apple pie, topped with imitation cream. 'I was up most of the night with those sods. Halfway through *Cagney and Lacey*, when the fire-bell goes off. They're only in the Boot Room, melting down some shoe polish to have themselves a sniff of it. Set fire to some paper in a tin, and smoked us all out.'

'The body was in a field under a clump of trees. Marianne Gaines' brother, aged nine. The father and the rest of the family have gone missing. They'll have to suspend me.'

Joy rose from the table, placed her arms around Jean, and held her for a considerable time. Eventually both women became aware that Michael had also left the table, and was filling the kettle to make coffee.

Today was Thursday. On Thursdays Michael shared Jean's bed, and had now done so for six months. She had told him, 'Never more than once a week,' and he had agreed. He wore a condom, and didn't insist on a lot of enthusiasm.

It had begun one night after he had arrived at the door of her bedroom in one of his anxiety states. She had been tired, and had allowed kind words and cooching (her word for hugs) to develop too far. During that first night she had caused Michael to laugh, something almost unknown in him. She had made him withdraw, and climax on her stomach, and had then pressed her nose against his, and whispered in her Greta Garbo voice, 'That was lovely, and there's plenty more, but let's ration ourselves to once a week.' And he had laughed.

She still hoped that one night he might laugh again, or even smile, but he never had. He had presented himself at her door every Thursday night, complete with condom (which she bought for him, because he was too shy), and had approached his weekly treat with the seriousness of a schoolboy studying for Remedial Maths. Perhaps she had imagined it, perhaps he had never laughed at all.

It was not the intention of the Charitable Trust which had brought these four people together, and now subsidized their rent, rates and electricity, that they should become sleeping partners, nor would the rabbis, priests, doctors, psychiatrists and other minor clergy who were the trustees of the Trust have considered it an appropriate way for a forty-six-year-old Social Worker to bring a forty-nine-year-old burned-out schizophrenic towards independence. Jean had never understood why 'burned-out' should be used to describe Michael's condition, since what it suggested was someone all of whose circuits had been blown by electro-convulsive therapy, whereas the actuality was no more than that Michael had ceased to have hallucinations and that his condition, if monitored, could be controlled by drugs.

She lay in bed, waiting for Michael to join her, and wished her regular Thursday-night wish, which was that Michael's ritual of straightening the pictures on her walls and realigning the ornaments and mementoes on the shelf above the blocked-up fireplace would cease, or at least be replaced by another less intrusive and less time-consuming. If she had thought of it sooner, she might have locked away those things she didn't want him to handle, but now he would miss them, and become upset by her sudden secrecy. It was too late, and she must endure his sifting through her pile of photographs, snapshots of children she had known, past and present.

Only the pile of boxes which took up one corner of her room was worth fighting over. There was no cupboard large enough in which to hide them. The first time Michael had approached the boxes, she had spoken sharply, asking him not to touch them since they contained the materials of her work, that only she knew what was where, that she had packed them so nothing could be lost. She had stressed how important it was to her that they remained exactly as they were, and Michael had nodded; he well understood how important it was that things remained exactly as they were.

The box did contain materials of work, mostly past work

and mostly unsuccessful. There were abused dolls, neglected Teddy Bears, her Fisher Price toys, finger-puppets and glove-puppets, including the famous trio, Crocodile, Witch and Policeman, fresh from their unsuccessful whirlwind tour round the high-rise flats of South London. There were finger-paintings and doodles, Plasticine models of penises, one or two breasts, but no vaginas, unless one counted a cave with stalac-tites into which a jelly-baby had been thrust to save it from the wolves. There were complete Plasticine families, painstak-ingly pressed by tiny fingers into orderly lives which might be contained inside a shoe-box, incestuous fathers, neglectful mothers, abusing brothers, depressive sisters, often in a semi-circle always and forever facing a television screen, with a dog or cat which never died set on a carpet of white cardboard which still had to be paid for in weekly instalments.

'Come to bed, Michael.'

The heavy thumping beat from Joy's record-player came up to them from below. Joy would be stretched full length on the settee, or would be dancing alone, glass in hand. Too much food, too much alcohol and loud music were a necessary part of the ritual of Joy's unwinding from the job. Joy was always either wound up or unwinding; there was nothing in between.

With everything in Jean's bedroom now arranged symmetri-cally, Michael lowered himself stiffly into the wickerwork chair, and studied the toe-caps of his shoes. So far he had not even removed his jacket. He said, 'I think I should go so far as to say that the use of Christian names should be strictly rationed to those people who have known each other well for a long time. If everyone goes around using given names when-ever they like, they become devalued in my opinion. It stands to reason that I am not "Michael" to a girl in a shop, serving behind the counter. The simple knowledge of my Christian name does not confer an automatic right to use it.'

'Come to bed, Michael. I'm sure the girl didn't intend to be over-familiar, nor to upset you, and it did happen more than a week ago.'

Below, Meatloaf had finished singing 'All Dressed Up and Nowhere to Go', and had been replaced on the turntable by Motorhead, the words of whose song could not be distin-guished by a listener in the bedroom above. All Joy's records had been given to her by young people who had outgrown them. All had been played and replayed, most had been fought over, buckled and scratched; many became stuck at a single musical phrase and had to be moved on manually after much repetition of that phrase. The young Police Constable who had stood almost to attention in the living-room that morning had seemed interested in the record-sleeves scattered about the room, *The Oppressed*, *Madness*, *Angelic Upstarts*, *Feed Me to the Lions*, *Killer in the House* and *Dog Eat Dog*.

'What would be interesting would be to know how that particular girl in that particular shop came by the knowledge that I am called Michael.'

'Perhaps she'd heard me call you Michael. We've been in that shop together often. Please come to bed.'

'It had a tone about it. Her use of my name.'

'What kind of tone?'

'Of condescension. As if she were humouring a child or a handicapped person.' Thus Michael, who would only leave the safety of the house if Jean accompanied him, who insisted on keeping hold of her hand or linking his arm in hers even at those moments when it was necessary for her to receive shopping or count change! Thus Michael, who wore a suit and tie, and carried a neatly folded overcoat over his free arm even in the warmest weather, and who was regarded with special interest by all passers-by, from bus-conductors to dogs! The condescension of tradespeople was the least of his problems.

Jean said, 'Perhaps she's handicapped herself, Michael. Had you thought of that? Perhaps her dad had told her to stop biting her nails over the Russian Salad and be more pleasant to his regulars. Being out of practice, she went a bit overboard; that's all.'

At last Michael began to remove his tie. The knot, as usual, was too tight. The collars of all Michael's shirts curled up at the corners under pressure from that knot. Trying to flatten the tips of his collar would preoccupy him for minutes on end. He said, 'You're telling me not to be over-sensitive, is that it?'

She would not be trapped. This was the soft option everyone had taken with Michael when he was in a state. He had once told her that, if he had a shilling for every time the word

25

'sensitive' had been used to describe him, they could live in the Hilton Hotel. 'I'm saying I don't think it's worth getting into a state about.'

'This suit needs cleaning already. I hate the smell of the cleaner they use at Sketchley's. We must find somewhere else.'

Soon they lay side by side, with the bedside light on and only the backs of their hands touching, as if they were childhood sweethearts sharing a room for the first time. Below, Motorhead had made way for Dire Straits, and Joy could be heard greeting the arrival of Tony, and hugging him until his ribs cracked. Jean said, 'I want you to go out on your own tomorrow, Michael. It doesn't have to be far or for very long, but I'm worried about how dependent you've become.'

'I don't think I can go out.'

'I know you can, or I wouldn't ask. We'll take it gently in stages. I'll think of something we need from the greengrocer's in Paulden Street, just one item so as not to confuse you. It's no more than two hundred yards.'

'Can I decide tomorrow?'

'No, I want a promise now. I know you. I'll give you the correct money, and I'll come and find you if I think you're taking too long.' Jean stroked the side of his face, feeling the sweat break out on it. She thought of the Doré illustration to *Little Red Riding-Hood*, in which the little girl sits up in bed next to the Wolf, the girl fascinated yet repelled, the Wolf placid and resigned, appearing to be very much the sort of person whose good opinion one might seek. 'Do I get that promise, Michael? You do need the exercise.'

'I've got my machine.' He had bought an exercise-bicycle by mail order on hire-purchase.

'But you never use it.'

'Only because it makes me dizzy. I get dizzy in the street too, even when I'm with people. Specially in crowded places. You should be more careful.' This was a reference to one of their 'family outings' on the Sunday before, which had been to Kew. Such outings, although Jean and Joy insisted on them, usually led to a quarrel. Kew Gardens had been the worst for some time, since it appeared that the world and its dog had chosen that Sunday for a visit. They had lost Tony four times in the crush, and Michael had stood beside Jean in one of the hot-houses, next to the insect-eating plants, and had shaken from head to foot as he had tried at great speed to explain to the dying flies inside one of the plants about his own problems, which were worst in the spring when the sap rises.

The sheet was now damp with his sweat. He buried his face in the pillow, and used his little-boy voice. 'Why did you have to go and spoil it?' Michael's anxiety-states were real enough, mostly a fear of losing control, of a depersonalization which feeds on itself until suddenly there is no sense of identity, no knowledge of place, and even the pavements and the sky become subjects for conjecture. He had grown used to the routine and the invariable walls of hospitals, but thrust out alone into a bed-sitter had not left it, and had been found after two weeks, sitting inside a wardrobe. He had been without food, heating, money or any sense of time, and so they had brought him here.

Francis and Emily Thompson had been his parents, in their early forties when he was born, and had died within five days of each other when in their mid-sixties. Michael had often heard his parents referred to as 'that childlike couple', though, unlike other children, they had seemed to accept him. They had never found it necessary to answer any of his questions directly, but had referred him to biblical texts, some of which had been embroidered in silk on linen, and hung on the wall. The reason why a horse should be able to run much faster than a cow turned out to be that God moved in a mysterious way. Indeed this turned out to be the reason for most of what happened in life, particularly the more unpleasant happenings, so Michael had rejected the world God made, and created his own, but he had very little confidence in it, and it was for most of the time even more unpleasant than God's.

Jean said, 'I didn't mean to spoil things, Michael, but you have to move forwards. We've got to get you a bit more independent. I may not always be here.'

His parents had sometimes told him that they might not always be there, and then had not been. Outside the walls of the house, Michael never left Jean's side. He was always touching her arm or holding her hand, staring about him as if seeing everything for the first time. Sounds still came to him oddly; sounds from different places and at different levels all seemed to reach his ear at the same time and the same level. It was not surprising that he sometimes replied to the questions of strangers on distant buses, not surprising that, like Red Riding-Hood, he was both fascinated by and terrified of the outside world. Sometimes Michael would make deep guttural noises, which others might think to be laughter, but they were not laughter; they were the noises the Grandmother made when first she saw the Wolf.

Below Joy was now singing along with Meatloaf in a rendering of 'Heaven Can Wait'. Michael gave no promise, but switched off the bedside light, leaving the condom he had placed by it in its wrapper. Jean said she was sorry, and dried the sweat from the side of his face with a tissue. He began to sob into his clenched fist, making the sound made by wellington boots when extracted from mud. Jean was grateful that 'Killer in the House' had not been played downstairs that night.

The large piece of good luck of which the Inspector had spoken turned out to be merely that the shirt the dead boy had been wearing bore the name 'J. A. GAINES' on the inside of the collar, being yet another item of clothing which had first belonged to his elder brother. All the police had needed to do was to telephone the Casework Administrator who held the District Child Abuse Register, in which there would not have been many entries under 'Gaines', and against Marianne's name would have been those of her parents, with their address, and of her siblings, James and Adam. The Register would also have contained a record of the telephone number of the family's Key Social Worker, together with the names and addresses of any other adult who visited the family regularly.

'We got nowhere with that. Nobody but you and the Health Visitor ever went there. There's no record of any relatives, and nobody in that dump of a house will admit on principle to knowing anything about anything. They must have had some friends in the area.'

'If they had, I never heard about them.'

'Living in two rooms! What did they do to get a break from each other?'

'He'd go for long walks; she'd stay with the children. Once

a week, the whole family had an outing.' He looked up sharply. 'They'd walk three miles to the cheapest supermarket to shop.'

'And it was he who collected the kids from school?'

'Most of the time, yes. The older boy's twelve now.'

The Inspector picked up and glanced at the album cover of *Frankie Goes to Hollywood*, then set it down again on top of the pile Jean had hastily made. It was now 5.25 am. The curtains of the front room were still closed, and the room itself filled with smoke from the Inspector's small and cheap cigar. Jean had not slept. The Inspector's discreet tapping at the front door had brought her downstairs from the bed in which she hoped Michael would still be asleep. Joy and Tony slept through anything, even police-raids.

He had left the police car two streets away, had sent it back to base, and would telephone for it to meet him at a different point later. It was the Inspector's experience that the Press had a bush-telegraph system of finding out that something juicy was on; they would employ small children to spot the numbers of police cars parked anywhere unusual and phone them in to the Night Desk. Jean had forgotten that the newspapers would be involved. The Inspector said, 'They'll make you feel like a celebrity; they'll be all over you while this inquiry is on. "Jean" this, "Jean" that! How about telling us about your parents, love, and where you come from? Then we'll take a picture of you in the garden. Have you got a pet? – a dog or a cat? – a sun-dress or a pair of shorts? Then they drop you like a ton of bricks when we find him. We usually keep a case like this under wraps until we need the media, but there's always a leak from some-where, someone at the mortuary, some local where we found the body, and occasionally – it hurts, but it has to be said – one of our own men. Just for a few quid towards a holiday in Benidorm, or a couple of tickets to the England/Wales International.'

What Jean and the Inspector were now engaged in doing was 'putting together the full picture'. The Inspector needed this picture, which would help him in his inquiries, which so far had been unproductive. He had not slept either, and had no intention of doing so until he had a lead.

'Why would a woman like that, living in squalor, go to the trouble of stitching name-tags on her son's shirt?'

29

'She wouldn't. Didn't. Their father did anything like that.'

'Where would he have learned needlecraft?'

'I told you. He was the youngest of three boys, without a mother for most of the time.'

'So he was the hausfrau?'

'He was the smallest, bullied into doing whatever the others told him to do.'

'Unfortunately we don't have an address for either of his big brothers.' He waited. Jean had already explained that Steven Gaines had not seen or heard of his brothers for over ten years, and had not wished to. The Inspector said, 'What I was actually asking was whether he was the hausfrau in his own home. Did he do the cooking, make the beds, sweep the floor, bath the children?'

'He cooked sometimes; I don't know about bed-making. He bathed the children for several very good reasons. First, they shared a bathroom with two other floors, and the door had no lock on it. For privacy a chair had to be placed under the handle of the door by an adult; a child might have locked itself in. There was a gas-meter requiring fifty-pence pieces. The boys shared a bath for economy, and would have mucked about if not watched.' Under the Inspector's close gaze she became more defensive. 'He insisted that all the family bathed twice a week, even though it cost them three pounds, a large dent in the family budget. Until Marianne was removed, she shared a bath with her father.' The Inspector waited. 'After she'd gone, the father bathed, then the boys used his bathwater, saving fifty pence, which they would be given as pocket-money. Lots of children bath with their parents until puberty. There's a lot to be said for it; I had no reason at first to suspect sexual abuse; that kind of closeness between parent and child could be seen as healthy. You can't stop a father from supervising the bathing of his sons.'

Now it was her turn to wait, as the Inspector checked yet again that he really did only have one cigar left, knowing that the shops would not be open for another three hours. He took from his pocket some anti-smoking chewing-gum, placed a wad of it sadly in his mouth, and said, 'No justification needed, Miss Davis. On the rare occasions I'm to be found at home, I have been known to bath my children; I know what you're saying. Now, about Maureen Gaines and her depressions. I suppose any woman would get depressed if she knew what her husband was doing.'

'The depressions began long before the first child was even conceived.'

'You don't have much time for her, do you?'

The question was intended to catch her off balance. Jean took time to answer. This small room, pathetically furnished and decorated as it was, constituted part of her home; she was not in the Detention Room of a police-station, being interrogated. She said, 'Social Workers, like everyone else, are prone to human failings. One of mine is that, if a woman who knows her daughter is being sexually abused does nothing about it except keep quiet, then that woman has to work very hard to regain my sympathy. Unfortunately, Maureen Gaines was always far too depressed to be interested in anybody's sympathy; I was a necessary evil among many as far as she was concerned. Needless to say, I did my professional best to keep my feelings towards her objective.'

More questions followed, more brush-strokes towards the full picture which would replace the grey, urine-stained blankness of a child's mattress, which still took up so much of the wall-space of the Inspector's mind. Where had Steven Gaines met his wife? How long had they been in London? Where were they before that? Had they ever left London? Where had Maureen Gaines come from originally? Had she any relatives, and if so where?

When the phone rang, Jean rushed into the hall to answer it before it woke the sleepers upstairs. The Inspector was at her elbow, knowing that the call would be for him. She returned to the front room, parted the curtains no more than an inch, and opened the window. No signs of life were visible in any of the houses opposite. Behind drawn curtains people would be waiting for the bells of alarm-clocks to ring. It was not a street to which newspapers were delivered.

It was fully light now, with the mist that promises a scorching hot day. A black and white cat rubbed its hindquarters against a gate-post, checked that the coast was clear, and delicately polluted a pocket-handkerchief of neatly turned earth. Jean had noticed a woman with trowel and bag of peat working for a full hour on that patch of soil.

From the hall she could hear the Inspector giving instructions. 'And then a door-to-door inquiry at all the roads near the foster-parents' home. Did anyone see a man and a small girl getting into a vehicle at about five on Wednesday evening? The girl wore nothing over her dress, and there was torrential rain. That's the sort of area where every house has a woman posted behind net curtains for most of the day. A car *or* a van, could be either, could be a bloody articulated truck or a motorcycle with sidecar. I want the make and the colour; it's probably too much to expect a number.'

Jean had never managed to be all that objective about Maureen Gaines, or to conceal her disapproval. Steven Gaines had not often talked about his feelings for his wife. He had said, 'I know she stands outside things, and doesn't get involved. She should've let you know what was happening between me and Marianne, but Maureen's not had it all that easy herself, you know. She had these foster-parents in Bournemouth, and they doted on her, but her own real mother kept turning up to upset her, telling her that her real father had been a loony who'd hung himself. She'd been a bit wild, Maureen, giving her foster-parents hell and staying out all night, but she was still a virgin when I met her; you can't fake blood. I was the first she gave herself to; the rest was all show. It did a lot for me, that.' There was no point in telling the Inspector about the foster-parents in Bournemouth; they would not go to Bournemouth.

It was after the marriage things had begun to go wrong. Maureen had not wanted to be touched, no foreplay, no cuddling. 'She'd allow me – you know, to do it – because she knew I needed the release for my health, but she wouldn't take part; she'd just lie there. When the kids came, she'd pull them onto her knees by their clothes so as not to have physical contact with them. She knew she ought to hug them, but she got frightened if she touched their skin. I did most of the physical contact. Babies need that; even animals do. I didn't want Maureen to go to outsiders for help, other than for Valium. She was mine, and I thought they might take her away. Anyway I could help her with the depressions as much as they could. I know what depressions are like.'

Jean moved through the hall into the kitchen. The Inspector

was still on the telephone. 'I know he's had two nights and a whole day to travel, but I still want those Motorway Service Areas watched. Tell them to concentrate on the Petrol Bays. Unless he's done a bank job on top of everything else, that family won't have the money to eat in the cafeterias. And they won't all leave the vehicle at the same time. Two adults, 1 M 1 F, early thirties; he's a body-builder, six foot – I don't know what it is in metres; work it out. Boy of twelve, girl of seven and a half, looks six. Good idea! Hang on,' he put down the phone, and moved to the door of the kitchen. 'Miss Davis, my colleague's just come up with an idea. Marianne must have been soaked to the skin. They'd have had to change her clothes. The description we've been giving of her so far is useless. When she moved to the foster-parents, did all her clothes go with her, or were some kept back for her father to drool over?'

'One dress was left behind. Pink and blue vertical stripes with a white collar.' Jean stirred both mugs of instant coffee as if she were doing the Inspector an injury.

He relayed the fresh description, replaced the telephone on the receiver, and went to use the bathroom. Jean wondered whether Tony had been the last person in there, and if so, whether he had pulled the chain. The Inspector returned. His expression gave nothing away; she would never know whether Tony had pulled the chain or not.

'You don't happen to have any other clients living in the same road as the Gaines', do you?' Jean shook her head. 'Anyone in the next street or thereabouts, anyone who might just happen to be on friendly terms with one of the neighbours? Whatever vehicle they used had to have been parked in or near that road, and he must have been seen loading it, yet nobody's talking.' He paused, sipping his coffee, looking at her over the rim of the mug. 'Not to us, they're not, but they might to you. After all, you have a perfectly justifiable reason for asking around. They're your clients. You want to know where they've gone.' He set down his mug on the pile of long-playing records, and shook his head. 'I keep on seeing that bloody mattress with the dent in it. Perhaps I'm wrong. Perhaps we should let the Press in, get them to tell the world what Steven Gaines has done. Then maybe we might get some cooperation.' He smiled. 'You don't seem to have a pet for the Press photographers, not unless it's asleep upstairs in your bed.'

Was it an innocent observation, or did the man know who was upstairs in her bed? At this stage of the investigation he would sweep in information, any information, like a vacuum cleaner sucking up dust. Jean said, 'Did you have any more questions? Concerning Steven Gaines?'

'Not that I can think of at the moment. But there will be more, lots more until we find him. By the way, I spoke with your superior – Team Leader, whatever they call themselves these days. There'll be a Case Conference on the boy tomorrow. Obviously we're going to take up a lot of your time until this is sorted out, so she's agreed to split your case-load between her other people for the time being.'

'Am I to be suspended, then? Officially?'

'Your boss didn't take me that far into her confidence, Miss Davis. My guess is that it would be just paid leave to begin with. But that's not my department, thank God. Let's just see what the Case Conference spews up.'

'Yes, I will.'

'I'll try to be there. Put in a good word.'

He stood up, and so did Jean, thinking that at last he was about to leave, but at the door he turned, and thought for a moment as if preparing himself for a long speech. 'Someone said that Child Abuse is like suicide. The abuser is full of guilt, trying to hurt himself; he wants to be found out and punished. But then your lot spoil all that by trying to take away his guilt, convincing them that it's all due to something that happened in his childhood. You talk about – what is it? – negative self-image. But guilt's a very positive thing, Miss Davis. So is fear. How else do you think my own kids have learned to behave themselves?'

Jean looked at the Inspector, trying to form in her mind an image of his children, and wondering what their view of him would be like, but all she said was, 'Gaol doesn't teach you to love. Not yourself. Not anyone.'

The Inspector removed the anti-smoking chewing-gum from his mouth, replaced it in its wrapper, and thereafter in his pocket. 'Never chew in the street. Hangover from my days as a pavement Bobby. Diminishes the confidence of the public.' It was now five past seven in the morning, and he still had one cigar left. He telephoned for his car, and Jean could hear a fresh set of instructions. 'Try again with the people on the other side of the road from the Gaines house. Lean on them. Take Fletcher with you in case they start rabbiting to each other in Punjabi or Rastafarian. Tell Fletcher to hint at what we want Gaines for, how serious it is, but not to spell it out; I want another day before I start tripping over newsmen. Miss Davis here will need a little of our protection when that happens; the first Flash Harry to set up home in her outside toilet gets his camera confiscated, alright?'

His last words to Jean before going were, 'This is a terrible occupation, Miss Davis. My kids have got so used to not setting eyes on me from one month to the next that the only time they ask where I am is when it's coming up to Christmas, and they've made out their shopping-lists. If I believed in Father Christmas, I'd want him to get me the number of that van or whatever that Gaines must be sitting in right now.'

She left them asleep, Michael curled into a ball with one hand covering most of his face, Joy snoring on her back, Tony lying face-down on the covers, naked apart from his socks, his legs slightly parted, his arms by his sides, the fingers touching the buttocks, an image of passive compliance with what the world had done to him so far and what he expected it would continue doing. These were her pets. Had the Inspector checked them over during his visit to the bathroom?

There was space to park outside the Gaines house, but habit caused her to choose a place further down the street, so as to allow herself time to gather her thoughts, and force herself to get out of the car. As she walked towards the house, the air grew thicker, as it had done the very first time she had visited the Gaines'. Then as now, part of this thickening was apprehension in her, part was her knowledge that she was under observation from the neighbouring houses. In an area largely inhabited by what the Council called 'problem families' any arrival by an outsider is noted.

At the house itself, where she had expected there to be at

least one policeman present, the bell brought no response, and she bruised her knuckles on the door. Finally the door was opened by a small Asian boy from the family living on the ground floor.

'No policeman today, Fazul?' The boy shook his head, smiling shyly. 'Is it alright if I come in?' He stood to one side, extending one arm in imitation of the doorman at the Ritz. Other questions followed, each answered by a shake of the head. He had not seen the Gaines family leave, nor had he witnessed the loading of the car or van. No, his parents were not at home. Jean had tried many times to persuade Fazul to speak, had often sat on the stairs making one-sided conversation. He had always seemed interested and polite, smiling, nodding or, as now, shaking his head, but had never committed himself to words. Occasionally an expression had crossed his face which suggested that there was something he would like to say to her, but dared not. Today she watched for this expression, but it did not come. This was an area in which even Asian children were not immune from sexual abuse. A few years ago several old men, some of them religious leaders, had been discovered testing their libidos regularly on small girls and boys. The local community had known what was happening, but some of the parents had considered this special attention given to the family to be an honour.

Padlocks had been placed on both doors of the Gaines' two rooms, and a paper sash stretched across each. Written on each sash was the same message that the room had been sealed by the police, and that unauthorized persons were forbidden to enter. Jean imagined herself as some local dignitary, or the star of a soap-opera, waiting while scissors were produced so that she might cut the sash and declare the Gaines flat open as a place of public resort. What was she doing there, standing with her back resting against the stair-rail, her eyes fixed on the doorway in which she had first seen Steven Gaines?

It had been an evening in winter, the staircase dark because none of the lights in the common parts of the house ever worked. She had stood waiting for the door to open, and when it had, she had found herself facing a man in his early thirties wearing only a pair of jockey-shorts. She had asked if they might talk inside the room, and he had replied, 'No way!', standing there, framed in the doorway with arms outstretched as if about to demonstrate some body-building exercise which her knock had interrupted. It had seemed to her that Steven Gaines was enjoying the first few moments of that meeting, flexing and reflexing the well developed muscles which looked as if they had been anointed with baby oil.

She had explained who she was, and that the hospital doctor who had treated Marianne Gaines that afternoon for bruising had asked her to call and discuss with the little girl's parents how that bruising had occurred. Steven Gaines' pleasure had subsided. He had begun hitting the door-frame with the palm of his hand, as if urging himself to more extensive violence. He had asked why the doctor had not discussed the bruising with him, and Jean had explained that such a discussion was the business of the Social Services, and Mr Gaines and his daughter had left the hospital before a Social Worker could be found.

He had told her (wrongly) that since this was not Council accommodation, she had no jurisdiction there. The Council had done fuck-all to help them, and he had found these two rooms himself. There was nothing to discuss. The girl had fallen down the stairs. Jean had begun to list Marianne's injuries, the swelling on the left side of the head, the bruises on both upper arms like grasp-marks which could hardly have been caused by a fall, and he had said, 'I shook her. When I found her at the bottom of the stairs I was angry, worried that she might have broken something. She knows those stairs are lethal.' And Jean had stood her ground, saying that, unless she were allowed to see Marianne and talk to her, she would have no alternative but to involve the police. Many of her calls turned out to be false alarms, but she had to be sure.

Up to this time, Maureen Gaines had remained motionless inside the room, with her face turned away from Jean. Now she moved behind her husband, placing one hand on his naked back. At no point then or later did she make eye-contact with Jean. Then there was a silence, during which Steven Gaines, his eyes widened in a trance of rage, stared through the Social Worker, until his wife spoke his name, when he struck the frame of the door again violently with the palm of his hand, shouting, 'Think they'll give me remission for cooperating?'

before moving aside to allow his wife to pass him and lead Jean up the lethal stairs to the room in which her children slept.

Jean had taken her time, had sat on the edge of the mattress talking quietly to Marianne, telling her that the doctor had wanted to make sure she was getting better. The table-lamp on the melamine table had a picture of the Sleeping Beauty on its shade, and Jean had asked Marianne if she knew the story of the Sleeping Beauty, and whether she could name all the Seven Dwarfs, and said that they would have to move closer to the lamp, so that Jean herself would be able to look at Marianne's bruises, and that Marianne would have to remove her vest and knickers to allow Jean to do so.

At this point, Maureen Gaines had uttered a noise indicating disgust, and had pulled the two boys out of their beds and pushed them from the room to stand on the landing. There had been no time for Jean to check either of the boys for bruising, but they appeared to be well nourished.

The little girl had made no protest, had neither blinked nor threatened tears, and had not looked to her mother for guidance or protection. She had stood, and placed herself near the light, had removed her clothes, had turned on the spot when asked to do so, had moved away from Jean, then back towards her, had allowed her arms to be manipulated, her bruises to be touched, had opened her mouth wide so that Jean might look for missing teeth, and had stood motionless while Jean's fingers felt her head for bumps or scars.

She had answered none of the questions Jean put to her, and her eyes had never left Jean's face. It was not quite the expression well documented in the literature as 'frozen watchfulness', but nor had it been that of a normal child. It had been the expression of a totally passive mature woman, and Jean had felt as if it was she herself who was the infant.

After the girl had put her clothes back on, and the boys had been let into the room, and had jumped into their beds shivering, Jean had made as if to leave, then asked Marianne casually what had happened to cause her bruises. The girl had walked to the door, and pointed to the stairs, and the older of the two boys had laughed, and said, 'She's a thickie, didn't she tell you? Can't even tie her shoelaces yet.' Both boys had giggled, and dived under their bedclothes.

All Marianne's bruises, except for the grip on her arms which her father had explained, had matched those likely to have been caused by a fall down the stairs. But a reason had to be found for Jean to visit Marianne Gaines again, and to continue visiting until the child told her what Jean already knew.

She had found several reasons, some legitimate, some mere subterfuge. They included Marianne's reluctance to speak, her bed-wetting (the upstairs room stank of urine), the general state of the two rooms and the common parts of the house. She had begun writing letters to the landlord's agents, and had told the Gaines' that their living conditions and the lethal stairs would be used as ammunition in the long on-going battle she was having with this particular landlord. It was at least a half-truth, and no more shameful than many of the thousands of promises she had made to clients in the past, and been unable to keep.

She had talked with the teachers at the school which all three of the Gaines children attended, had learned that Marianne did not form relationships with her classmates, was not liked by other children, and that she daydreamed. She did speak, but only when absolutely necessary, and had never been seen to cry. Some bruises had been noted, not often, and her brothers had explained their cause. The teachers, when asked, could not be certain whether Marianne masturbated; they clearly considered the question to be in poor taste. It was true that Marianne wet herself, no matter where she was, and this led to her scratching herself or holding her knickers where they were wet, but whether this constituted sexual arousal the teachers really could not say. She was certainly a slow girl, but this was natural when she had two lively elder brothers to contend with; Marianne would come into her own when her brothers moved to another school.

At first when Jean visited, Steven Gaines had either been out or would leave as she arrived. It was not until the third visit that the children's mother spoke to her, and then only with a 'Yes' or 'No'; usually Maureen Gaines answered Jean's questions with a shrug of her rounded shoulders. She seemed always to be standing by the window near the stove, turned away from Jean and looking out. She rarely left that spot.

James and Adam would approach their mother, and whisper conspiratorially to her; they were her messengers and protectors. If Jean were to offer to make a cup of tea, the offer would be refused, but the tea would be made and brought to her by one of the boys. Once the elder boy carried a hard-backed chair the length of the room to place it by the window for his mother. Jean saw her squeeze his hand in thanks, but no words were exchanged.

Words were exchanged between Jean and the boys, but she had to work hard for them. If pressed they would answer questions about school, football, snooker and programmes watched on television. Once when their mother had removed herself to the room above, they told her how greedy Marianne was, that she stole food, and never stopped eating. They told Jean how embarrassing it was for them at school to have a sister who wet herself, and held their noses and sniggered to indicate that sometimes Marianne had fouled herself as well.

Marianne had been present, had listened to all that was said about her, but had not responded. Jean had still not heard her speak, or been able to involve her in any kind of play. None of the toys and materials in Jean's box of tricks had held Marianne's interest.

Five weeks after her first visit, Jean had been sitting in the lower room with the children while their mother was said to be lying down upstairs. The boys had been watching television with Jean sitting behind them, pretending an interest in the programme but actually watching Marianne, who sat on the floor in the corner behind the television, with the side of her face resting against the peeling wallpaper.

Jean had been wearing trousers. At a point when the two boys were particularly engrossed in the programme, Marianne had slowly risen to her feet, and had walked unsteadily and with great difficulty towards Jean. She had reached out an arm to steady the child, and Marianne had taken it, allowing herself to be steered between Jean's legs. She had then lowered her head until her mouth was touching the cloth of the crotch of Jean's trousers, and had made sucking noises. One of the two boys had heard the sucking noises from his sister, and had turned from the television, red-faced and furious, to scream at her, 'Filthy cow! Stop that! Wait till I tell him! Stop it!'

Which boy had it been? Had it been Adam?

Jean had lifted Marianne onto her knee, and had hugged her for many minutes, had held her there until the boys had regained their interest in the television, and had then stood up, still holding the child, and had left the room with her, carried her down three flights of stairs, and left the building, while behind her she had heard the elder boy shouting to his mother to tell her what was happening.

Examined at the hospital, Marianne had been found to have what had been described as 'extensive internal damage, corresponding to that caused by persistent vaginal intercourse with a large adult male'. No semen had been found in either vagina or anus. Jean herself had received an official warning of suspension for removing a child from the bosom of its family without having first obtained a Place of Safety Order.

As she turned away from the door with its padlocks and sash, she remembered the weight of Marianne Gaines in her arms. She had been afraid that they would both fall down the stairs, afraid because what she was doing was illegal, and she had known that, unless Steven Gaines had abused his daughter during the last twenty-four hours, no semen would be present, and a blood-test would be useless. As had happened.

She had told the Inspector that Steven Gaines had been relieved to have been found out, glad to have been stopped, and finally that had been true. With no positive proof against him, he had denied it, but she had worked on him long and hard, had harassed, bullied, lied, begged, threatened, had employed tactics far removed from anything she had been taught in training, until finally she had recognized his weak point and had told him that, unless he accepted responsibility for what he had done, and therapy to help him avoid re-offending, she would make sure he never saw his daughter again until she became an adult. That Marianne had been regularly abused was not in dispute, and that it had happened while she was in his care made him unfit to be her guardian. Unless he accepted the responsibility for what had happened, shifting the guilt from his daughter, she was likely to be psychologically scarred for the rest of her life.

He loved his daughter; that had been the key. He accepted responsibility to her, to Jean, to the psychotherapist, though not of course to the police. Sitting beside Jean on a bench in the park beneath trees, he had cried, spoken of his own childhood, of his brothers and his father, the abuse he himself had suffered, and finally of his own self-disgust. He had told her things she knew had never been told to anyone else, and she had sat there, listening, knowing that she herself would not tell anyone else, not even the Team Leader. She had risked her job (Jean had never thought of it as anything so grand as a career) and behaved unprofessionally in order to deserve his trust, gambled her livelihood for the sake of one six-year-old victim, just the one among so many of her clients. But it was important, she thought, that one didn't always play safe. A cold wind had dried the tears on his cheeks. He would not talk to her indoors; he had to be away from his wife and the two boys; there had to be space between him and anyone else who might hear what was said. And they had met out of doors, week after week.

Self-disgust! That accounted for the body-building, of course.

Descending the last flight of stairs, she heard a door on the ground floor being closed. It would be Fazul, playing games. She turned her face in the direction of the sound, expecting the door to open again and Fazul to peep around it, grinning, so she did not at first see what her hand touched as it came to rest on the banister rail, and knocked the object onto the floor, whence it spun into a corner by the front door.

She bent to retrieve it and to return it where it had been left. She saw that it was a toy, then that it was a toy van about the size of a matchbox. She looked at the toy in her hand, and at the paint which had come off on her fingertips. It was a toy white van, a Ford Transit, but it had recently been painted blue.

The woman's lips were trembling as she opened the front door. She had recognized Jean's car, and had been standing behind the pane of frosted glass, ready to unhook the three doorchains. 'I thought you might telephone.'

'Sorry. Didn't get a chance. The police have kept me busy.'

'They've been here several times. I told them I saw nothing.

No van, no car, nothing. I never let her out of my sight, you know that.' The woman replaced the three door-chains.

'Yes, I know.'

'Yet she was out in the garden. In all that rain. I couldn't explain it; I've been going mad trying to figure it out. I thought she was upstairs. How could she have known he was coming for her? He couldn't have planned what he was going to do to that boy.'

'No, he couldn't have planned it.'

'The police told me not to speak to anyone about it. The newspapers mustn't know, not yet. When they do, they'll come round here. Christ, Jean! I can't take any more of this.' Later Jean would see the woman on television, talking to a reporter. She would be wearing a new dress, and have curled her hair.

They were standing in the hall. The woman stared into a wall-mirror, set amongst gilt cherubs; the sight of her own reflection seemed to intensify her distress. Jean placed an arm round the woman's shoulder, and led her into a lounge which smelled of lavender polish and cut flowers.

'She'd just started to relax with me, you see. Geoff swears that he got a smile out of her the other night when he was reading her *The Wind in the Willows*. It's taken time, but you warned us it would. We thought she was doing alright here . . . in the circumstances. She was, wasn't she? Be honest. I rely on you, you know that. You'd have said, wouldn't you, if we were making things worse for her?'

'You did fine.'

Jean remembered conversations with Joy about Marianne and her foster-parents. Joy believed that Jean had become too involved with the person to whom Joy invariably referred as 'the girl', which was her way of reminding Jean that Marianne was just one client among many. Jean had said, 'She's a little gem, and she's doing alright. She's making them work for it,' and Joy had replied, 'Sounds to me as if she's dead emotionally. Some animals die during the sex-act, you know. Maybe that's what's happened to her. Now, do we sit here getting wet-eyed all evening, or do I get a lift to the pub?'

The woman now sitting opposite had worked hard to form a relationship with Marianne, and her husband, the antithesis of Steven Gaines, had impressed Jean as the kind of man any

43

child would be lucky to have as a father, comfortable, cuddly, easy-going, a man with a job he enjoyed and a wife on whom he doted. She said, 'Oh, yes, I'm sure they'll find him. They usually do.'

'Before anything else happens?'

It seemed best to Jean to answer such a question with a question, so she asked whether Marianne had taken anything with her, and was told that this was a question the police had also asked. Marianne had taken nothing, not even a raincoat, no doll, no teddy bear.

'Did the dress she was wearing have a pocket?'

The woman was puzzled. 'I'm not sure. I think most of her dresses have. Why?'

Jean backtracked hastily, saying that the police had asked her whether any of Marianne's clothes had been left behind at the Gaines home, and that she had not been able to remember what Marianne had been wearing that afternoon. 'It would have been soaked whichever it was. I hope they had something else for her to wear,' and then, moving the subject away entirely from the pocket and what might have been in it, 'I expect the police will want a photograph.'

'They took the two we had. One was indoors with a flash, sitting at the table, wearing a paper hat; it was rather dark, and she'd pulled the hat low. The other was on the steps that lead down to the lawn. She was squinting into the sun, and I don't think Geoff had got the focus right. He's not the best photographer in the world. All our films used to come out black, because he didn't put them in properly, and they never used to wind on. We must have wasted a fortune and missed all the fine weather.'

The foster-mother was more relaxed now. She had drifted into a reverie, the sort of lassitude which often follows extreme anger or emotional excitement. Jean said, 'So you were in the kitchen, and you thought Marianne was upstairs?'

The foster-mother nodded slowly, but did not tell again the story she had already told and retold. Instead she said, 'Have you any idea where they've gone to?'

It seemed to Jean as if everyone expected her to know the answer to this question. She shook her head.

'I think Geoff would go looking for them if he knew where

to start. The police can only do so much, though I suppose, now that it's murder, they're bound to make an effort.' Her voice trailed away. She was looking past Jean towards the french windows, and so into the garden from which Marianne Gaines might have been taken (but one could not know, since nobody had seen her taken), and when she began to speak again, it was slow aimless talk, much of it to herself and for herself, talk of not allowing herself to sleep in case Marianne came back and couldn't get into the house, of lying awake going over and over in her mind what she had done on that day and which room she had been occupying at any particular time. She had even managed to remember what she had heard on the radio, and how long she had spent in the toilet, how much of a magazine she had read, and the details of an article about a man who built dolls' houses, in which every item was authentic; even the backs of the mantel ornaments were painted, and the drawers of the tiny chests were dove-tailed, and provided with working locks which required the tip of a pin to operate. She had remembered that she had looked out into the back garden several times that day, remembered one occasion, and timed it by the radio as being at ten to four; it had been the moment when a sudden downpour with large hailstones had hit the window, giving her a start. She had watched the hail whitening the lawn as if a huge tablecloth had been spread out for a picnic, and had thought to herself how Marianne would enjoy the garden once the weather had improved. 'She did a painting at school of the back garden, as seen from her bedroom window. Brought it home some months ago. I've been hiding it from you. Best you see it now. It's not very flattering.'

There was a hedge forming three sides of a rectangle, done in brown powder-paint applied with circular strokes, more resembling coils of barbed wire than privet. A patch of blue represented the tiny pond for ornamental fish, with a few thin strokes of green for the weeping pear and seven dollops of grey for the rockery. Painted over the whole picture from top to bottom were six broad evenly spaced vertical lines of dark grey. The foster-mother said, 'The bars of a cage. They can't be anything else.'

Jean carried the painting over to the french windows, and

looked out into the back garden, which was bathed in sunshine, and from which birdsong could be heard. She herself had made many unsuccessful attempts to persuade Marianne to paint. 'What did you say to her when she showed you the picture?'

'I hope that's not one of those trick questions, Jean. I'm not feeling up to that sort of thing today.' The foster-mother leaned back in the chair, placing one hand over her eyes to shield them from the sunlight. 'What did I say? . . . I said it was lovely. I said I particularly liked the fish-pool. Then I changed the subject. She nodded when I asked if she wished me to keep it. She may even have given half a smile. She has quite a powerful presence about her sometimes, as I think you know. What would you have said to her?'

'I'd have taken her upstairs, stood her by the window, opened it wide, and asked her where the bars were. She wouldn't have answered, but she'd have understood the reason for my asking.'

'Even if I'd thought of that, it would have been a bit difficult, since only the small top window opens; the others are jammed shut with paint. We've never loosened them for the very good reason that she's tall enough now to climb onto that window-sill, and we feared an accident. Alright, I know I'm supposed to be professional about it – treat fostering as a job – give just so much and not too much – "mother but don't smother". How the hell do I do that? How can anyone ration their feelings? You tell me.'

The woman had been attractive once, with a strong interesting face. A plump puppy of a man, who giggled a lot, had worshipped her, and had won her. The face was still interesting, but now it was in its late thirties, and, after four miscarriages, the laugh lines were already too deep; the joke had turned sour. The mouth, once generous, was not defensive; the teeth had been clenched too hard and too often. The eyes, at present red from lack of sleep, were still large and well shaped, and only occasionally expressed more fear than is suitable in a person fostering a small child. Jean thought, 'What would you look like if you'd been rejected by as many children as I have? Sitting there, cringeing from the light! What sort of state will you be in when you get to my age?' but what she said was, 'If I could have told you how not to get emotionally involved, and you had been able to follow my advice, you probably wouldn't have been the right person for Marianne. She knows what she's about. She knows that her best defence is to unnerve the opposition, and we're all that to her. I did warn you about that. We're all fair game to her, all adults, every one of us, and after what has happened to her, why shouldn't we be?'

Another mistake perhaps, to have placed Marianne with this insecure woman, but how was one supposed to strike the right balance? Maybe a fat and fifty-year-old mother-hen, who had seen everything and stood no nonsense, would have been a better bet, but women like that were not thick on the ground, and usually already had a household of rough-and-ready kids who would have swamped Marianne.

She left the foster-mother, and wandered upstairs, hoping to be alone, but the woman followed her and remained in the doorway as Jean looked about Marianne's room. Jean had been in this room with Marianne many times, sitting on the carpet with her box of tricks open and the toys spread out on the floor. Marianne had lain on her back with her legs bent, ignoring the toys, gently rocking from side to side, and gazing at her own reflection in the emerald green tiles which surrounded the blocked-up fireplace. Jean had read her stories, or made them up; they had been all the same to Marianne, who had asked no questions, made no comments. Jean had drawn shapes on paper, but Marianne would not add to them, and when asked to draw for herself, had looked away, and made perfunctory scribbles from which no meaning could be deduced. Marianne's other favourite position in the room had been to stand at the window with her back to Jean, looking out.

From the window all the back garden could be seen, and certainly the back fence and narrow public path beyond. It would not have been necessary for Steven Gaines to have made contact with his daughter before he arrived to carry her away, only for him to have known the address where she was living, since if he had stood on that path and waved to her, she would certainly have gone down to him.

'Don't touch anything!' The woman spoke sharply. Jean

47

had been opening and closing drawers, searching for something, and it was as if the woman, realizing suddenly what Jean was doing, had come out of her trance. 'You mustn't.' Jean had a hand still inside one of the drawers. It was possible that the object her fingers were touching was the one for which she had been searching, and which otherwise might have been carried away in the pocket of Marianne's dress. 'The police asked me if I'd touched anything, and said not to. Just in case.'

'Just in case of what?'

'They wondered if her father might have got up here, and any evidence in a case of murder is important. I told them he couldn't possibly have done so. Never mind fingerprints, he'd have left mud all through the house; it was pouring down outside.'

'Well, if it's fingerprints they're worried about, mine would have been here already. I have worked with Marianne in this room quite a lot.'

'I do dust and polish between your visits, you know. Today's fingerprints would be new. I shouldn't be able to explain them.'

'Tell the police the truth, that I thought I'd left some toys and work-materials here that I needed for another child, and before you knew what I was doing I'd had a good old rummage. I still have a job, if only just. As it happens, the things I need aren't here.' The object Jean's fingers were touching was not the object she wanted. She removed her hand from the drawer, and closed it. She crossed to the window, and looked out again, down into the garden.

'Geoff said I mustn't let them get to me, but they seemed to think I must be lying to them, to cover something up. I think they believed I'd left her alone, and gone out somewhere. They kept saying, "But how could she have gone out into the garden without passing you, if you were downstairs?"'

'Perhaps she didn't go out the back way. Perhaps she saw him from here, waving to her, and went quietly downstairs and out of the front door to meet him in the street.'

'She couldn't have. She can't reach the chains on the front door.'

Jean had forgotten the chains. 'And the back?'

'The chain in the kitchen would have been off, because I'd been in the garden earlier, but I was in the kitchen myself. And the french windows in the lounge are always locked unless Geoff's at home.'

'It's clear, then,' Jean said. 'She couldn't have got out by the front or the back. She couldn't have got out of this house at all, and she couldn't have been taken away. I suppose what's bothering the police is that she was.'

Without rising from his desk or looking at her, the Inspector pointed to a chair as he continued reading what Jean took to be a report. She waited. There were charts on the wall, and she attempted to deduce meaning from them, and failed. The alternative to this intellectual diversion was aesthetic, a wall-calendar across which at this time of the year the torso of Miss July was stretched in full colour. Clutched tightly in Jean's right hand was a toy van of a size to fit in a matchbox, the paint now dry, and that hand remained in Jean's pocket.

Finally the Inspector closed his report, and raised his head to look at her, indicating without words that he was waiting for Jean to speak. Jean said, 'I did as you suggested, and asked around the street.' He waited. 'All I could find out was that a couple of people saw a blue van they hadn't seen before.'

'What sort of van?'

'It might have been a Ford. They couldn't be certain.'

'Who saw it?'

'A couple of elderly people. I was talking to a group of them, can't remember which of them mentioned it first. Of course they may have made it up. People of certain cultures often say what they think you want to hear. They like to please.'

'Not in my experience. You're talking about Asians, are you – these people you can't put a name to?'

'It was in a shop. If I'd asked for names, I'd have got nothing. They were of mixed races, and they kept butting in, interrupting each other. Two of them said they'd seen a blue van parked in the street that evening.'

'But no number?'

'No.'

'Or even part of a number?' Jean shook her head. 'And you rang up and made an appointment to come in and tell me this?'

'I didn't know how busy you were or how important it was.'

'It would have been more important if you'd phoned it in the moment you heard. You were seen near the Gaines home an hour after I left you.'

'I'm not a detective, or even a policeman. It's a little more difficult for me to assess what is or isn't worth bothering you with.'

'And since you knew he'd already got a thirty-six-hour start, and wouldn't be foolish enough to stay with the same vehicle for long, you didn't rush. It's a little difficult for *me* to assess whose side you're on, Miss Davis.'

'The little girl's side. Does that surprise you?'

'Did they have anything else to tell us, this nameless bunch of Dolly Mixtures?'

'If I'd pressed them too far, they might have suggested that the next time their windows are broken or dog-shit pushed through their letterboxes, the police might take some action.'

There was no reaction to this. The Inspector did not even blink, but continued as if she had not spoken. 'The DHSS have promised to let us know if he turns up at any of their branches to get money. Of course he won't. His alternative is to turn to petty crime. Bit of a come-down after he's started so high in the big league! In your opinion, Miss Davis, how would this father of three – two now – go about getting the money to keep his family?' The Inspector was using a pencil to tap out a slow regular beat against the edge of his desk, as if he were reminding a dancing bear of the rhythm it needed to begin its act. 'Well, let's play a game of make-believe, let's be Mr Steven Gaines contemplating a job, and by that I mean that we're trying to decide between conning a few old ladies out of their pension books or holding up a Building Society. We're trying to balance risk and reward, Miss Davis; we're not contemplating collecting the empties in a pub or sweeping up at some Holiday Camp. Now, of those two options, which, do you think –' He stopped in mid-sentence. The pencil, halfway through its downwards stroke, went flying across the room to make contact with Miss July. The Inspector placed the flat of his hands against the desk, and wiggled his fingers up and down in a semi-official transport of delight, repeating the word 'Funny!' several times with varying intonations.

Jean was genuinely puzzled as to what all this might mean, and the Inspector, now affable again, explained. 'Funny how easy it is in this job to forget that it's the holiday season. The unemployment figures shrink, and all over Britain Insurance Cards are left at home, and no questions asked. Casual employment, Miss Davis. Summer season! Where better to hide than among a crowd of half-pissed, semi-sunstroked yobbos? Right! What can he do? What are his talents? He's a body-builder, isn't he? Can he swim?' Jean nodded. 'He's not the jolly type, though, is he? Reassure me! Tell me he's not likely to be taken on as a Red Coat, and put in charge of the children's games at the Junior Swimming Pool, with all those little bundles of temptation floating around on waterwings.'

'I don't think they'd be in any danger.'

'I don't imagine that you thought his son would be in any danger, or you'd hardly have left the two boys with him, but you were wrong, Miss Davis. Nevertheless I'd like you to join me in this game. Share your insights with me. I would have had you down as a joiner-in, even a little over-competitive maybe. Am I wrong?' He smiled, showing teeth whiter than the Wolf would have displayed to Red Riding-Hood. 'Not been taken off injured, have you? That hand of yours, the one you keep in your pocket, not giving trouble? Don't tell me you've burned it, or trapped it in a door somewhere.' Jean removed her fingers from the toy van, held up her hand, and wiggled her fingers. 'Well, then, what do you think? Is our man that clever? Has he got that sort of nerve? Or would he avoid the crowds?'

Jean stared at the wall-charts with their coloured triangles, squares and circles, all signifying she knew not what. 'I promised myself long ago never to play guessing games with people who know more than I do.'

'One thing he will know is that we don't have a photograph of him for the newspapers. He'll guess that we might get one from the school of the older boy, and he won't know that the only photographs the foster-parents took of the little girl are worse than useless, so he'll keep the two kids under wraps as far as he can. One guessing game we shall ask you to play will be to help with one of those ludicrous Identikits when you've finished here. Now, forgetting all past promises made to yourself, which route would he take? Busy holiday resort? Isolation in some derelict barn or the middle of a forest? Does the man have balls and gamble, or does he hedge his bets?'

'I'm not a psychiatrist, Inspector. Or a bookie.'

'What a lot of things you're not today, including being co-operative! It's a wonder you came in. But you could pretend, Miss Davis; you could try a bit of make-believe. Isn't that a useful talent in your line of work?'

Jean put her hand back into her pocket, and gripped the toy van until she could feel its sharp edges. 'If Steven Gaines did go to the seaside, it wouldn't be to look for other children. His obsession, if that's the word, is with his daughter. Nor am I sure he'd be much good at pretending to be on holiday; he wouldn't know how to go about it.'

'You just pack up the car, and head for the coast, or so my more fortunate colleagues tell me. How long is it since he had a holiday?'

'When he was a child, eight or nine, maybe ten. With his father and his brothers. They would have been fifteen, sixteen.'

'The seaside?'

'Yes, I think so. I don't remember his saying much about it, or where they went.'

'That's odd, don't you think? I mean, people don't usually say, "That was the year we all went to the seaside," without naming the place. They say, "We had a terrible time at Bognor that year. It rained every day," or "Blackpool was scorching. Even the rock melted, and mother came home with third-degree burns.'''

'People may say things like that. He didn't.'

'And was this a happy time for him? Paddling his tootsies in some unknown sea?'

'None of his childhood was very happy.'

'If I were in his shoes, knowing that it's probably only a matter of days or weeks before I was caught, I'd want to go somewhere I'd once felt safe, even if happiness had always been beyond my reach. What do you say?'

'If there were such a place, maybe.'

'And if this place where I'd built my sand-castle, and felt secure, was unknown, even to my confidante and moral mentor, I might not feel like experimenting with places unexplored, unless, of course, I knew a way of leaving the country without a passport. These day-trips to the Continent have meant a lot of extra work for us, you know. But I don't see our man arriving at Dover in a blue van packed solid with furniture and abused children, do you? We've had to cover the ports anyway, just in case he dumps the family and tries to make it alone.'

Suddenly the Inspector was on his feet, and Jean found that she was also standing. He was smiling at her, and had not smoked even one small cigar during the interview. Jean wondered if he were manic-depressive, and this the beginning of a manic phase. He was speaking again, but in a different tone, maintaining his grin, and being friendly; it was quite unnerving. 'Well, that was a very interesting chat, Miss Davis, and not too painful for you, I hope. I feel much better about our relationship now; you and I might just have the makings of an above-average team. My sergeant, who is usually found to be hovering outside that door, will take you down to the Jigsaw Department. Don't take the game too seriously. No one ever really looks like eight Happy Family cards cut to pieces and reassembled on a different principle.'

What Jean had expected to find in Marianne's room, and had not found, was a replica of a button from an Army officer's uniform; it could be broken into two by the use of a fingernail. Inside had been a scrap of paper on which was written Jean's home telephone-number. Jean had given the button to Marianne at the beginning of the fostering, and had explained its use. She supposed, and hoped, that Marianne had taken it with her.

There had been boss-eyes, jug-ears and noses of many shapes from Roman to snub. There had been chins to fit lantern jaws and chins to fit fighting jaws and chins to fit other chins, chin upon chin, doubles, trebles and quadruples, enough chin-chins to keep one going until 'Last Orders'. Some of the chins had receded so dramatically that they could have been classified as necks, but necks were another category, and had their own problems, dew-laps and scrawniness being but two. There had been hair-lines and hair-lips, eyebrows plucked to a thin blue line and eyebrows which might have been exhibited at Cruft's.

In spite of the generous array of choices, or perhaps because of it, Jean had been unable to fit together an Identikit picture which resembled Steven Gaines. They had told her not to hurry, to take time and ponder, and suggested that she might begin by making a little portrait sketch as a reminder. They had offered her many pieces of card, each identified by both letters and numbers – A1, B7, C5 – until she had begun to see everything in triplicate. There is a standard textbook, *The ABC of Child Abuse*, which also uses letters and numbers to an almost confusing effect, and Jean began to muddle the cards with the book. '*What stage is the child at now? (One is good, five is bad.) Attitude of child to the world? Is it being scape-goated? Has it experienced good bonding? Was it a wanted child? Did its arrival disrupt the marriage? How good is the child's emotional resilience? (One is strong, five is weak.)*'

She had shaken her head so often that the muscles of her neck had begun to ache. Partly to relieve the feet of the people standing behind her, and partly to rest those muscles responsible for shaking, and bring others into play, she had begun to nod, and had continued nodding. A picture had been built up. Jean's principle in making it had been to use no numbers from one to five and none of the letters S, G or M. The picture had, she privately considered, resembled a living person, a well known television personality, but not the man who had walked with her by the canal, talking of his childhood holidays by the sea.

Now she faced other faces, three-dimensional and often in movement; these faces were alive, though she would not rush to call them real. The Case Conference was in session. Jean had been placed neither at the head nor the foot of the table, among a collection of public employees all of whom were trying not to stare at her, and all of whom were failing.

The room was airless, even with all the windows open, and the sound of traffic from below was louder than she remembered from previous meetings. The people around the table, usually given to all talking at once, were unnaturally silent. Jean remembered her first Case Conference, and how upset she had been at the amount of aggression displayed. The faces around the table then had sometimes been hostile and belligerent, each of them seeing the client in a different light, and each of them wanting something different, something for themselves not the client. Some of the faces had sulked, some yawned openly while others spoke, or grimaced when something was said with which they disagreed. Some had been the faces of natural bullies; some were faces with private grievances which they had dragged into the discussion; some stood on their dignity and would not budge. As a new girl, Jean had been a liability, and the faces made sure she felt so. Liabilities know better than to speak their minds; Jean had not spoken her mind, but had watched the faces watching her, some of them showing off for her benefit, though little was the benefit she had gained from that. She had watched them speculating how long she would last as a Social Worker, how soon it would be before she made some mistake they would have to clear up. No, she had not spoken her mind, but had gathered up her notes fifteen minutes into the Conference, and had left the room. The audacity of it had silenced the faces. She had been told later by her Team Leader that as a one-off gesture it was fine, but never to attempt an encore. She had been a Trainee Generic Social Worker then, allotted thirty clients in her first week, with another eighty-four by the end of her first six months.

Here today there were more silences. The talk, when it came, was desultory, stilted, interspersed with the sound of the traffic below. The people round the table wished that they were somewhere else. This was a Case Conference about the dead Adam Gaines, but it seemed to Jean that it was as much, at least beneath the talk, about the live Jean Davis.

Adam Gaines' form-teacher doodled on her notepad. The whirls and scrolls did not seem to be abstract, but looked like a design for some ballet or opera. Jean had watched Adam and his brother pirouetting round the room in imitation of some ballerina on television, while Marianne had remained sitting on the floor close to the wall, studying a thread of cotton stuck to the tips of her fingers. The teacher's doodling was a way of keeping her wristwatch in a position where she could see it. When she had designed the scenery for the last act, she would make her excuses and go. Perhaps it was not a stage-set at all; one can be deceived by looking at something upside-down. The doodle was more like some rococo Folly at the end of a pier. Steven Gaines had mentioned a pier and a building at the end of it, a small elaborate hut which was always locked. It had been a short pier, unsuitable for serious fishing, but inside the hut there had been something he wanted to look at; he had been able to see it through the window, but not to get close enough.

The solicitor for the Council sat behind his thick pebble glasses, saying nothing as usual, but saying it today with a small edge of excitement. The Health Visitor manoeuvred an extra-strong peppermint delicately from behind her hand into one corner of her mouth, where it lay like the swelling of an abscess. She had been on a diet intended to reduce obesity for as long as Jean had known her, and believed that the sucking of sweets would deaden the appetite, provided that the sweets were nasty. She had begun giving her report as though she were under the impression that Adam Gaines was still alive, and had spoken of his health and cheeky manner, then had remembered the occasion for the Conference, and had fallen silent. The face of the Health Visitor bore a resentful expression behind the peppermint; she felt she had been tricked.

The Inspector had sent his apologies in the form of his sergeant. Jean imagined the Inspector now at home, rushing around the bedroom searching for a bucket and spade, and explaining to his well disciplined offspring why they were not to accompany him to the seaside. The young sergeant sat holding himself together behind folded arms. He had lunched, and diluted alcohol was exuded from all the pores of his face, disguised as sweat, and ran down features which had already begun to practise the expressions of middle age.

By the time the Team Leader had begun her impression of Brown Owl attempting to instil confidence into a pack of trainee Girl Guides, the atmosphere within the room had changed from being a mixture of cheap talcum powder and diesel fumes to one closer to that of a Changing Room after Inter-School Rugby.

'No one could foresee such a terrible tragedy. I challenge anyone to fault this Department or my team in our handling of the Gaines family.' ('*Alright, girls, we've done our tracking, found the hidden treasure, and practised our knots. Next week our guest will explain how to feed and clothe a family of fourteen on eighteen shillings a week.*') Jean stared at her notes, some type-written, some hand-written. How many words had she written over the last sixteen years, how many dates, times, places, objectives, subjective criteria, assumptions, recommendations and guesses? Probably enough to fill a small Public Library. 'We're not talking here about an inexperienced Social Worker. This is no young kid, stuffed with theories, fresh from college. We're talking about one of my very best people.' ('*Pick your own team, Jean. Who would you like on your side for the inter-family tug-of-war?*')

Steven Gaines had talked about a Public Baths, a Swimming Pool with Slipper Baths which he and his brothers had found a way of getting into free. He had spoken of the penny-pinching boredom of those holidays (more than one, then), always to the same place. There had been no surprises. Thirty slatted benches painted in Local Council green, all set along a sleepy promenade and facing out to sea.

'The only fault I have ever had to find with Jean, and I've said this to her face so I can say it again now, is that she gives too much of herself. She just works too bloody hard.' What better cue to lead into the 'paid leave' speech? Had suspension been discussed and rejected? Unlikely; the motto of the Union was, 'Innocent unless proved fallible.' Steven Gaines had said, 'It seemed as if I had to follow them, had to be with them for some kind of safety; I hated being on my own. Yet all the time with my brothers I was scared in case they turned on me, in case they got funny and wanted to muck about with me. A few times, they did it to me outside in public, once in the Changing Rooms at the Baths, a couple of times on the beach among the sand-dunes, once in some bushes. I was terrified that someone should see me while they were doing it. It became a joke that afterwards they would each give me a threepenny piece. They said sixpence was all I was worth.'

He had smiled at that; it had been one of the few times she had seen him smile. The smile had not been at her but to himself, and she had wanted more than anything to touch him, to hold him close to her, to tell him about her own childhood. Laughing and crying at the same time, she would have blurted out, 'I sometimes got more than that, and I'll bet you were prettier.' Instead she had retreated behind her profession, and waited for him to continue.

'Are you alright, Jean?' Jean felt her shoulders moving up and down as if she were imitating Edward Heath. She was laughing, quite violently. The Identikit faces around the table were nodding, as she had nodded when she put together the picture. The spectacles of the Council solicitor (Number 8B) caught the sunlight, and dazzled her until the light shifted to reveal behind them piss-holes in a featureless snow of infinite complacency.

It was the end of a non-event. She was to take paid leave until the matter had been cleared up, a phrase which reduced 'the matter' itself to something no more tiresome than an unmade bed.

Now the Identikit faces were standing, shuffling chairs under the table, pushing about the dust of past clients to accommodate the legs of the chairs. Some of the faces were turning in profile. There was lantern jaw with gumboil (3C) saying, 'Do go somewhere nice, Jean,' and meaning, 'There but for the grace of God go I,' hooded lids with contact lenses (4D) telling her to build up her strength, and all the other Identikit phrases of the Identikit faces, 'Use the time well', 'Get away from it all', 'Send us a postcard', and the hypocritical 'Wish I could drop everything right now. You are lucky, Jean.'

She was to drop everything and everyone, and retire to a safe distance, so that the shit when it flew would be out of range. She had lighted blue touch-papers all over this Borough, and must now stand well back. Cascades of multi-coloured emotions, rockets of anger, Catherine wheels of blame were fountaining and shooting and whirling on their axes, and fire-cracker words spat from the tiny mouths of delinquent infants. Who would pick up the empty containers, douse the remaining sparks, and wait for the smoke to clear?

There were mothers and children whom it had taken her months to get on terms with, children separated from parents and parent separated from child for whom the months had turned into years. She was the only interpreter between such clients and the outside world. *'None of us is God, Jean. We're all part of a team, I hope.'* As if each of us were not his own God and his own Satan, and as if 'being part of the team' wasn't an excuse behind which to hide when things became too difficult. When was the last time the entire squad at Leeds United or Aston Villa talked anyone down from the top of a high building?

During the first week her clients would wonder where she had got to, would feel neglected, but would cope. By the end of the second week there would be the beginnings of grief. By the third week, the new minder might or might not have shown her face, but would have even less time than Jean had had to spend with each of them. Each child would be expected to start all over again with this new person, and most would feel betrayed, and go into retreat. By the fifth week the shutters of every child would be back up, with a sign indicating that this shop was no longer open for business. The new minder would shake her head, blame the previous Social Worker, and conserve her energy for the old clients, with whom she had a cosy relationship. Everyone is human. Everyone needs a cuddle. As Joy would, no doubt, say.

The Identikit faces had departed to assemble themselves around other tables at other meetings, where they would discuss the living, who were merely walking wounded, and not the dead. Jean tidied her notes, and stood for a moment by the window, to breathe in diesel fumes instead of the under-arm odour which had built up in the room. Steven Gaines had said, 'What hit you first were the carbolic smells, three different sorts of carbolic, because the sheets had been sent to one place to be disinfected, the pillows to another, and the blankets to a third; I never knew why, unless it was easier to owe money to three places than one. It's the smells I remember most about those holidays, the carbolic smells and the human body smells. As a child, I was very fastidious, Is that the right word?' His thumb and forefinger were sliding backwards and forwards along the crease in his trousers, and he flicked his fingers as if brushing away imaginary crumbs. 'One good thing, though! Nothing could go on in there – in bed, I mean. Dad would have heard them if they'd tried while he was around. It was all one room really, that caravan.'

A caravan. They had always stayed at a Caravan Site, and since they had always taken their holidays at the same seaside town, it must always have been the same Caravan Site.

'Are you doing this bonding with me?'

The boy was eight years old. He and Joy sat together in the Waiting Room of the Child Guidance Unit on a sofa covered with torn grey plastic. The boy had stopped biting the knuckle of his left thumb, which was already raw and bleeding, and waited for her to reply.

'That's what they tell me. Do you mind?'

The boy shook his head, and returned to the study of his knuckle, bending and straightening the thumb in order to make the wound open and close in mimicry of a mouth which might be talking to him. The Elastoplast placed on the knuckle by Joy before they had left the Children's Home had been removed slowly at various stages of their bus journey. Now her own left hand turned the pages of a magazine long out of date, while the knuckles of her right stroked the back of the boy's neck.

Everything about the child added to Joy's own self-dis-satisfaction. If one discounted his injury, the rest of him appeared immaculate. He was squeaky-clean, his skin glowing with health. His eyes, although a little too bright and knowing for his years, reminded one of cornflowers or pale gentians. His hair, washed and styled by himself at seven thirty that morning, was chestnut-coloured, with highlights added by the sun, not from a bottle; nothing from a bottle, save dandruff shampoo, had been applied to this child's hair. He wore short grey trousers, neatly pressed by himself, a bright red short-sleeved shirt with a dolphin motif, and expensive-looking trainers without socks, it being the fashion among his peers to go sockless into the world. The boy was of average height for his age, and his well formed limbs were sun-tanned, with fine blond hairs which glistened. He turned his cornflower-coloured eyes towards Joy, and behind his head the sun made a momentary halo out of the dust in the Waiting Room. 'What's it mean – bonding?'

'It means I become your key-worker and your special person. We're supposed to get to know each other really well, so that you feel you can trust me, and come to me with your problems. And I have to find out as much as I can about you, so that I know how to help you when you're in a state.'

'Funny name for it – bonding!'

'I knew you'd think it's something to do with glue-sniffing. Well, it's not.'

'Am I supposed to find out all I can about you?'

'Yes, if you're interested. That's only fair.' The boy's question, together with the smile on his face, gave her prior warning that his right hand, at first hidden in his left armpit, had moved towards her, and was now resting on her breast, which it began squeezing and stroking. She removed the hand. 'Watch it, sailor.'

'I know one thing already.'

'What?'

'You're not very liberated for a middle-aged woman.'

'Who says I'm middle-aged, and how do you know I'm not very liberated?'

'You still wear those things on your tits.'

Joy flicked over another page of the magazine, and tried to outstare an anorectic model in a leotard doing the splits. 'These boobs have got used to being given a bit of support while they're carried around. They wouldn't thank me if I let them loose. Being liberated isn't all it's cracked up to be, you know. Chances are they'd feel like you and me right now – displaced persons. Where the hell's that bloody therapist?'

'He'll come. You can't hurry them.'

Joy forced a longing for a cigarette and some strong coffee to the back of her mind. There were signs forbidding the first on every wall, and the hot-drink-dispenser had been out of order for weeks. Today would be a turning-point in her life, had to be. She had watched this boy get himself ready for the trip across town for his therapy, had admired the precision, the method, the meticulous tidiness. Then, as he had adjusted the knife-edged crease of his shorts in a full-length mirror, she had seen herself standing behind him, a red-faced, sloppy, fat peroxide-blonde.

The relevation had disgusted her, and she had remained disgusted for the entire bus-ride. The cleanness of this child made her itch. A forest of new leaves would have to be turned if she were to rid herself of the itch and of the sour morning-after taste which coated the inside of her mouth. The children and young people with whom she worked called her 'the Blonde Bomb-Site'. It would not do. The hair of the woman who had looked back at her from the mirror had been dry and frizzy. Usually pulled back, and secured with an elastic band, it had broken free, so that every split-end competed to draw a veil over the woman's face, and hide the pockmarks, open pores and blackheads which grew in number with each passing year. The woman's check shirt and loose baggy trousers, bought and worn for comfort and ease of movement, might do well enough for gardening, but were not the thing for travelling across town by bus, holding the hand of an eight-year-old in razor-creased, bum-hugging shorts. Nor were the sandals appropriate. They were old and much loved, but did nothing to disguise the over-large feet, of which the toe-nails, once painted dark blue in a fit of high fashion, were now cracked and chipped like neglected pottery. The sandals had cost five ninety-five, and had been made in Taiwan. They deserved a decent burial. Changes must be made.

As always it was the therapist himself, a young man with thick spectacles and neatly parted hair, who came to collect the boy. As always he nodded in Joy's direction, but concentrated his smile and all the body-language of which his small frame was capable on the child. As always the boy expressed his own body-language by shrugging his shoulders, leaving the sofa, and moving without hurry or apparent interest out of the room and down the corridor. The therapist followed, and Joy waited to hear the sound of the door to the Therapy Room closing behind them before standing and making her own way down the corridor to mount five stairs and enter a different room.

The room she entered was dark, and remained dark. Each of the chairs in it had a flap attached to one arm. These flaps, when lowered, would support notepads for those who had mastered the ability to make notes in the dark. She sat, located a steel waste-paper bin with her feet, checked that it contained no waste paper, and lit a cigarette. If there were signs forbidding smoking, the darkness concealed them, and her addiction to tobacco was one leaf which would have to wait to be turned.

The room was a Viewing Room; the therapist had insisted on her using it. She could see through a panel of one-way glass down into the room next door, where the boy and the therapist now sat. Videos of therapy sessions below were sometimes made from this room to assist in the training of other therapists, but would not be made in this case. Sometimes the room was also used for the counselling of families. One counsellor would sit in the room below with the family, and other counsellors would sit in the Viewing Room, and would make helpful suggestions by means of the internal telephone. Usually the family concerned would know of their being there, and had agreed to be watched as they revealed, or refused to reveal, their thoughts. The eight-year-old boy did not know of Joy's presence, and would not know. If the rectangle of glass through which she watched were to attract his attention at all, it would cause him to wonder why a large picture of a cottage garden had been placed too high on the wall.

For the first five minutes of the session, the boy remained in his chair, leaning forwards, hugging his knees, and staring at the toe-caps of his trainers. A tray with his name on it, Daniel, had been brought from a cupboard and placed on the floor close to him. Upon it were crayons, Plasticine, paper, scissors, glue, miniature animals both wild and domestic, some of wood and some of plastic, and a set of tiny cloth dolls to make up a family. These remained untouched. The therapist talked, asking questions about what Daniel might have been doing at school or at the Home, but the boy's replies were non-verbal, a shrug of the shoulders, a shake of the head, all given in a tired world-weary way. Daniel's predecessor in the room had arranged a group of dolls, five of normal size, in a line, each doll with both arms resting on the doll in front like chorus-girls about to leave the stage. The therapist broke up the line of dolls. His reason for doing so was merely to break the pattern, so that Daniel might, if he wished, make a new one, but once he had begun to break the pattern, he realized that there was no way of leaving the dolls which would not suggest a pattern of his own. This embarrassed him, so he went to the sink to wash his hands. Daniel watched the rearrangement of the dolls and the retreat from them with interest, then joined the therapist at the sink, and asked for a drink of water. The cold tap was running hard and fast. The therapist gave Daniel a glass of water, and Daniel, once he had drunk it, placed his face into the stream running from the cold tap, and held it there for thirty seconds. Then he turned the tap off, and began to play.

What was in progress was a war. With a sudden and furious energy, Daniel marshalled his armies. Inanimate objects were given characters, morals and ranks, and other inanimate objects to use as ammunition. Within a very short time he had created a nightmarish fantasy-world, using the entire room from the sink to the interiors of cupboards. Windows and window-catches, chairs, tables, dolls, Plasticine, paper, scissors, bricks, toy animals, the therapist himself, even the chair on which the therapist now sat taking instructions, all were transformed and pressed into service.

Daniel himself changed characters like a chameleon, at one moment neutral, another a conqueror, another the victim of atrocious tortures. The therapist's attempts at interpretation persistently lagged behind events, since one skirmish followed another so quickly, forces changed sides in mid-battle, and Daniel's own movement about the room was so rapid. Moreover the therapist's own involvement in the war required considerable concentration, since he would be required to change from general to tea-lady with no more warning to prepare him for demotion than a tea-towel plonked on his head.

Central to all the action was a small group of Plasticine phalluses, which Daniel called 'little men' – daddy's little man, mummy's little man, Uncle Jeff's little man, and so on. Though different in colour and size, each had been shaped into an erect penis, upon which a circumcision ritual had been performed at the opening of hostilities. The ritual had been performed with solemnity and excitement, with much brandishing, flicking and jabbing with the top of a pencil, ritually sharpened. The members of the Plasticine family at war also warred amongst themselves. Periodically Daniel would dash from the battlefield to the interior of a cupboard containing non-toxic paints, there to shape and re-size one or another of the little men after heavy losses of both infantry and cavalry. It was at these moments of comparative quiet that the therapist would attempt his interpretations, but Daniel ignored them, maintaining a steady stream of military despatches which included the fact that his own little man was growing in size, while those of the rest of the family shrank.

'A zoo's been bombed, and the animals have escaped, There's a fire in the jungle, More animals surrounded by fire. Floods in Iceland coming south might put the fire out; don't know yet if they'll reach it in time. Scotland's under water. This drawer here is a fort. It holds sixteen million red-coats, they've no rations left, and they're just about to mutiny. They've just fired a general from a cannon. He's landed in the Arms Store; it's exploded. Twelve hundred injuries, twenty-four dead. No time to bury them; put them under this.' (A sheet of black paper.) 'Keep the flies off them for a day or two. What's happening up there, Captain?' (Promotion again for the therapist, who is not, however, given time to reply.) 'It's a space-ship of monsters. Look at it! It's huge. Ray-guns and de-sensitizers. Take cover!' Actions, sounds, noises, Daniel rushing around the room with outstretched arms, pretending to be a light aircraft with engine trouble.

Balls of Plasticine were thrown, and they stuck to the ceiling of the Therapy Room, limiting briefly the dimensions of Daniel's war. Noises were made to represent rifles, rocket-launchers, cannon, and even the uneasy buzzing of an injured fly which Daniel had permitted to escape the final atom-bomb by hiding in the stomach of a dead sheep. His own little man, doubling as a space-taxi, was hurled into orbit, but got no further than a large picture of a cottage garden, where it stuck for a short time before dropping to the floor.

Slowly the war wound down without conclusion. The remaining Plasticine little men were fused together into one multi-coloured lump and cast aside. The sheet of black paper was removed from the dead bodies, drawn upon, and then refolded into the black dove of peace. But the dove did not satisfy, and with a curse was turned into a flower from a graveyard, a lily.

Into the centre of the black lily Daniel placed a green crayon to represent the stamen.

In the slow melancholy ceremony which followed, the therapist was asked to accept the lily as a gift on behalf of all who had recently died. He hesitated, guessing at some of what might happen next. Then the eight-year-old boy began to undo the buttons of his own trousers, which fell to the floor. The black flower was in the therapist's hand. The boy removed the green crayon from it, held it to his nose, smelling the scent of the flower of death, then inserted it into his own anus.

Daniel now lay on the day-bed, his face to the wall, the lower half of him still naked, his trousers still where he had left them, the crayon still where he had placed it. Though asked many times to do so, the therapist refused to remove the crayon, suggesting that Daniel might prefer to remove it himself. Minutes passed. The therapist sat where he was in the chair, while Daniel continued to lie on the bed. Asked what he was thinking about, Daniel replied that he was thinking he would like the crayon removed.

'Aren't you cold?'

Daniel admitted that he was. The therapist took a blanket from the cupboard, and spread it over the boy's lower half. Daniel jumped up, grabbing for the front of the therapist's trousers, and causing him pain.

The therapist now discovered himself to be under attack from all sides. Daniel moved swiftly front and rear, grabbing, and the therapist had too few hands to keep the half-naked boy from investigating pockets, hair, waistband of trousers, fly-zip. The buttons of his shirt were ripped off, his buttocks clutched and squeezed, his underarms tickled, the back of his neck kissed, his trouser-legs rolled up, belly punched. Finally his spectacles were snatched, and Daniel danced away, waving them in the air, then stood precariously on the window-sill, waggling his naked bottom to the world outside, and making sucking noises with his mouth and lips towards the half-blind therapist, ignoring all protests and requests that he should be careful and return the spectacles.

As the therapist approached him, Daniel threw the spectacles onto the day-bed, then the boy's arms encircled the man's neck, the naked legs were clasped about his waist, and thus

66

the two bodies moved like ballroom dancers about the room in the general direction of the spectacles and the bed, while the boy pressed his face against the man's, and whispered that he would only behave when the man had removed the green crayon and replaced it with his own cock. 'Go on. I know you want to. No one will know.'

Joy had left the Viewing Room, and now stood in the corridor outside the Therapy Room, knocking on the door with the side of her fist so as to make as much noise as possible. After a longish wait, the door was opened slightly, and the grateful tearful face of the therapist blinked at her. 'Thank you.' Joy moved to the Waiting Room, to be ready when Daniel emerged. The interruption could have been made by a cleaner or someone else needing the room. In fifty minutes, she had smoked five cigarettes.

Sitting beside each other on the top deck of the bus going home, neither Social Worker nor child spoke to each other. The bus passed the end of Joy's own road; she could see the house if she craned her neck a little. She did so, and saw, as she had expected, a group of reporters stationed outside the house. Jean would be inside with the doors locked and curtains drawn, irritated equally by the entreaties through the letter-box and the drone of complaint from Michael, locked in with her.

The bus passed a cricket ground, then a reservoir with its waterworks, the canal, and another cemetery. Joy said, 'I think the whole of London must bury its dead on my doorstep. Not that I mind. It means I've got a choice of walks on summer evenings.' The boy lifted his right hand to his nose, pressing on the tip, and held it there with his elbow resting on the other hand. That thumb would have to be bathed in antiseptic the moment they arrived back at the Home. She wondered if the green crayon was still where he had put it, and if so, how it was to be removed.

For a year before arriving at the Home, Daniel had been inserting pencils, wooden bricks, Lego and even an asthmatic's inhaler into his bottom. He had attempted to do the same for his younger sister and several other small children. His parents had been unable to control either him or his rages. Punishment only made him more secretive, and body-searches before and after each of his visits to the bathroom had always revealed that something had been inserted into his anus, and that he was walking around with it still there. At school he hung around the toilets, annoying other boys, and had once, under some heavy-handed questioning, accused an older boy of buggery. In class Daniel had no concentration, and alternated between baby-talk and a knowing sophistication to gain attention, asking the teachers embarrassing questions about their private lives, and latching onto long words which he would repeat endlessly. At other times he would sit staring at his hands, or sniffing his fingers, and if aroused from such a state, he would fly into a rage, and have to be sat on by an adult until calm. Six months earlier he had been the subject of legal proceedings, when he admitted to having inserted the handle of a baby's rattle into the behind of its owner, aged fifteen months, who had been left outside a shop in a pram. Shortly afterwards Daniel's mother had been admitted into hospital to receive treatment for a nervous breakdown, and Daniel's father had asked for his son to be taken into Care, saying that he feared he might lose control and injure the boy permanently.

'How are you going to find out?'

'What?'

'As much as you can about me. So I can feel I can trust you, and come to you with my problems.'

The boy looked directly at Joy, then stared out of the window. He must know that she would have seen his file. Children always knew about files, and most of what was in them.

'I'm hoping you'll tell me when you feel ready to.'

'Don't they have files on kids like me?'

Joy slipped an arm over the boy's shoulder, and gave him a hug. 'Nobody's like you, Danny Boy; you're very special. One day we'll take out your folder, and have a look at it together, eh?' The boy made no response.

He would have to be watched, day and night. There were older boys in the Home who would be more than happy to play 'Find the Crayon' with him. Like so many others he was in the wrong place, but where was the right place for someone like Danny?

She had been in the job too long, been in the same place too long, standing still. She had watched frightened children arrive for what they had thought would be a six months' stay, and six years later they were still there, still frightened, but now of leaving, their only prospects being a shared room at a Barnardo's hostel, an early marriage with a pregnancy to get them on the Housing List, and a life thereafter on Social Security. She had watched them walk backwards and forwards over the same patch of grass, growing taller but seldom growing up. Some had changed the colour of their hair many times in attempts to find out who they were, an indulgence unheard of until television advertising suggested it, but even with tri-coloured heads they still lacked identity, When not pacing like prisoners taking exercise, they would stand in groups for safety, hands in pockets, heads lowered, nodding sagely like delicate bedding-plants caught in a breeze. When they stood alone, it was often for self-punishment, and they would watch a punc-tured ball being kicked about, and claim that they knew how the ball felt. Dogs had punctured those balls, dogs belonging to Joy's colleagues, who had been working at the Home for longer than she, and actually lived on the premises. Many of the children had known these dogs as puppies, and had watched them grow into canine geriatrics who fouled the grass on which they themselves were expected to exercise and build their characters.

The children were 'in Care', a holding operation which would usually last for the rest of their childhood. Lately some-one had coined a spanking new term to make everyone feel better, since 'Care' had with the passage of years grown a little shabby. This was 'in Trust'; they were children and young persons in Trust. Joy imagined them in rows like oven-ready chickens, plucked, trussed and stuffed, with the tasty bits re-moved to be handed over separately in plastic bags. 'In Trust'! It was a new name for a very old condition. What these chil-dren really were in was the shit.

There were ugly children, beautiful children like the one now sitting beside her, plain children, overweight boys who had prostituted themselves in the toilets of railway stations and underweight girls who had done the same in the backs of cars, or had merely been used as the in-house resident prostitute in an extended family. There were children who had grown too wise ever to be children again, in Trust or out of it. Sometimes, after a telephone call from a parent, step-parent or foster-parent, who professed love and a longing to have them home again, the children would 'do a runner', and have to be collected from a Police Station next day, since the professed parental feelings seldom lasted longer than the telephone call itself, and a further call would be made the moment that the loved one had been seen ringing the front-door bell.

They had odd notions of what children not in Trust were like. They feared boredom more than pain, cold, rape or hunger, yet suffered it persistently. Some were mentally ill to degrees not certifiable; some of them merely mirrored the behaviour of the Residential Care Workers amongst whom they lived. They would tell Joy themselves that their only two uses were to give work to Social Workers who might otherwise add to the unemployment figures, and to introduce the magistrates of Juvenile Courts to what most of them seemed to have missed out on, the real world.

'Here we are!' Theirs was the next stop. 'I want to bathe that thumb when we get in, and if you're very good I might just rub a wet chammy over the rest of you while I'm at it.' Joy began her progress to the back of the bus in order to allow time for the tricky manoeuvre of descending the stairs while the bus was in motion. When she turned, Daniel had thrown something through an open window. The something bounced off the head of a cyclist, and rolled under the wheels of a car.

Daniel came down the aisle to join her.

'Now, what was that?'

'Just a crayon.'

She had spent hours looking from an upstairs window, always through a net curtain and standing as far back as would yet allow her to see out. Sometimes an optimistic photographer would point his camera towards the net curtain, and fire his flash-gun. Whenever this happened, Jean put a hand over her face.

She had watched the two dusty flowerbeds in the pocket-handkerchief of a garden opposite being turned and re-turned

by a trowel specially bought for the occasion. The woman
wielding it had been interviewed at least five times, and had
been photographed against her garden gate. Jean had never
spoken to this woman, but the woman had chatted at length
to her interviewers, had nodded gravely and authoritatively
and had used the trowel to point out Jean's car, Jean's bedroom window, and, if one might speculate from the direction
of her generous gestures, a number of local places of interest,
such as Brockley Cemetery and the quaint old shop in Lady-
well Road where the best pie-and-mash in the locality was to
be found. This woman had changed her dress five times the
day before, and in the evening had put the trowel away, placed
a cushion on her front step, and sat on it sipping orange juice
until sundown.

They had shouted up at the window and through the letter-
box. 'We just want to find out something about your background.' 'Where do your parents live, Jean?' 'You're not a
Londoner, are you?' They had come in all shapes and sizes,
and every colour it was possible for human skin to be, though
white males preponderated. There was one of them who
looked Chinese, a punk photographer with blue hair, and an
enormously fat man wearing a pinstriped suit with white plimsolls. Their voices, as they chatted to each other about where
they had found lunch and how severe their hangovers were,
drifted up to her; their accents ranged from Lewisham to the
Gorbals, and there was one woman in a Paisley turban whose
silver spoon seemed to have lodged sideways across her soft
palate, causing her to speak in loud gushes, and gulp for air.

'What are your politics, Jean, just for the record?' 'What's
your favourite food? TV programme? How much do you earn?'
'Do you have a police record? Would you describe yourself as
militant?'

They were at every downstairs window, and at every door.
She could not use the kitchen, and relied on Joy to bring in
cold food. 'Did you yourself have a happy childhood?' 'What
made you specialize in Child Abuse?' 'Have you had any personal experience of being abused?' 'What's your own father
like? Is he still alive?' One of them had explained that what
they were offering her, out of the goodness of their hearts and
a desire to ensure fair reporting, was a chance to tell her side

71

of the story. Another had begun with, 'I hope you're going to be very careful how you handle the other boys, Jean, because what they seem most interested in is to start a witch-hunt.' Of course, such remarks are likely to sound more tacky when spoken through a letterbox.

'Why did you never marry, Jean?' 'Are you gay, Jean?' 'Did you have a close relationship with the Gaines family? Which particular child did you get on best with?' 'This house is owned by a charity, isn't it? Have they threatened you with eviction? Are they supporting you through all this?'

'No statement', 'No comment', 'Nothing to say'! These were phrases she had heard on the television News or Channel Four's *4 What It's Worth*, which investigated abuses of another kind, such as the selling of non-existent houses in Spain to old-age pensioners or damp-proofing which left houses damper than they had been before. Sometimes she had felt sorry for those investigated, at other times been made angry by them. She had watched them trying to cover their faces with their hands, hold newspapers over their heads, turn their backs on the camera and run, while short fat highly paid persons with video-cameras had pursued them. She had seen cameramen filmed by other cameramen, close-ups of pavements and running feet, rooftops and pigeons taking to flight, sudden bobbing microphones appear from nowhere. She had heard shouted swear-words, bleeped out by studio technicians, doors shut in the face of the investigator, studio presenters' reassurances that the matter would not be allowed to drop. Jean had never harmed a consumer in her life. Why should she now be pursued?

'Did I get this wrong, or did I hear somewhere that you yourself were in care for a while?' 'Where's your mother now, Jean? Will the news of this upset her? Being as she's quite elderly, might it not make her ill, don't you think?' 'Are you very close to your mother, Jean?'

At first she had left the telephone off the hook, but British Telecom, who would usually have taken days to answer a call for assistance, began immediately to send bleeping noises down the line. Next morning at eight thirty, a van with two telephone engineers arrived, saying that the switchboard had been jammed with complaints that her telephone was out of order. She had asked if she might change the number and go ex-directory, but was told that such desperate measures take a deal of time. 'What people do nowadays is to get themselves an Answering Machine, and just ignore it till they feel strong enough. Then they sit down with a stiff drink, and play back all the loonies who never bother to listen to the message. Some of them go on for hours giving you an order for Chinese Take-away, or complaining because their stretch-covers haven't arrived. Answering Machines seem to attract wrong numbers. The lonely like them too; it's halfway to having a real conversation. Best thing in your position would be to have it on the short-tape mode, where they just get enough time to leave their name and number.'

As it happened, they did have just such a machine in the van. Its name was Robin, It was not the best or the cheapest, but as Jean was in a pickle, it could be the answer. The senior of the two engineers recorded a short message, and Robin was placed by the telephone in the hall, where he began to click, buzz, whirl, re-wind and flash his lights almost as soon as he was switched on.

Unfortunately there was no machine which could silence the shouted questions or take messages from the newspersons who continued to clutter the street outside the house. Joy fought her way through them whenever she left for work, sometimes taking a handful with her to the Home, where they hung about questioning the children. Did they know if Joy was lesbian? Had they ever met Joy's friend, Jean?

More worrying was to watch Tony accept money from the newspeople. Later he reported that they had asked whether Jean drank wine or ate chocolates, not to accuse her in print of such vices but to discover whether she could be softened up by gifts. Three bunches of flowers were placed on the doorstep, and quickly wilted in the heat. Tony improved in appearance, by shaving every day and bathing twice a week, but deteriorated in character. 'Shall I go out there again, and tell them to bugger off? I only got two miserly fivers out of them last time. Why do we have to have the curtains closed all day? It's like a morgue in here.' A photograph of Tony leaving the house had appeared in several of the tabloids. 'Child Murder Case-Worker Silent', 'Child Sex Murder. Social-Worker Barricaded in House.' 'A close friend of child-abuse Social Worker, Miss Jean Davis (46), said last night that she was unavailable for comment.' Tony had said that she was planning to watch television and wash her hair, but this had been freely translated by the reporter into a statement that Jean had been suspended and a suggestion that her silence could only be construed as an admission of guilt. The question which the reporter's tabloid was fearlessly and frankly asking was what this Social Worker had done to cause the rape and murder of yet another child and the abduction of that child's brother and sister, and it demanded an answer.

The van of Rosario, the icecream vendor, could be seen across the road, manoeuvring around the newspersons. Icecream had seldom interested Jean; now she discovered her mouth watering. Tony would get her one if she asked, but would take so long that it was unlikely that there would be much icecream left when it reached her. She imagined the van's slow progress along Sharadoe Road, heavier now with the weight of the coins contributed to Rosario's profits by newspersons, who, she observed, were great eaters of icecream. The van would pass the church of Saint Mary Magdalen and the Turf Accountant's with its cinammon-coloured brickwork. It would pass the Anglo-Irish Food Store, Britannia Antiques, the Koo Fong Takeaway, the Mysore Curry House and the Pulcinella Pizza Parlour. It would pause outside Saint Cyprian's Social and Bingo Club, so that the children of the tower-block Housing Estate could come running down the stairs of Holly House, Cypress House, Laurel, Acacia and Juniper, the lifts being out of order. Gentrification was taking its time to reach this part of London. Battalions of stripped pine had moved south of the river to Wandsworth, then east, skirting round those parts of Clapham and Balham which refused them entry, pushing out towards advance-posts already established in Camberwell and Peckham, soon to join up with the battalions moving west from Dulwich, Greenwich and Blackheath, Eltham already penetrated and only Deptford standing out against them with a counter-force of cut price furniture, dressed up for battle in inflammable plastic foam. But so far only a very few Victorian wash-hand-stands were to be seen on sentry duty in the shops of Malpas Road.

Were they really called that? Wash-hand-stands, for the washing of hands after standing on them. Jean had learned at school to do that. She had placed her hands on the asphalt of the playground, and had thrown her legs up and back, to set her feet against the grey stonework of the Primary School wall. Rosario would be almost at Deptford by now, parked by the church with the neon sign, 'Christ Died That We Might Live and to His Glory.' Michael was sitting on the floor behind her, working on a giant jigsaw. He had accepted that the presence of the newspersons outside meant that Jean would not go out and leave him alone, so he had ceased to complain. Was standing at this window, looking down on a crowd of reporters, anything to do with what Christ had in mind? 'We want to get to know you, Jean, but you're making it difficult for yourself. You have to believe us; we're on your side.'

What she had seen while standing on her hands was a world which was upside-down.

'Hello, Jean! My name is Colin.' They were in the kitchen, the time was not yet five am, and she had not slept. There was a round chubby face, with a dark brown moustache, twinkling at her. The man was a dwarf, couldn't be more than four foot eight. 'I'm here to tell your story for you.' His accent was Welsh. Jean knew the Welsh to be a devious lot, but materializing through a back door bolted in three places must be exceptional.

'How did you get in?'

'The clue is one you may have noticed. I'm not very big for my size, see?' He pointed to a window the size of a breadboard. The glass had been expertly cut out of the frame.

'You're trespassing.'

'Yes, I know. I'm not usually the criminal type, but I thought you needed someone on your side.'

'No, thanks.' Why did they never come up with anything new?

'I'd do the same in your shoes, you know, try to hold out for Jean Rook or Bernard Levin, but I happen to be here on Special Offer, thrown in, you might say. Also I'm more user-friendly. Any chance of a glass of water? I've been hiding in the cupboard under the sink all night, didn't dare turn a tap on in case you heard the cistern going.' Jean turned on the cold-water tap, and the man placed first his mouth into the flow of water, and then his right hand, where Jean saw a cut around which the blood had dried. 'Used to do that for a living, replacement windows. A bit out of practice at the moment. Not got a drop of TCP, have you? This is the hand with which I'm hoping to take down your particulars.'

Jean pointed to the First-Aid Box. It was out of his reach, so she handed it to him. 'How long did you say you'd been here? Just so that I can get my facts right for the police.'

'Took me about half an hour, working very slow, see? That would have been about two pound forty-five, less stoppages, where I used to work. Got into the cupboard about 0200 hours. Desperate situations require desperate remedies. Replacement windows have fallen in, see, in the last few years. I'm for the dole-heap, if I don't make something out of this assignment.' Jean looked away. 'Thought my lot was up, when you turned out to be publicity-shy.'

'You knew I was what you call "publicity-shy" before you broke in, Mr . . . er . . .'

'Col or Colin, Tubby or Titch, anything so long as it's not Taf or Taffy. I was supposed to have elocution lessons, but my mam couldn't raise the four and sixpence a week.' Jean filled the kettle and placed it on the stove. The Welshman took this as a sign of hospitality and raised himself onto a kitchen stool. 'I took a gamble with the window, see? Gambling's easy when you've not a lot to lose. Thought to myself, "If I get in without a burglar-alarm going off, or shredding my arm into oven-ready chips, she won't rush to call the police. They won't be her favourite people; they haven't bothered to keep the crowds from her door. What must it be like, surrounded by us lot? She and I can have a quiet little chat, then I'll mend the window myself, won't even charge her."' He was twinkling with good intentions like a Garden Gnome, or perhaps a hobbit. 'Behind every front door there's a tragedy, just waiting to be let out. That was in the brochure for the Correspondence Course I took in Journalism. Did it every evening after work; kept me out of the pubs for a while. Since turning pro, I've seen the inside of more pubs than I ever did in Penarth. And then I was abused as a child myself, see, so there's the special interest; that's how I come to have this assignment.' He had thrown in the last remark as if still discussing his consumption of alcohol. Did he really think that Jean could be so stupid as to believe that any News Editor would know so much about the private lives of his junior reporters? It was the current cant, of course, the received idea of the Eighties, that everyone had been abused as a child.

'How abused?'

'How? You mean, how badly?'

'I mean what form did the abuse take.'

'You want details?'

'I'm a Social Worker.'

She waited, watching him. He lowered his head, and moved it slowly from side to side. Finally he said, 'I find it very difficult to describe. Very painful. I never talk about it.'

Jean put down her mug of coffee, and moved decisively to unbolt the door. 'Quite right. Neither do I. One shouldn't mix business with pleasure. You'll excuse me if I rush you, but a trained person should look at that hand. There's an excellent Casualty Department at the Hither Green Hospital. Did you leave a lot of blood in my cupboard? Will Flash shift it, do you think, or should I use something biological?'

The little Welshman slid his bottom slowly from the high stool until his feet touched the floor, and stood where he was, trying to look like an orphan about to be cast out into snow. 'All I need to save my job is one line, one little quote that nobody else has. Believe me, I know what you feel like; I've landed myself in a shitty profession. Just something, some small thing, about the boy who was murdered. Or his father. Anything, anything at all you can offer me. I'm being honest when I say there's a lot at stake for me. A small man shouldn't have to hide in cupboards. Big men could afford that loss of dignity. Please. If you can think of something.'

Jean closed the back door, and replaced one bolt. It was now five thirty. A trickle of reporters was usually getting into position by six thirty or seven. The Welshman said, 'Or perhaps something about you? How you feel right now.'

'What I feel is irrelevant.'

'That's your mistake. By avoiding the Press, you've got the

public more and more interested. They see pictures of the outside of the house, and know you're inside. Some of them identify. "How would I feel if something had gone wrong in my job, and suddenly there I was, unable to get out to the shops or visit the dentist?" That's what they're all asking. It's the Greta Garbo thing all over again. You've done the opposite of what you intended. They long to know what sort of person you are.'

'I had the impression they'd already made up their minds that I was their latest Aunt Sally.'

'How do you feel about that?'

'I've decided not to accept the part. It lacks subtlety. All I want is to get back to work and my clients.'

'How many times have you been physically attacked by clients?'

'Quite a few.'

'Can you give me details?'

'No. That's something else Social Workers don't talk about very much, not even to each other. The moment you try to describe something like that, or worse still write it down, it changes its nature. Newspapers and television don't know how to report Social Work. How can they possibly cope with all those grey areas? News works best in black and white.'

They talked, which is to say that she talked and he listened; it was the reverse of the conversations with Steven Gaines. A tape-recorder the size of a wallet was taken from his pocket, and shown to her, and she accepted that anything she said would be used or unused, for or against her, cut, edited, taken out of context, misquoted or misunderstood. The little Welshman was no bigger than a large child, and it was part of Jean's job to comfort children.

Murdered Child's Social Worker Breaks Silence.

When he had gone, Jean knew that she must go. It was impossible to remain in the house, and unwise; she had unbuttoned her lip, and would find it difficult to button it up again, and keep it buttoned. 'Send us a postcard,' the Identikit faces had said. 'Wish I could drop everything right now.' She must get away; she was on paid holiday, and expected by her

78

Department to do so; they had said she must rest, and she could not rest while under siege. Of course the police would not like her going, but she was not under house-arrest. They had not positively told her not to go, presumably because they had not imagined that she would go. Jean was not to be blamed for a failure of imagination in the police. She would go, and she would not tell anyone where she was going, because if the reporters knew where, they would follow her, and if the police knew where, they would also follow her.

There would be a problem with Michael. Joy could not handle both Michael and Tony on her own; Jean would have to take him with her. How? Getting Michael into her car and keeping him there would be a major obstacle to flight, particularly as the only safe time to leave would be at dead of night when the road outside was clear.

'Getting him out of the house is only the start of it,' Joy said. 'Wherever you take him, you're going to have to share a room; he's not going to sleep on his own in a strange hotel. Then there's the hand-holding. The sooner you wean him off that the better. He's a bit long in the tooth to be carried into the Ladies with you every time you're caught short in public. I wish I could be there to see it – you wetting your knickers, and him clinging on to you while a crowd gathers. Perhaps you could take some of those bags incontinent people use.'

Well, there would be problems, but she must deal with them; problems existed to be solved. Joy said, 'You've got to take him. We're in full agreement about that, because if you sneak off and leave him with me, I'll book myself into a YWCA for the duration. So, if you're set on going, make passionate love to the little bugger tonight, and drain him of his juices, so that he sleeps all the way to Scarborough, or wherever it is.'

'It's not Thursday.'

'Tell him it is. It can be Thursday whenever you say so; that's the meaning of love. And after you've done the deed, pop a few tranquillizers into his mouth as a fail-safe. I'll pack his case while he's out of his room, and help you get him downstairs and into the car. It's the only way.'

Perhaps it was not the only way, but it was a way, and might work. Scarborough! Odd that Joy had mentioned Scarborough. She had no idea where Jean intended to go, and had not wished to be told, since she might be tempted to sell the information, she said, to *The Daily Arse-Wipe*, though she trusted that Jean would telephone from time to time without giving away where she was phoning from. If Joy didn't have half a dozen adolescent nymphos of her own to look after, she'd come along as well for the ride, leaving Tony to live it up in style at the expense of the media. And Jean said that she herself had no idea where she intended to go; what was important was just to get away. This was only partly the truth because, during the day, she had begun to know, if not where she was going, then at least why, and the why would decide the where.

Scarborough! It had always been the same Caravan Site at the same seaside town. Steven Gaines' father had lived in the north. The family had been poor; they would not have travelled far for their annual holiday by the sea. North-east or north-west, it must be north. How many Caravan sites with a twenty-year history of poverty were there on those two stretches of coast? Jean did not know, and was not sure how to find out, but she knew that, unpursued by police or Press, she intended to find Steven Gaines, and to receive back from him, whether willingly or unwillingly given, his daughter Marianne. Jean's job was Child Care; there was a reason for that. She intended, paid leave or no, to do her job.

PART TWO

Past Imperfect

ONE

There's a river at Bedford, the Ouse, with walkways on either side under horse-chestnut trees. Near it there is, or was, a Boating Lake for children, with paddle-boats, all of different colours like shrunken Mississippi steam-boats, except that the paddles were worked, not by steam, but by the active legs of children, who assisted their legs with flailing arms. I do remember someone actually shouting, 'Come in, Number Seven. Your time is up.'

In the old days, grown-ups used to take punts out on the river, moor them to the exposed roots of a tree growing at the edge of a small island, and picnic there. I used to consider this the posher part of town. Swans and ducks would waddle up for bread. That, for a child, was like living in perpetual summer. The ducks and swans are there still, but now they share their nests with plastic cartons from McDonald's and empty cans of Stella Artois. I'm not sure about the Boating Lake, because I haven't looked. I don't want to discover that it has been filled in to make the foundations for a block of high-rise offices.

The Bus Station once had a Waiting Room like those found on the stations of branch-line railways, cream and green walls with old wooden benches and plenty of graffiti, the kind of Waiting Room which gets steamed up if more than three passengers try to use it at a time. I spent many hours in that Waiting Room, though I seldom caught a bus, and now remember it mostly in the rain and at dusk when all the lights came on outside, blurred reflected coloured lights from the spilt oil in the puddles of rain on the tarmac, blurred reflected light from the shiny uniforms of the drivers and conductresses, all of whom seemed to chain-smoke Capstan Full Strength. They'd take your money, punch your ticket, and hand it to you covered in ash which had dropped from the fag dangling at the corner of the mouth, and when they spoke of the rain, they pronounced it as though it were the name of a river in Germany, 'It *do Rhine, don't it?'* Smells of fish and chips mixed with the smell of petrol. Or would it have been diesel, even then?

The new Bus Station is mostly glass, and seems ten times bigger. When I visited, the Waiting Room was empty, except for myself and one other woman, younger than I, but by no means young. She was tall, and carried her handbag in an ungainly way over one arm. Her skirt, blouse and head-band were all in pink. I wondered if she were on the game, and waiting for a customer, or whether she had merely been stood up. A Sunday afternoon wouldn't have been the best time for trade, and was certainly a time when men who have made promises find they are forced to break them, incapacitated as they are by lunchtime drinking.

John Bunyan still stands on his plinth, clutching his book, and directing newly arrived pilgrims to the nearest cinema. He is the town's main claim to fame, and the old jail is much as he left it. I made my bob to him that Sunday afternoon, and went to the Market Square, close to the main bridge over the river. That was empty also; it was a fairly empty afternoon in Bedford. I stood in the centre of the Square, imagining a Saturday morning in the late nineteen forties, the Square chock-a-block with stalls and shoppers. The stall-holders would be shouting – 'Caulis, lovely caulis! Look at this for a pair of knockers!' or the very latest nylon stockings, their heels decorated with black arrows, hearts, ivy, cobwebs, even spiders, 'How about a pair of these to crawl up the back of them shapely legs, me dear?', or someone would hold a full tea-set high in the air above his head with one hand, and thump his stall with the other, pretending to stagger, rattling the rest of his stock and causing old women to squeal with delight.

Between the ages of six and eleven, I used to be taken to visit Bedford once a fortnight. This was the period during which I was being fucked four times a week by the man who might or might not have been my father. This same man, on these fortnightly visits, would buy me as consolation prizes small objects I neither wanted nor needed. I supposed even then that these gifts were part bribery, part conscience-money, and as time passed I began to help him to choose the gifts, telling him what I'd like.

Usually he'd wait until my mother had gone off to buy something, then he'd take me by the hand, and guide me towards the colouring-book or ribbon. Sometimes he'd tell me that the gift must be hidden from my mother (as if I needed telling); he had very little money, certainly none for presents. He would crouch down beside me, his face alight with pleasure, explaining that the hair-ribbon or brooch was because he wanted me to look pretty, when I would happily have settled for looking

84

as unattractive as possible, desperately wishing I had been born a boy. I didn't know then that being a boy might not have saved me from his attentions.

The presents which were supposed to be kept secret somehow never were. I can remember at least two public slanging-matches. One was in the middle of Woolworth's, and I managed to edge away, to be hidden behind a counter by a friendly salesgirl until the shouting stopped. The other happened very suddenly in the Market Square, and was caused by my mother's wish for a new pair of stockings, and discovery that there was not enough money to pay for them. The stall-holders fell silent as this new voice shouted, not about the quality and cheapness of vegetables, but about the cheapness and lack of quality of the man at her side. Again I looked for somewhere to hide, expecting that at any moment the accusations would include a description of what was happening at home, but the shoppers had formed a circle around us, and put down their bags to listen, folding their arms and leaning against the stalls as if they were at a show. Several stall-holders stood on boxes to get a view. My own view of my mother's angry red face shouting, of her finger pointed at me, naming me as the reason she was forced to wear cardboard in her shoes and gravy-browning on her legs instead of stockings in all weathers, and as the reason why she couldn't buy meat from the butcher because she already owed him too much money, was a view I'd gladly have exchanged.

The row ended in anti-climax. My mother, having run out of names and of examples of poverty, slapped the face of the man who may have been my father, and pushed her way through the crowd to catch an earlier bus home, and I led him to the Boating Lake, where he sat for twenty minutes watching me in one of the paddle-boats.

On the way home, he laid his raincoat across both our laps, placed his hand between my legs, and felt and squeezed me until he had worked my knickers loose enough to place two of his fingers inside me, while I looked away out of the window at the Bedfordshire countryside rolling by. There were passengers standing in the aisle. The bus-conductress leaned over, squinting sideways at me, with a spiral of smoke from her cigarette making her eyes water, and a long worm of ash threatening to drop onto the raincoat which covered both our laps, and asked in a hoarse throaty whisper, 'Whose little girl are you, then? You look like Daddy's little girl to me.'

Such was the conspiracy of adults! I was convinced that people knew what was being done to me, but simply chose not to speak of it. I *couldn't look at them, was incapable of meeting their eyes, was constantly on the verge of tears but always biting them back, since the consequences of such a display were unpredictable. It was like walking around with my head in a storm-cloud, a cloud that moved with me, keeping my thoughts separate from my body, since my thoughts were my own and must remain so, while my body belonged to him. A crook of his little finger, and I would have to go to him. If he told me to go upstairs and wait for him, I knew what to expect, and he would take his time before following. 'Undress!' I would do so, and he would watch me. 'Bend over!' I would bend. 'Part your legs wider!' I would part my legs.*

The bus terminated its run in the middle of our village, but we lived in the woods, a distance of four and a half miles. If there were just the two of us walking that distance, he would lead me behind a hedge for what he called 'a rest'. He never asked me if I minded. What he said was that we were 'showing her' – 'her' being my mother. It was a phrase he used hundreds of times during those years. I had no idea how he knew of my own need to 'show' my mother, but he did know, and knew that this need matched his own. Neither of us ever thought of any different way in which we might 'show her', but from the time I was six until the time I left home, aged eleven, the compulsion to do so never diminished.'

She had been very small when she first began to wonder why they had come to live in the middle of a wood, when she realized that there were farm labourers' cottages nearer civilization. Later she would guess that he had chosen the middle of a wood in an attempt to keep her mother away from other men, yet he must have known that, once the wheel had been invented, this was a vain hope.

Each morning her mother would wait for him to go off to work. Then Jean would hear her mother counting slowly to a hundred under her breath, would watch her pretend to busy herself while doing nothing in particular. 'Fifty-four, fifty-five, fifty-six!' Her mother would walk a little way in the direction he had gone, just to make sure that the coast was clear. 'Seventy-two, seventy-three, seventy-four!' She would turn on her heels and walk back. 'Eighty-nine, ninety.' A last look after him. 'Ninety-seven, ninety-eight!' She would run hell for leather towards the push-bike hidden under a hawthorn bush.

It was an old bone-shaker, what used to be called a 'Sit Up and Beg'. And daughter would watch mother pedalling away from her along the cart-track, and would turn and go back into the house she had been instructed not to leave, there to wait as Snow White waited for the return of the Seven Dwarves. Six-year-old Jean had believed that her mother's bicycle trips were necessary to fetch tea and bread from the village shop. Eleven-year-old Jean had known for some years that what drew her mother like a moth to a flame was the Prisoner of War Camp in the opposite direction.

Wood End Cottage, one room upstairs, one room downstairs, and miles from anywhere; the roof was made of rusty sheets of corrugated iron. It was a glorified barn, plonked down in the middle of nowhere, freezing in winter and suffocating in summer. The wooden outside toilet contained a bucket, the contents of which had to be emptied and dug into the ground. The only running water ran from a pump, also outside. The amber-coloured liquid squeezed from it had to be boiled before being drunk, and in winter, when it froze, snow would be melted for washing and drinking.

Most of the glass had disappeared from the rotted window-frames of the cottage, and had been replaced with sheets of cardboard or squares of old raincoats fixed with drawing-pins. In the upper room, Jean's parents slept in an iron bedstead, and Jean herself on a small horse-hair mattress on the floor, with one blanket and a collection of coats to cover her in winter. ('*The two boys had slept on single beds on one side of the attic room, Marianne Gaines on a mattress laid out on the floor at the other side ... Yes, that was the mattress on which Jean Davis, Social Worker, had first interviewed the possibly abused child, Marianne Gaines.*')

Sometimes when Jean attended the Primary School in the village, dried soapflakes would be stuck to her skin to conceal the flea-bites. She assumed that her mother must have shown her what to do with the soapflakes, but could not remember her mother's ever touching her once she had learned to dress herself. Whatever had happened between mother and daughter during the pregnant nine months when one had carried the other inside her, had not made for a lasting friendship. Small daughter watched mother a great deal, as though waiting for something, but unsure of what, sensing that this watchfulness was an embarrassment to both of them, but unable to stop, since she was fascinated by everything the larger woman did. The more Jean was ignored, the more fascinated she became; the less interest her mother showed in her, the more she watched and waited, determined to be with her mother in case this unknown something should suddenly happen.

Much later, asked to describe her mother, Jean would say that she never thought of herself and the two people with whom she spent her early life as being 'real people', but merely as indifferent actors pretending to be a family. The expression being then fashionable, she would say that her mother was 'out to lunch', not really in touch, not really there, that she would have been just as effective maternally if she had been stuffed and mounted. Of course she was both mounted and stuffed several times by assorted POWs, but that was probably her only way of proving to herself that she existed.

Jean would remember that her mother's hair and skin were always a little greasy, but would explain that it was not easy to keep clean when one had to heat water in a kettle to wash. She would say that her mother was neither plain nor pretty, but had a good figure, that she liked to feel the sun on her skin, and would in summer spend much time sitting outside naked to the waist, while her daughter watched from the window; that the insects devoured Jean the moment she stepped out of doors but left her mother alone was another cause for resentment. Jean's mother wore blouses with straps instead of sleeves, because she had good shoulders, and it annoyed her to have to put on a bra to ride to the village, but in those days the Post Office would have been barricaded and troops sent in, if Jean's mother had ridden her bicycle to get bread with her breasts swinging free. The local people privately called Jean's mother 'The Village Bike', on which everyone got to ride.

Jean had no way of knowing whether the man who lived with them was her father; the man himself may not have known. He was a tall man, over six feet, strong, weather-beaten as one would expect, never with a proper beard but always the makings of one, smelling of tobacco, wood-smoke, pigs and occasionally alcohol, which would have been home-brewed beer from the farm where he worked, there never being the money in that family for anything grander. Though he called himself a gamekeeper, he was a farm-labourer, who fed and mucked out the stock. The pheasants and foxes were also his responsibility, so he allowed himself the more interesting job-description. Not that he kept or conserved very much, though the skins of animals would be hung to dry outside the cottage. Jean never discovered what he did with these, or how he had managed to miss the war, whether it was because of his job, or because one of his legs was shorter than the other. He didn't have much of a limp, except when he chose to put one on for effect.

As for the Prisoner of War Camp, it was no longer used as such, but housed cheap Italian labour, together with a number of displaced persons – Poles, Ukrainians, and even Yugoslavs – who seemed to have nowhere else to live. Since the routine of the Camp, with its roll calls and work-parties, was very similar to what it had always been, the villagers continued to think and speak of its inmates as POWs, particularly since many of the Italians had actually been POWs, some of them at that very Camp. All the inmates were male, all bachelors. Even the married Italians were bachelors, since their conditions of employment did not allow them to bring their wives with them.

The First Time
One day in 1947, the year after the last true POW had been repatriated, when Jean was six, she was left alone in the house at Wood End. She had been left alone before, of course, but most of the period before this particular day has been blocked out from her memory.

It was one of those overcast days, the sort of day on which small children become convinced that the world is about to end before they have grown tall enough to be let in to the cinema on their own, a hot sticky day with motionless dark clouds curled up like dragons waiting to breathe fire. There was thunder too, but that was in the distance at first. She knew that lightning without rain was dangerous, had heard someone say that a roof of corrugated iron would attract it, and that if it didn't fry the lichen and set the house on fire, it would strike a tree close by, which would fall on the house, crushing it.

There always seemed to be dead or dying flies on the window-sill. She hated the sound they made when they had fallen on their backs, and couldn't right themselves. It reminded her of the noises her mother's bed made. It was always called that; her mother would say 'my bed', and the man would refer to it as 'your mother's bed' as though he were a lodger. The sound the flies made as they battered themselves against the cardboard of the window was like that of the bed-springs going up and down. Not that they were springs exactly, but wires bent into a diamond trellis and stretched across the iron frame.

She hated insects which could fly; they seemed to have an unfair advantage over her. Nobody had invited them into the house, yet they made such a fuss about trying to leave it. She would see them in the mornings as she watched her mother leave, millions of them gathering under the trees, preparing to enter a cottage which they would only die in trying to get out of again. She imagined that some day under those same trees she would stumble across the remains of picnickers whose meal had gone on too long, and who had become the prey of these creatures, a group of seated skeletons, their flesh picked clean by flying ants, wasps using the empty Thermos flasks as echo-chambers to attract other wasps, bluebottles sunning themselves inside plastic tea-cups still held aloft, midges crash-landing on the bones of little fingers still extended in the direction of Buckinghamshire. She hated flying insects.

She would be without food until her mother returned, and possibly even then, since her mother's performances as a bad actress trying to remember lines and moves often included a scene of distress and self-reproach at having forgotten to buy food. Her mother had threatened that, if Jean wandered into the wood, she would get lost there forever, that she would starve to death slowly and painfully, her cries for help getting weaker and going unheard, until finally she would only be able to cry inwardly, would cry for the merciful release of death. Her mother had managed to give even this gruesome warning a fine romantic sound.

Even inside the cottage there was an area forbidden to her. She was not allowed any closer to her mother's bed than the one brown shoe placed beside it on the floor by the man who may have been her father. This shoe, which he never wore or moved, and which did not seem to have a pair, contained his pocket-watch; it rested against the heel of the shoe, and faced her mother's bed, marking the line which she was not allowed to cross. The dial of the watch was tarnished, its numbers difficult to read. Only by counting the dead bodies of flies on the window-sill could she remind herself that time was passing.

Today they were not dying quickly enough. She had counted the bodies several times; each time the number was the same. Time appeared to be standing still. There was no noise now from the flies, nothing but silence. Then it was cooler, and had begun to get darker. The clouds were thicker and lower, almost touching the tops of the trees, and were no longer in motion.

As if someone might hear her, she tiptoed up the stairs, edged her way towards the brown shoe, and tried to read the hands of the dial. A cloudburst, hard and sudden with hail-stones, hit the corrugated iron above her. Then there was thunder, very loud and close, as if the trees were being ripped up by their roots, and the cottage was disintegrating beneath her feet. Rain began pouring into the room in one corner where the roof was rusted, and Jean wet herself where she stood, into the brown shoe and over the pocket-watch.

Mopping the shoe, the watch, and the floor around them with old rags from downstairs, she began to shake and then to cry. Outside, a plank fell over, and she froze again at the noise, her back to the bedroom door, convinced that he had come home, crept up the stairs, and was standing behind her.

Nothing. For a very long time, nothing. She could see the hands on the dial of the watch now, see the second-hand moving, watched its jerky movements, expecting each jerk to bring a sound from the man who would be standing behind her. She waited, but there was nothing. He was playing with her, must have come home early because of the rain, and must be standing by the door, watching.

Again she began to sob. Among the tears, words formed. She was sorry. It had been an accident because of the thunder. She had been frightened; it wouldn't happen again. She held her breath, trying to control her sobs, tried to listen for the sound of his voice. But there was no sound of his voice. So, without turning to face him, she began slowly to move, to slide herself across the floor towards her own mattress, crawling onto it, and pulling the horsehair blanket over her head.

Two hours later she was still alone. She had been without food all day, and could not remember what she had eaten the day before, but knew that it would not have been enough to stop her feeling hungry. Now it was dark outside. She was going to starve to death slowly as her mother had said she might, and without even having left the house. They had gone away together, and were not coming back for her, had plotted to leave her, to meet somewhere in the village and just go off somewhere without her.

She moved the blanket which covered her, and felt the coldness of the room after the storm. She crossed to the chest-of-drawers, slid one drawer open, and felt about for her mother's clothes. They were still there, but perhaps they had been left to prevent her guessing what was planned. Without her, the runaways would have more money, and could afford to buy new clothes; the man had even left his precious pocket-watch to make her believe that they were coming back. Her mother's counting to a hundred and following him a little way before going off in the opposite direction had all been a pretence.

Then there was the tiredness, a kind of tiredness she had never felt before, as though she were about to fall over. She moved back towards her mattress, arms outstretched, feeling at the blackness around her, sensing that her legs would soon be unable to support her. Her feet touched the mattress, and her knees sank into it. The coarse blanket felt so heavy that she could hardly lift it over her head. Then there was nothing until he woke her.

He was asking her if she had been left all day without food. She lied, saying that she had eaten some bread, but he knew that he had taken the last slice to work with him. He was asking what time her mother had left. She shrugged, but he told her she must know. Had it been morning or afternoon? Morning. How long after he had left? She told him that her mother had gone to get food, and he pointed out what she already knew, that the shops in the village would have closed hours ago. She asked him if he had brought any apples from the farm, but he had not.

92

He left her, and went downstairs. She could hear him moving about, and talking to himself. He was saying, 'Show her,' and piling furniture up against the door, nailing planks across the window.

The rain outside was not so heavy now, the sound of it on the roof almost lulling. He had taken the candle with him, leaving the room in darkness. She turned over, closing her eyes, not wanting to hear what would be said when her mother returned. At least they hadn't left her, and the man seemed worried that she had not eaten all day.

Much later shouts from outside woke her. The first thing she saw was the flickering candle, the first thing she felt, his hand covering her mouth, preventing her from crying out, then his other hand, moving in circles over her stomach, as though trying to rub away a pain, before moving lower to between her legs.

The candle-flame illuminated his left shoulder and part of his naked chest. The rest of him was in darkness, except for his eyes which were bright, too bright, and watching her. There was sweat on his shoulder, and running down the side of his neck. His body was shaking, so that she began to shake. She heard the rain hitting the roof, and her mother's voice outside, shouting to be let in. His jaw was set, his teeth clenched; he was whispering the words 'Show her' over and over again.

There had never been rough-and-tumble games, no physical contact between them, even when clothed. Now his body was pressed against hers, with his fingers up inside her, and it was going on and on, his fingers moving backwards and forwards trying to get deeper, his hand over her mouth, pressing down hard. He was hurting her, meaning to hurt her, but there was nothing she could do. The more her mother shouted to be let in, the more nervous and excited he became, and the higher his fingers seemed to be reaching up inside her.

With her knickers pulled down and off, her dress pushed up around her neck, and her six-year-old, undernourished body wriggling and struggling to be free, she listened to the sound of her mother's voice, to the man's breathing and the repeated words, 'Show her! Show her!' She heard also her own sounds, the noises she was making through her nose, pig-like noises, grunts like a runt piglet with a blocked snout, trying to get its breath.

The sounds her mother made changed, became those of a woman sobbing, a woman begging and promising good behaviour, without having admitted to any bad behaviour. Then silence, and the face leaning over her, a candle-flame reflected in each eye, listening.

Slowly his fingers were withdrawn from inside her, and she watched the muscles of his face relaxing. She felt the soreness where his fingers had been; she felt his left hand still covering her mouth but less tightly. Perhaps he was about to leave her, would rise from the horsehair mattress, and cover her again with the blanket. His head turned now towards the bedroom door, still listening.

A stone hit the front door. More shouts, more screaming, more calling of names. Her mother's anger returning too soon, spoiling everything, getting it wrong. Fists banging against the door again, and the tightness of his hand over her mouth again as he pushes her legs apart, unbuttons his trousers, repositions himself, and with his teeth and jaw clenched hard again thrusts something much bigger than fingers into the soreness that fingers have already made.

She is struggling again. His hand has been removed from over her mouth, and she is making noises, but these are muffled by his chest. She has tried to bite an arm she could not reach, has grabbed with her hand where she has seen boys in the playground at school grabbing at other boys to make them cry, has felt a warm soft part of him, but her hand has been wrenched away. Now he holds both her wrists in one of his hands, pushing her arms back over his head, brushing his chin, the stubble of his beard against her fingers.

She has stopped fighting. She listens to the rain against the roof. He thrusts his body against hers, saying, 'That's right. Don't struggle. You'll get to like it soon.'

What she will never tell him, now or ever in the five years to come, is that she has liked it from the moment he removed his fingers and placed himself inside her, not what he has been doing, which has hurt her, but the fact of what he has done, that he has not left her alone to die, has worried about her, and together they are 'showing' her mother.

The man who may have been her father stopped moving up and down inside her, withdrew himself, and lay beside her.

94

She reached down with her hand, and touched the stuff running down the inside of her leg. He hugged Jean, and kissed her on the face, touched Jean's face with his lips, kept doing it, and Jean watched his face, seeing panic there, and felt the coldness of the sweat amongst the hair on his chest. He placed his right index-finger to his lips, and Jean thought, 'He mustn't do that. It's dirty. That finger has been inside me. It's full of germs.'

There was no need for him to indicate that they now had a secret; she knew that well enough, and knew that secrets are to be kept, unless they are to be used.

He dressed himself quickly, went downstairs, and removed the furniture from the door. She heard the argument between her mother and this man about the wet bread, the milk bottle which had been dropped and broken, the puncture and flat tyre her mother claimed to have had, about there being no fire, and no dry wood, nothing to heat water, and no prospect of their lives' ever improving.

He had left the candle, and she stood unsteadily and moved closer to it, kicking the brown shoe containing his watch to one side. She wanted to see the stuff she had received from inside him, but there was only blood running down her leg, not his, but her own. He had not bled. She had watched him getting dressed. There had been sweat on his body, but no blood.

She used the rags with which she had earlier wiped urine from the shoe to clean herself, and turned her mattress over so that her mother would not notice the stain; there was blood on that too. She felt disappointed at not being able to examine the sticky soothing stuff which she had felt shooting out of him, but either the stuff had stayed inside her, or had become mixed with the blood. He had made noises like a small child when the stuff had come.

For days it was painful for her to walk. Jean told her mother that she had hurt her ankle, and her mother pretended not to hear. When she sat, she pressed her thighs together to remind herself of the pain and of what had happened.

Years later, the Social Worker, Jean Davis, in her early thirties and wishing to know whether it would be possible to have a child, consulted a gynaecologist, and was told that it would not be possible. She supposed that what had happened to her insides during that first occasion might have accounted for the impossibility, though, of course, there were many other occasions during the next five years, many of them more violent and more sadistic.

This Social Worker came to realize that it was unfair to present a six-year-old child with so much power. Not only had Jean won the man who may have been her father away from her mother, but she had a friend of sorts, her only friend. Later she wondered at what age children are old enough to know what is expected of them.

Now, when I walk up the gravel drive on Visiting Days, it's usually my mother's face pressed hard against the window, looking out. Since this is an Old People's Home, flies and bluebottles aren't given much free parking time on the window-sill.

My mother has begun to talk to me a little, but it is mostly whingeing and complaint. She hasn't really progressed much, just grown old. She's sixty-nine now, going on six years, two months.

The other old people at the Home have been allowed to keep mementoes of their youth, just a few, not enough to crowd the room – wedding photographs, snapshots of children and grandchildren, certificates showing that they competed in the school sports, passed an exam, read a poem aloud, could do ballroom-dancing, the waltz and the veleta. My mother has none of these things.

I don't mention the past, and my mother only occasionally refers to her own part in it, a role she claims not to have enjoyed. Of the twenty or so years in which she and I neither saw each other nor even communicated, very little is said. If she had any more children after I left, they are not mentioned.

She sits always in the same chair, the shoulders of which she was once so proud hunched forwards, covered with a cardigan or shawl. She seems to have shrunk, and her hair is thinner, not greasy any more; the staff tie what is left of it up in a pink hair-ribbon similar to the ones which used to be bought in Bedford for Jean. I've asked the staff not to do this, told them how institutionalized it makes my mother look, but they say that she threatens not to eat if they take the ribbon away. They tell me that my mother likes all the food which is bad for her, such as chocolate, cream cakes, potato crisps, pickled onions and icecream.

Every time I visit her, my mother tells me in a manner which suggests that she expects something to be done about it that she can't stand the blacks and the coloureds, the Irish and the Jews, dismissing the entire staff of the Home in one sentence. I smile and nod, wondering if she expects me to come up the drive with a tommy-gun hidden under my coat to wipe them all out and rescue her. I never remind her of the Prisoner of War Camp, and that once she would screw any nationality she could get her legs round, never remind her of all the Ukrainians and Poles, scared shitless by the prospect of repatriation, whom she allowed to jig-a-jig on top of her, while she lay dispensing comfort and trying to remember all their names.

There's always a moment during every visit when she goes silent, and I wait, watching in my mind's eye my mother turning the pages of an old script, underlining the moves she can never get right. Then the line comes back to her, always the same line, 'You never helped me, did you? You could have tried to stop him.' What this means is that neither I, from the ages of six to eleven, nor my much older mother tried to stop the man who may have been my father from hitting her, and I admit that I didn't, shake my head, tell my mother I'm sorry, and prepare to leave, blinking away a mental image of a six-year-old child pushing a large pram in which sits its female parent.

The staff tell me that Mother brightens up after I've left, and goes into a different but equally old routine of telling the same dirty jokes, misremembering them, like a child performing in front of adults in a last-ditch attempt not to be sent to bed. The staff say that, when she's on form, my mother could be all Seven Dwarves rolled into one. And I say, 'Better late than never,' which appears to confuse them.

TWO

I drove back there a few months ago, to Wood End, not sure what I hoped to find. They were building a bypass around the village where I went to school. It had never been more than a church, the school, a pub, the blacksmith's and a Sub-Post-Office smelling of cats and cheese, which the sub-postmistress ate – the cheese, not the cat – all the time she was serving; the cat's responsibilities included window-display. Now suddenly the village had been elevated to bypass status.

When I left in 1951, there was a small newish prefab estate outside the village proper. Now there are two depressed-looking Council estates, one of them where the prefabs used to be; the Council had just carted away the tin homes, and built brick ones over the old sewage pipes. Somehow they've found the space to add a row of lock-up garages, the backs of which have been decorated with one huge mural of clouds, angels, exotic birds and spacemen stepping out of rocket-ships; a collection must have been taken up to pay for that amount of spray-paint. Incorporated into the middle of it was a notice to the effect that ball games were forbidden. The nuclear age had arrived in rural Bedfordshire just in time for the banning of ball games. I expect there's now a special room at County Hall for the burning of books, not that any County Council can afford to buy books these days, or at least none that would be good enough to be worth burning.

The only children I saw on the estates were standing at windows, looking out at the rain. I suppose I gave them a subject for speculation – a middle-aged woman standing in the middle of the road, gazing about as if I'd come to buy the place.

There were more signposts pointing to Wood End than I remembered. I began to wonder whether I might find myself driving over the Wood End flyover, and peering down on it, but at last there was this narrow, winding single track, and I knew where I was again, which was just as well since the rain was pelting against the windscreen, and the inside of the car had completely steamed up. There were not many houses along this road, and had been none at all when I used to tramp along it twice a day to and from school. One had a sign outside, 'J. Truscot. Panel-beating. MOT While-U-Wait'; next to the house was a scrap-yard, containing many well-beaten panels and the best part of an old fire-engine. Further on there was a house made of corrugated iron – not just the roof; all of it – and aptly named 'Iron House'. It had been painted all over in violent yellow ochre, as if the occupants were saying 'Don't forget we live here.'

The road petered out into a dirt track, as I expected it would, more a mud track on that day, with clay-lined pot-holes. I'd gone quite a distance before I realized that there was going to be nowhere safe to execute my three-point turn, and that I'd have to hang out of the window, and reverse down the track; my rear-window de-mister was having one of its rest-periods.

By the time I stopped the car and got out, the rain was so heavy and the mist so thick that it was impossible to see if the wood was still there. I'd brought nothing as practical as wellingtons with me, but I was determined not to be beaten, so I left the car and walked on, until I came to the end of the track where there was an official black and white pole barring the road to vehicles; it was like one of those barriers they have at frontiers, only not quite so grand, lacking guard-dogs and armed soldiers in beaver hats and trench-coats. On the other side of the barrier, there was yet another notice. This one read, 'BEDFORD THRIFT CONSERVANCY. ACCESS TO PERMIT-HOLDERS ONLY'. A bypass and a Nature Reserve! That's the nineteen eighties for you.

I read the sign several times, giggling and laughing like a lunatic while the rain soaked further into the sensible tweed suit I'd chosen for my long-delayed return to Nature. I tried to multiply three hundred and sixty-five by the number of years it had been since I was last at Wood End. Out of the thousands of days I might have chosen, surely some of them must have been fine and with a visibility of more than five yards? By the time I got back to the car, I was crying with laughter. I had mud up to my shins, and my shoes had shrunk and were gripping my feet like Hansel and Gretel, expecting at any moment to be abandoned in the wood.

So I sat there in the car, shivering with cold, still sniggering some-times, and sucking an acid-drop I'd unstuck from the side of the glove-compartment, watching the rain slide past the windscreen, all too well aware of my forty-six-year-old body stuffed into wet tweed, trying to convince myself that the little Jean who wandered the woods at will beyond the black and white pole, long before Nature Conservancy was even a gleam in some planner's eye, was really myself. Two words, 'Children bounce', stuck in my head, going round and round as if on a loop of tape, along with a memory which I can't be sure really is a memory, because if it is it would certainly pre-date my being six, and it's unlikely that I'd remember anything before then. This memory is recurrent; I'd had it before, and I still have it. What I see is a child of about three, sitting on someone's shoulders and being carried beneath tall trees through which sunlight is filtered. The person carrying is running, and the child bounces up and down, squealing and laughing because it thinks that what they are doing is chasing the sun and may catch it. I've no idea who the grown-up is.

'Children bounce' is almost the first thing I was told when I came into Child Care. It means that, if you find a baby with a fractured skull or long bone-fractures, the chances are it didn't get either just by falling out of its cot. Why I should have thought of all that then, I don't know, especially when there was the problem of getting the car out of the mud.

Perhaps I expected the rain to ease, or maybe I didn't want to leave without having set foot inside the wood. I turned on the windscreen-wipers so as to see out, knowing full well that what I was doing was running the battery of the car down, and that soon there'd be no heat in the engine to warm me. Three times I started the engine, and three times I switched it off again. I could not leave yet. All I could do was to sit there, watching the wipers go back and forth as if they were counting off the years.

Then suddenly I was sitting in school at my desk, staring at the lines of jam-jars on the window-sills, all filled with dead or dying wild flowers or crumbling dried grasses, wondering whether I should have the nerve, when the moment actually came, to hide in the broom-cupboard until everyone else had gone home, so that I could stay in the building overnight, and not have to go back to Wood End. I did manage to do that several times, when I knew in advance that she was going to be absent without leave for most of the night, and he'd pretend to go after her, leaving me alone in the dark, and then return. Doors would be made to creak, and there would be footsteps outside. He'd stand under the window, whispering to himself in two different voices, each with a foreign accent, pretending to be a couple of POWs who had escaped to *find a woman. He'd make animal noises, unspecific howls or else the sound of a fox on heat; for years he'd told me that there was a wolf somewhere in the wood, and that he himself had often come across gnawed human bones. I would lie there, waiting for the sound of the latch being lifted. He never hurried himself; everything seemed to take forever. Once he tied a couple of sheepskins around his body, and crawled upstairs in the dark on all fours, breathing like a large animal, sniffing and even purring. Once he brought a damp piece of leather with him and a chicken's foot, and what with those being pressed and scratched against my leg in the dark, and the sniffing and purring noises getting louder and closer to my face, I fainted. He'd thought it all out; he was very good at that; it was a game, a preliminary ritual, but it also had to be real. I would have been eight or nine then, and already wondering how to escape.*

At that age I never asked myself why he created these elaborate games; I thought it was just to frighten me, that it gave him pleasure to inspire fear, that it was part of a sadistic process that continued on the mattress, that it was part of the pleasure of sex for him. Now I wonder whether it might not have been something else, that his object in frightening me might have been that I should come to him for protection, cling to him, whether the whole game may not have been intended to elicit tenderness, not that it ever did; he failed in that, as in so much else. I also think now that the words 'Show her' are capable of more than one interpretation. They could mean, as I then believed them to mean, 'Punish her. Show her what happens when she neglects us. Show her how much we hate her,' but they could also be taken to mean, 'Show her what tenderness means. Show her what love means. Show her how to show me affection.' He never was tender, of course, not at those times; maybe he didn't know how to be; maybe he wanted to be, but his anger got in the way.

Ah, Social Workers, Social Workers! How we complicate the most straightforward issues!

Staying in school overnight was also frightening, but at least it didn't end in sex. When I could be sure that everyone else had gone home, I'd wander from classroom to classroom, looking at the pictures on the walls, and lifting the lids of all the desks in case someone had left fruit or sweets behind; now and then I'd find a sandwich of cheese or fishpaste. My first port of call would always be the Cloak Room in the hope that at least one child would have gone home without its coat, so that I'd have something to cover me. In the Main Room, usually divided into two by a screen, there was an ancient coke-stove, which would go out at two thirty every afternoon, since it was calculated that the children would have generated enough of their own body-heat by then to see them through until four. All the rooms were high; I don't think they had ceilings, but just went up to a point under the roof. From the moment when all those little legs marched from their desks and sprinted towards the gate, the floorboards, beams and all the woodwork started to groan and creak as the temperature dropped.

My corner for sleeping was the one where the rush mats were kept. I can't remember what they were used for. Would it have been Music and Movement, or just for covering the floor to sit on? Certainly the boards were filthy, with years of dust, Plasticine, spilled powder-paint and food ground into them. The school had its own small kitchen for School Dinners, and Dinner Money was collected on Mondays. That was another traumatic experience. The moment my name was called, I would have the long walk to the teacher's desk empty-handed. There, in front of the whole class, I'd try to whisper my excuse, while the teacher clicked at me teeth which should have been sent back to the National Health for readjustment. Then I would have to face the class as I walked back to my desk. I used to practise walking backwards, but never dared to do it when the moment came.

One of the more enjoyable moments of life at that school would come during Morning Playtime, when I would stand close to the kitchen window with my face in the steam, listening to the clatter of aluminium pans and watching the Dinner Ladies in white overalls rushing around inside. They were always laughing, even when (particularly when) they dropped trays of steamed pudding or pans of mashed potatoes.

I'd sleep quite well on those rush mats beneath the blue gabardine raincoat of some forgetful child. I'd wake early with the light, but I'd bedded down early, so that was all right. I'd arrange everything as it had been, then dart across the yard to the Girls' Lavatories, and sit in a cubicle until I could hear other children, early arrivals, playing, when I'd make my entrance, and join them. Well, not join them exactly, more leaning against the wall and watching.

During my nights at school I'd change all the water in the jam-jars on the window-sills. The teacher who was always telling us to bring her wild flowers, buds and grasses would forget about them once they'd been put in a jar, and the water would evaporate, or just turn green. She only noticed this if the window-sill was full when she had to make room for a new arrival. Later, when I did escape, which was done by simply coming out of the school gate and walking in the opposite direction to Wood End, I began searching the hedge-rows and banks for flowers to brighten up those window-sills, thinking I'd get a Red Star from Mrs Edgely. I collected quite a fistful before I remembered I wasn't going back.

I always felt safe in the village itself, perhaps because I knew it so well; I only went home when I had to. I knew the best places to hide, which lilac in which garden smelt the strongest in springtime, which field had fewest cow-pats, and where bluebells grew thickest. I had three separate places where I knew I could sit for as long as I wished without being disturbed. I must have spent a great deal of time in the corner of one field or another.

The occasional times I stayed out all night never seemed to bother my mother much, though he would become hysterical, and get his revenge in various small sadistic ways. He'd got it into his head that I'd gone to the bad, and was allowing village boys to have their way with me. None of them had, or did. Usually I was ignored or called names, indicating that I was dirty, which I often was. In summer I'd be covered with insect-bites, plus the occasional bite-mark made by him, and in winter my nose and lips would be blistered and chapped. Once a year, a nurse would come to the school to check heads for lice. My tests were always positive, which may be why I was given a desk to myself; it was at the side of the room near the radiator, so I didn't mind. The nurse would hand out evil-smelling stuff to put on the lice-ridden scalp, and would comb my hair with a fine-tooth comb. My hair was always tangled, and handfuls of it would come out. The process was extremely painful, and made my eyes water, while all the other kids would just sit there giggling. Talk about child-abuse!

My mother would go to Jumble Sales, and bring back any old thing for me to wear. I was no good at needlework, and she'd never sewn a button on in her life, so everything was either too long, too short, too baggy or too tight. I remember Mrs Edgely bringing me one of her daughter's skirts, because the one I'd been wearing had a slit up the side where the seam had gone. Perhaps she'd recognized love-bites for what they were, and thought that my showing less leg might prevent them.

I don't think I very much wanted to join in with the others when they played, or when they walked around the village, pairing up and pretending to have girl-friends or boy-friends. All that seemed infantile to me. Since it gave them pleasure to exclude me, and I preferred my own society, we all got what we wanted.

I suppose that mine was a classic case, in the sense that I always believed that what was happening to me was my own fault. Even after that first time when I was six, I remember thinking, 'I mustn't wear that dress again.' 'I must stop going behind the shed and crouching down to pass water.' I'd seen him watching me, standing there and grinning, so I knew it was wrong, but in the middle of nowhere, when the privy stinks to high heaven summer and winter alike, squatting over a bucket isn't the most pleasant way to pass the time, and anyway most of the time it was I who had to empty it.

All the abused children I've ever met have been convinced that there's something rotten and nasty inside them. Try to bring it into the open and talk about it, and they'll try to lock it deeper inside them. It can be frightening for both parties. Unless you're very sure of yourself, know that you can give yourself all the time it takes, and already have an emotional rapport with the child, it's better not to begin.

Even children who have not been abused need to associate power with goodness. How else would they make sense of their own arrival into the world? There was the interest I got from him, the attention, the cuddles and gentle touching I got from him sometimes. A child has to get these from someone somehow, even if at other times that person is hostile or brutal.

Later I came to the conclusion that these other times were also to do with sex, that the power he had over me turned him on. Part of the time, he was challenging me to tell on him, trying to provoke me into doing so. She already knew; I'm sure of that. She would have to have been deaf and blind not to know.

I've also wondered about those cuddles and tiny presents. How real was the interest? Was there really any affection, or did I imagine it because I needed to? Recently I read a comparison of an abusing home to a hijacked aeroplane, where the captives find goodness in their captors because, if they didn't, their fear would explode their heads before a trigger had been pulled or the pin removed from a grenade. The comparison was extended to the inmates of concentration camps, where there is prolonged contact between victims and victimizers. The ego of the victim protects itself by identifying with the authority-figure; the gaolers end up by being regarded as parents. The passengers in the hijacked aeroplane are also said to exhibit that 'frozen fear' or 'frozen watchfulness' which we're told to look for as a sign of the abused child. It acts as a protection, whereas panic in the form of an hysterical outburst would be highly dangerous.

We had the poor man's opiate at school, of course, though I've never been a serious user. We had Assembly, with prayers and a rousing hymn, and we had either RE or RI – certainly R something; I can't remember which it was in those days. We had 'texts', tattered rolls of oilcloth, which the teacher would unfurl with a flourish, and drape over the blackboard. Presumably the pictures of Christ getting His feet washed were intended to have an added significance for those of us who came from homes without hot water. Christ was also shown turning water into wine, there was Judas looking as though he had just raided the larder, and a picture of four soppy-looking men in a boat watching a backlit Someone skipping over the waves towards them. The phrase 'Suffer little children' was used a lot, though it was not explained to those of us who did suffer why we should be doing so. We were needed as sunbeams, yet we were made to play in the yard in all weathers. Vanity, vanity, all was vanity, but those of us who did not own clothes smart enough for Sunday School were despised by the others.

Nowadays teachers are told to keep a lookout for children who always seem to be tired, children with tangled hair that hasn't been brushed. (It's amazing what good bonding you can get with children, if they'll let you fiddle with their hair.) They're supposed to take special note of children with phobias or poor concentration-spans, children who shrug incessantly or click their teeth ritualistically, certainly of those who masturbate openly or come out with words which indicate that they know more than they should about sex. Most children do all or some of these things at some time, and if they were certain signs that abuse was taking place at home, then eighty per cent of the children at my Primary School were being fucked by their fathers instead of, as I believed, only one.

In the nineteen forties and early fifties, nobody asked such a child, 'Are you happy at home, Jean?' or set in front of such a one anatomically explicit dolls, to show how that child manipulated the dolls's genitalia. If a child were asked to draw a picture of its family, nobody took the child aside to ask it indirect questions which would show whether it hated its mother or was terrified of its dad. The most positive statement I made in those days was to scrape a stick along some iron railings in the churchyard. It was my coded message to God.

The iron railings have now gone, and one doorway into the church has been plastered up, while the other is protected by two iron grilles, one making a gate into the church, the other protecting the wooden door. Both were locked and chained, and there was a notice telling one where to go to apply for the keys.

The old Primary School is now a Residential Home, and the new one is a collection of Portakabins, set on a patch of well tended grass near the church, but there are locked gates there too, and of course a notice. This one threatens that 'Proceedings will be taken against any unauthorized person entering upon this land'. What sort of people live in the village now? They must all be church-desecrators and child-molesters. No wonder they need a bypass.

It was four o'clock one afternoon, when Jean was leaving school with everyone else to go home; she had no plans to sleep in the broom-cupboard that night. As they crossed the yard, dragging raincoats or ducking to dodge the swung satchels of those already committed to academic success, the church bell started to clang. One single note, tolling over and over: it was the sort of sound which vibrates to the roots of one's teeth. It was the sound to be heard on the soundtrack of one of those foreign films in which a village is being invaded by some enemy, and women in black pick babies up from doorsteps and run down narrow streets clutching them, or drop their washing into the well and turn wild-eyed to camera, while shutters are closed and heavy doors bolted. On this occasion, mothers not quite as wild-eyed had congregated at the school gates to grab their children, all having heard the news long before Fred Parrot, the only man permitted to handle the bell-ropes, had been located under a tractor and had pedalled four miles to do his Quasimodo impersonation. Only Jean's mother was absent from the assembly of wild-eyed mothers.

One rumour was that Hitler had not committed suicide, but had been taking a sabbatical, from which he had emerged to invade Britain. Airborne landings were to be expected in rural Bedfordshire as a preliminary to the attack upon London. The fact was that four POWs had 'escaped' from the Camp up the road, and were said to be hiding out in the wood. Jean's wood.

Once it became known that the invading army consisted of four undernourished Italian labourers who had failed to answer the roll call or report for work, new rumours were started to ward off the general feeling of anti-climax. One was that the POWs had stolen some rifles, and were holding Jean's mother hostage at Wood End Cottage; another, more likely, was that she had assisted them to escape. Someone claimed that a sheep had been abducted; this gave rise to the usual jokes about wellington boots. The POWs, most of them young and many of them attractive, particularly the Italians, were a constant source of speculation among the villagers. Even the children had heard that hair-curlers and a complete home-perm kit had been confiscated from one hut; nobody told the children why, so they assumed that these articles were used in the manufacture of bombs. Some of them were said to have been seen holding hands, which was a practice totally unac-ceptable even in London, let alone rural Bedfordshire. There were other stories, mostly involving cruelty to animals, sani-tary arrangements and eating habits. When Mrs Jefferson, the publican's wife, reported the loss of some underwear from her washing-line, it was assumed all round the village that the Ita-lians had taken them, although Mrs Jefferson was a woman whose figure brought a new meaning to the word 'smalls'.

Since nobody was there to collect Jean from the school gate, and none of those who were there offered her sanctuary, she began one of her walks. Jean seldom went straight home from school; it would have been unusual to find anyone there.

She passed a group of men outside the Post Office, seven of them, and they each had a dog. The men were trying to plan tactics, but could not hear each other because of the racket the dogs were making. These were not Alsatians or tracker dogs, not even sheepdogs, but a motley collection of mongrels, with two dachshunds and an Afghan hound.

Jean took one of her favourite ways home, towards the rail-way line and the footpath beside it. This was the path which led to the POW Camp; it was regularly used by those of them who worked at the local brick-yard. Between the path and the Camp there was at one point a deep dry ditch. Jean had often watched her mother search for coins in that ditch, dropped from the POWs' pockets on their way home. She knew exactly where to look, and often found a few coppers, once a half-crown.

Jean loved walking along that path by the railway line. It had been made by laying broken bricks so that the brick-lorries would not get mud-bound. She liked the dust which it gave off in summer. For some reason she felt safe there, walking over those broken bricks, red, yellow, orange, putty or biscuit-coloured, and the path's running alongside the tracks made her feel as if she were going somewhere. If one left the path, and walked about fifty yards through ferns and couch grass, there was a man-made lake, where once clay had been dug to make the bricks. Now all kinds of waterfowl and wading birds had taken it over. Jean never bothered herself with trying to find their nests. She just liked to sit, watching them land on the water as if they were on skis. When she was tired of watching, she would walk back slowly to the path and continue on her way, sometimes doing a little dance as she went, stomping over the broken bricks.

She reached the cottage, to find, as she had expected, nobody at home, circled it several times, threw a few stones, brought for the purpose, at the door, and shouted, just in case the POWs were hiding inside. So far it had been almost a game, but then she discovered that she was not as brave as she had thought, wondered whether perhaps they really were hiding inside, and did have guns. She began to imagine that there were faces at the window, looking out at her among the cardboard. The light was just beginning to go, and not for the first time, the cottage became a place of fear. She could not bring herself to approach the door.

For a while she sat at the edge of the clearing, watching the cottage door. It must have been late March or early April; the hawthorn was in bud. It was always difficult to move quickly through that wood, because there was so much hawthorn.

Nothing happened, and that in itself began to seem sinister. She decided to walk through the wood towards the farm where the man who may have been her father worked. Probably she would meet him on his way home, unless he had found himself an old dog, and gone to join the men outside the Post Office.

There had been a wet winter, then a dry spell, then more rain, and all the woodland paths were overgrown. Brambles and the suckers of briar, always at shoulder-height, reached out at her, or formed themselves into a tunnel, of which the roof kept getting lower. A few of the previous year's leaves clung to the beech trees, looking like potato crisps, and reminding Jean that she was hungry. The bark of other trees was mottled, as if someone had poured golden syrup down their trunks. It was impossible to move quickly; every footfall made a noise like a starting-pistol.

Then Jean heard a noise which was not the noise of footfalls, not her own, nor of the men and their dogs, who were probably still outside the Post Office trying to make sense out of each other's tactical observations. Jean knew and could distinguish every sound that wood made, from the cry of a fox to the whirr of a startled pheasant. This noise was none of those. It was the noise of her mother's voice, and then another voice, a man's voice, mumbling.

She moved towards those voices as quietly as she could, but when she found those who were making the noises, they were so wrapped up in each other that they would not have heard her if she had been practising the bagpipes as she approached. What she saw first was a man's bottom, going up and down. She could not see her mother, just the raffia bag she had made for her mother at school, and a pair of saddle-shoes. The thighs of the man were large and white, with a great deal of black hair on them, and around his ankles was a pair of grey tweed trousers. Jean recognized them as a pair her mother had brought back from one of her Jumble Sales. Jean had only ever been allowed to go to one such Sale. She and her mother had arrived an hour early, to be first in the queue at the Village Hall. Jean remembered that her mother had had the sharpest elbows in the hall that day, had walked around with them splayed out sideways like the fins of sharks, had bought up as much as she could; it was no wonder they never had any money. None of what she had bought found its way to the man who may have been Jean's father; Jean's mother must have kitted out half the POWs in the Camp.

She stood, only partially concealed by scrub, and watched the movements of the Italian bum. It must have been good at what it was doing, because its movement continued for a very long time. After a while she made out a body beneath the bum; she assumed that this body was her mother's, since it was making grunts and moans in her mother's voice, but she could not see the faces, and this annoyed her, because she wondered what sort of faces people pulled when they were doing what they were doing. She particularly wished to see her mother's face, because she wished to see how its expression would change when her mother saw Jean. If her mother were ever going to notice her, and to give her attention, this would certainly have been the time.

The bum continued to bump and grind, and to pump away as if it were prospecting for oil. One of her mother's hands seemed to be pulling the hair of the man's left thigh, and sometimes she would draw her fingernails over his buttocks, so that four pink lines showed up against the white. Jean had little doubt that her mother and the bum were enjoying themselves, but surely they could not have been very comfortable.

Jean had no idea what she intended to do, and so did nothing. If she was in any danger, it would only be from her mother, and she welcomed that. She wanted to see her mother angry, wanted her to hit out, call Jean names, any names she could think of, but a name, something positive. She wanted to see her mother cry with anger. She wanted that very much.

She need not have worried about making a decision; it was made for her. A hand came from behind her, and covered her mouth. She was pulled backwards, and turned to face away from the pumping bum, and the man who was holding Jean hissed at the bum, which must either in consequence have climaxed quickly or not climaxed at all.

Jean and her mother remained all night with the four POWs, with the youngest cradling Jean in his arms for warmth. None of them touched her, apart from that. Jean's mother did not hit her, but looked sideways once, and thereafter ignored her; she may have tried to convince herself that Jean had seen nothing; the look she gave was that of an actress trying to indicate that her colleague should not be on stage in this scene. To the four men, Jean's mother complained about the cold a great deal, pretending to be some delicate flower. She addressed them by their first names, and flirted in rather a bedraggled way. It is probable that by this time they loathed her.

At first light, Jean and her mother went home, and Jean was sent off to school. The POWs stayed in the woods for four days and nights, then returned voluntarily to the Camp, the men with dogs never having left the Post Office, and the Camp authorities being unconcerned to find them, since after all the war was long over and the men were only prisoners in an economic sense. Two weeks later, one of the four runaways committed suicide. It had been an odd experience for Jean, to have lain throughout the night cradled in the arms of a strange young man while (as she believed) other men with dogs and torches were hunting for them. It had been a strange experience to be treated as if she were a child, and very precious. It was a strange experience a fortnight later to be told that someone called Angelo, whose bum she had seen moving up and down on her mother, had hanged himself.

THREE

When Jean, just turned eleven, on an afternoon in 1951, walked
out of the school gates, and kept on walking, her parents had
become so used to her being out all night they did not report
her absence until three days later. It was the man who may
have been Jean's father who came to school looking for her;
her mother did nothing. Perhaps he needed a clean pair of
socks. Jean had become the general dogsbody by that time,
playing at being a housewife since nobody else would; she had
been washing most of his clothes and some of her mother's. She
had brought wild flowers into the house, set them in bottles,
jars and even empty cans as vases, and changed the water
regularly, had tried to make rock cakes and to mend the rotten
window-frames. Her mother had readily fallen into the role of
unruly daughter to Jean as mother. The only article of furniture
Jean was not allowed to touch was her mother's bed.

Jean's experience of the world outside the village did not
extend to beyond Bedford, so when the first man who gave
her a lift asked where she was bound, that was her answer.
She spent her first night at the Children's Boating Lake, where
there was a large wooden shed in which the paddle-boats were
stored and mended, and which was not locked – at least not
in 1951 – perhaps because multicoloured paddle-boats are not
easily resaleable. She made herself a nest of sacking and tar-
paulin, and slept among the mingled aromas of varnish, damp
wood and the grease which was applied to the boats' moving
parts. She decided that each differently coloured paint must
have a different smell, the blue of pear-drops, green of sherbet,
and that a freshly painted red boat with a yellow number on
its side smelled of icecream soda.

Next day she hung about by the side of the lake, and one of the men who worked there gave her some chocolate and a free boat-ride, then had a good feel up her skirt under the tarpaulins, and told her to make herself scarce before he did something they would both regret. Looking back with hindsight, Jean Davis, the Social Worker, may have concluded that the man should not be blamed, since Jean's waif-like state and the knowing way she looked at men must have provided a strong temptation, but Jean herself just assumed that everyone knew about her, and she accepted that she was fair game; the man who had given her a lift into Bedford had driven most of the way with one hand on the wheel and the other up her skirt. Jean could not understand why the man with the paddle-boats should get angry when she told him that she did not wish to leave.

After that she went into the centre of town, where she tagged on to a group of other children. At first they did no more than put up with her, but when they found out that she had run away from home, they showed their approval by saying that they would take care of her. Jean learned how easy it was to steal from the Market and from shops. Together they loitered at the Bus Station. where they did some sturdy begging, all carefully worked out and passably discreet. Two girls would approach a middle-aged man, and the prettiest would do the talking, or rather whispering, which went, 'You look nice, mister. Give us sixpence, give us a fuck.' Usually they would get the money, sometimes they got nothing, and very occasionally the man would grin and place his hand on his flies, when the two girls would run away.

The sub-culture of the streetwise child is sophisticated. Jean learned the rules. One was that they were never to mass in the town in any group larger than four, except on waste-ground. There were set times for meeting, and the venues were changed. Only one team was permitted to work the Bus Station at a time, each team being allowed forty-five minutes, after which it had to move to the other end of town; they timed themselves by the Bus Station clock. Jean was fascinated by the expressions which would appear on the faces to whom she suggested sex. Some would change colour; others would look down at these eleven-to-twelve-year-old importuners, and their eyes would come to life. Some of the girls would use that moment to wink, or stroke their lips with their tongues, but Jean found that, whenever she did so, it would have an adverse effect, and her takings dropped.

The rest of the gang were townies, who would cheerfully ride the tailboards of lorries or swing from the hand-rail of a bus, with an arm and a leg doing semaphore as the bus leaned over, going round corners. But Jean was not used to the town, and was almost run over several times. If she had been of a more carefree disposition, the whole of Bedford might have taken on the qualities of an enormous Fun Fair, but as matters were, she was terrified for much of the time.

Sometimes it amazed her how long she was on the streets of that comparatively small and sleepy town. She slept in derelict buildings unmolested, and ate much better than she had at home. Food was very important to the gang; they kept reminding each other that they had to keep their strength up. Mostly the food was stolen, but sometimes a group of four would pool what money they had, stride into a working men's café, demand a window-seat where they could see and be seen, and pile their sixpences on the counter for a round of meat and two veg.

During this period Jean twice saw the man who may have been her father. Once he was by the Boating Lake, just watching the children paddle round and round, the older girls holding their dresses down between their legs as their knees went up and down. The other occasion was in Woolworth's, when again he was just standing there, watching a family with small children. One of the children was playing up because it had dropped its icecream, and he stood half-smiling with his head on one side. On both occasions, Jean very nearly went over and took his hand, and perhaps, if he had recognized her, she would have done so, but he had not seen her, and even if he had been looking for her, would not have expected to find her with other children.

It was strange that she should, even momentarily, have wanted to go back to him, but in a masochistic way she almost felt safe with him; at least she knew what the dangers were. Living on the streets, she never knew, and spent much of her time in a state of anxiety and tension. An observer might suggest that this toughened her up and made her more self-reliant, but she did not feel self-reliant. Perhaps some of the others enjoyed the excitement, but they all lacked something. There was much talk about being mates, and trusting only each other; they considered themselves too young for love. The word 'friend' was hardly ever used. Perhaps, sophisticated as they were, they knew that there is no real friendship in large groups.

Jean cannot now remember what she was trying to steal the the first time she and her partner for the day were caught red-handed. It could have been baked beans or chiffon scarves; the routine was so invariable that the objects had become un-important. Anyway the sophisticated code of rules had let them down, and the police demanded their addresses. Jean was taken by the police to the address she had given, there to confront a bemused and indignant middle-class couple, who denied any knowledge of her, while she stood on the doorstep like one of the Bisto Kids, examining her toe-caps.

Does anyone now remember the Bisto Kids? Yes, because they have returned in the advertising. Jean could easily have looked smart, but for some reason refused to wear what she had stolen. She stood on the doorstep in a threadbare green raincoat, shoes worn down at the sides enough to sprain both ankles, a cut-down dress in a paisley pattern and a stained maroon cardigan which had passed through many traumatic experiences long before it reached the Village Hall Jumble Sale. She had spindly white legs and a flat chest. None of this touched the hearts of the middle-class couple, who said, 'She's not ours. I can't think why she gave this address,' and went back indoors to count the spoons. So Jean was placed on remand.

In those days Social Workers had cryptic titles. Jean was assigned to someone called 'the Boarding Out Officer', who had warts on his fingers, dandruff in his eyelashes (or ble-pharitis, as it is now called), hair plastered down with some kind of grease, and wore a fawn raincoat six inches too long for him. His name was Eric Morrison; Jean now feels consider-able affection and gratitude for him, although she did not feel that at the time. She appeared before the Juvenile Court, and so did her mother and the man who may have been her father, since they were summoned to do so. Jean had the impression that the man wanted her back, and that her mother had two wishes which were at odds with each other, one not to have Jean back and the other not to be thought badly of by the Court or the reporter from *The Bedfordshire Times*.

Since Jean's was a first offence – or at least the first to be found out – the Juvenile Magistrate said little except that she was a naughty and ungrateful girl to run away from home and put her innocence at risk on the streets of a growing and cosmopolitan town (she meant the Italians and the Asians, who had already begun to arrive). Jean was sent home, but was soon on the run again. Nothing much had changed, except that she had discovered how easy it was to take a few weeks' holiday, a rest cure from the man who may have been her father, but then her appearances in Court became too regular, and the Boarding Out Officer made a more prolonged appearance in her life as she was taken into Care.

Eric Morrison always seemed to be frightened of something. Jean never discovered what it was, but there was an expression in the eyes; he looked like someone who had been bullied at school. 'Boarding out' was literally what he did; children in Care were boarded out into the homes of paid foster-parents, and Eric arranged this. Once he took Jean to such a house, where they found nobody at home, so they sat on the doorstep playing Five Stones until a nosy neighbour informed them that the occupants would not be back until the evening, and Eric stepped out of character, said 'Bugger this,' and they went off to the cinema, where they saw *Pandora and the Flying Dutchman*, with Ava Gardner and James Mason. Eric sat through the film, his raincoat folded neatly over his lap, and the usherette, who had seen older men with small children in her cinema before, kept flashing her torch on the two of them to make sure that Eric was behaving himself, which he always was.

Afterwards in a Snack Bar, where he had ordered a pot of tea and toasted tea-cakes, he asked Jean why she kept running away from home. He was very apologetic about having to ask, and did not, he said, really expect Jean to tell him, but it was part of his job to try to find out. This was the part of his job which he liked least, not because it did not interest him, but because, having found out, he was never able to do much about it, except put in a report; Eric's reports, he told Jean, were seldom read, and never acted upon.

He was either very honest or very clever, or perhaps both, since this approach induced Jean, who had told nobody until then, to tell Eric about what the man who may have been her father was in the habit of doing to her. She thought he might reply that she was exaggerating, or even suggest that she had invented it, but instead he said nothing at all for a long time, but sat staring at the crumbs on the table, and then slammed his hand down on top of the crumbs, blurting out all the foulest words in the English language. Luckily there were no other customers in the Snack Bar, and the waitress had gone off to get the receipt counter-signed, since Eric was buying the meal on expenses. Jean was shocked to hear a grown man and an employee of the Council using such words, but Eric did not apologize; he continued to bang the table, first with his hand, then with his clenched fist, before attacking his own bony knees. He had run out of words by the time the waitress returned, but even so she gave Jean the receipt, thinking it to be safer, and Jean slipped it into the pocket of his raincoat as they left.

As they sat in the Waiting Room of the Bus Station, Eric said, 'I would very much have liked to have given you a cuddle, Jean, but I daren't now. I hope you'll understand.' Jean wished that she could charm the warts from his fingers, and lick the flecks of dandruff gently from his eyelashes, but such conduct would have been considered out of place at the Bus Station.

Then there was Dotty.

'If I hear another door being slammed in this house, I shall emigrate.' Dotty was not Jean's first foster-mother, but the others had all been what were called 'short-stay', hardly fostering at all, and certainly not mothering. Dotty was long-stay, a Home from home, five children, all girls, crammed by an ingenious use of bunk-beds into one bedroom of medium size, so that there were not in fact all that many doors to slam.

The children were not allowed to call her 'Dotty' to her

face; it had to be 'Dorothea'. She was a small wiry woman, who seemed forever to be attempting an impersonation of Old Mother Riley. They had to remind her when they were due a meal, and that they had not had a bath for three weeks, and that, due to the normal processes of growth which Dotty preferred to ignore, every garment they possessed was now two sizes too small. As to her threat to emigrate, it was doubtful whether any other country would have accepted her. 'Occupation, madam?' 'Substitute mother to delinquent children.' 'And what about references?'

In addition to the five foster-children there was Davy, one of her own making, fourteen and fat, who lay about on the sofa all day and every day, thinking up names for the different diseases which, he claimed, were attacking his body and preventing him from going to school. Reg, the man of the house, spoke in grunts, worked on the railway, and was a martyr to back-trouble. A typically domestic scene would be Davy stretched out on the sofa with a grubby towel held to his forehead except when there was food about, Reg in the armchair behind a newspaper with his feet on a beer-crate, and Dotty running this way and that between them.

She never walked; there was never time. Yet nothing got done, or not for her 'boarders'. They did it all, the cleaning, washing and cooking, did it all for bribes and because they would get disgusted at the mess. They did it because they didn't want the authorities to discover how they lived, and move them on again. When the Boarding Out Officer or anyone else paid a visit of inspection, Dotty would move twice as fast in order to impress, smiling a hideous basilisk smile and cooing at the children with watery eyes. A tablecloth, never otherwise used, would be found for the table, and table-mats and table-napkins would appear from a drawer which was at other times kept locked; there was even a chrome cruet-set. While the visitor was being dazzled by this show, a signal would be given for one of the children to run upstairs and give the bowl of the WC a good scrub, while another opened all the windows of the communal bedroom, and made the beds.

What made Dotty's residential care so attractive to her child-residents was the freedom; they treated the house as lodgings. Jean returned to her routine at the Bus Station, now with a new partner, Meryl, her first and closest friend, but with the onset of puberty this routine altered in one important respect; it was no longer begging, but prostitution, and the action soon moved, therefore, from the well-lit Bus Station to the darker alleys of the town.

'*Please, mister, give us a fuck.*' *The 'give' was meant to turn them on, and in Meryl's case it almost always did, but they never got away from her without handing over a shilling, or one and nine if it was raining. One and nine was the price of a seat at the cinema, and since Meryl didn't care to sit watching the picture on her own, or to have no one to whom to whisper her running commentary on the action, this often meant that she would have to go down the alley a second time to pay for me. 'I don't believe you're trying, Jeannie. You'll end up a kept woman; I can see it now.' Then back to the Bus Station to earn a bag of chips and a cream soda, or a Cornish pasty and dandelion-and-burdock.*

If I said that life was uncomplicated then, that wouldn't be true; it was very complicated, but, compared with other periods of my life, the complications weren't a problem. I was happy. I had someone whom I liked more than I would ever have admitted, and for the first time I had a sense of being liked. Meryl was in charge; I was her side-kick. That gave me status, and status is very important to a child.

Meryl had blonde hair, brilliant blue eyes, and small doll-like features; it was not surprising that she could lay hands on one and ninepence whenever we needed it. She told me that very few of her clients ever got as far as putting their cocks inside her; they were usually too nervous or excited, and would come soon after she'd touched them. She had a way of looking at them, and swaying from side to side, of unbuttoning their flies (no zips in those days) and grasping their balls in her tiny hand, which was never frozen. She kept talcum powder in her pocket like a tennis-player; a little rubbing with this, and a few moves to indicate that she was about to take the cock into her mouth would be enough to bring even the most self-controlled punters to climax. She collected the spunk in lace-fringed handkerchiefs, none of which she would ever throw away. They would be rinsed out when she got home, and placed in the water in the kettle from which her adoptant parents would make their early-morning cup of tea.

Meryl, you'll have gathered, was not one of the girls at Dotty's. She had been fostered for a while, then adopted by the foster-parents. Anything she asked for, she was given. I thought she had all the luck in the world, and could not understand why she played her new parents up or how she had to come to know so much about sex. After I'd known her some time, she told me about Uncle Alan who came to baby-sit once a week, and while her doting adoptant parents were supporting the Arts at the Grand Theatre, sitting spell-bound through Rebecca or weeping through Goodbye, Mr Chips, *Meryl was learning a hundred and one ways with a handful of talc.*

Though I was Meryl's side-kick, I was never an apt pupil. I used to pray for the men to tell me to bugger off, and if they said 'OK' I'd close my eyes and clench my teeth, which caused some of them to lose interest, button themselves up, and wander off. Some would do the business, and wander off without paying. 'Get the money first, girl. Grip it tight in your left hand, and do what you have to with your right.' I was supposed to say 'Money first!' but I could never bring myself to treat it as a business transaction. For me, saying 'Money first!' was like paying for a meal before you'd eaten it.

I often went home sore, and not being able to have a bath for weeks on end didn't help. It was a vaginal discharge that gave me away. Dotty woke me up one morning, waving a pair of knickers in my face. 'Whose are these?' Then it was certainly a bath, but it was in cold water, and she had poured into it a pint of San Izal, which was a powerful disinfectant, used for unblocking drains. Dotty leaned over me, crying and swearing, and telling me I was the first person in the house ever to have caught something nasty, and how she had never experienced anything like it in her whole life before. I forbore to point out that she seemed to have recognized the signs quickly enough, but in fact what Dotty had recognized, or thought she had recognized, was the gonococcal discharge in men, and the VD Clinic to which she sent me after having permed my hair, painted my face, and instructed me to say I was over eighteen and give a false name, diagnosed thrush.

I was propositioned twice on the way to the Clinic. Meryl laughed like Little Audrey when I told her, but decided that she had better introduce me to French Letters anyway, and demonstrated the correct way to slip one on while pretending to examine a broom-handle in Woolworth's.

It's ironic that it was Meryl who died of cervical cancer on October 30th, 1968, which was about the time I decided to put my experience of Child Care to some use, to start training officially, and to study to become a Social Worker.

FOUR

It's always a bit formal, going to see Mother where she is now, always a false situation. I'll never get to know her that way, sitting with her for an hour once a fortnight, and she'll never know me, even if she felt inclined to.

I sit there, watching her as she is now, the pink hair-ribbon, the folds of sallow skin, the eyes sometimes dead or far away, sometimes reacting to the slightest noise or movement at the other end of the room. Those eyes always express fear; even when they are as dead as pebbles, they express fear – 'Who's this? Is anything expected of me? What are they going to do to me now?' As I watch her I'm also watching myself, and making judgements on us both; I can't help it. Every time is the same. From the moment I get into the car, I begin lecturing myself about its being a social visit and how we must both enjoy it, about living in the present and not expecting too much. I'm still chuntering away to myself when I park the car and walk up the drive. Then I see her, and immediately I begin to watch her. She herself only gives me one moment of eye-contact, right at the beginning when she registers who I am. That flicker of recognition sends us both travelling back all those years.

During the months when I was looking for her, going from Reference Library to Reference Library, register after register, I kept asking myself what I was looking for and why was I bothering. I never managed an answer. Part of me hoped I wouldn't find her, or better still that I'd discover she was dead, which would have saved my having to make any decisions. Another part of me knew that I had to find her alive; we had unfinished business. When I sensed that I was getting close to her, I became very scared.

You know those little windows in the swing-doors of hospital wards? I stood behind one of them watching her for over an hour, a bundle of cardigans over a Bri-nylon nightdress, shuffling about the ward in broken-down slippers, first to one bed, then another, redistributing the magazines, swapping this and that, exchanging the occasional word, constantly chewing on a caramel, and dribbling from the left side of her mouth. At first I thought she was the Tobacco Baroness, collecting her dues, then she seemed more like the Lady of the Manor, visiting sick villagers. I thought to myself, 'That's me, That's what I'm doing – a Social Worker, poking my nose into everyone else's business, and pretending that it's for their own good. So that's where I got it from!'

I can't tell you how pleased I felt at having recognized some of myself in her, forgetting that ten minutes earlier I'd had to ask which was she among this ward of old women. The nurse had said, 'That's Mrs Davis. The one with the pink hair-ribbon.'

When finally I walked into the ward, I'd decided that I'd pretend I was visiting someone else, and see what happened. My legs were wobbly, so I fixed my eyes on a chair by a bed, and headed straight for that. It turned out that the woman whose bed I had chosen never had visitors, and didn't know what to make of me. I worried that I might be slowing, or maybe quickening, her pulse-rate, so I said quickly, 'Please don't worry. I haven't come to talk to you about God or the hereafter. I'm a hospital-visitor, like they have in prisons; I do this voluntarily.'

All the time I talked to the woman, I was watching my mother, and she was watching me. Not because she knew who I was; she hadn't a clue. No, she was the unelected monitor of that ward, and felt she had a right to know what was going on; if the old women in that ward saw one visitor a month, they thought themselves lucky. She was as curious as hell to know how the old biddy to whom I was talking so animatedly had found herself a relative. I didn't find it easy to fire questions at this complete stranger, and pay a decent attention to her mumbled answers, while a mother I hadn't seen for almost thirty years was leaning over the patient in the next bed, dribbling caramel into her hearing-aid as she tried to listen to our conversation.

Then I did an even naughtier thing. I asked the woman to whom I was talking if she would introduce me to the lady in the hair-ribbon, and the woman raised an arm very slowly as if it were to be her last gesture, and beckoned my mother over.

Both my names are common, but I still expected some recognition, or at the very least for her to say, 'That's a coincidence. My name's Davis, and I have a daughter called Jean,' but she didn't; she never mentioned me. What happened was that she shuffled over, clutching a bundle of magazines to her bosom, and stood there, glaring. I said, 'I see you keep everyone well supplied with fashion tips,' and laughed a silly self-conscious laugh while she waited. Then I said, 'I'm told we have the same surname, Davis, is that right?', and she nodded, and then said, 'It's common,' and I laughed again, and said, 'I suppose it is.' Then I did an even dafter thing. Before I realized what I was doing, my arm had been stretched out towards her, with the hand dangling there at the end of it, hanging in mid-air, while my mother looked at it; I was attempting to shake hands with my own mother. For a moment I thought she would walk away, leaving my hand suspended, without shaking it. Then I said, 'I'm Jean. Hullo!', she gave my fingers a perfunctory tug, turned on her heels, nodding, and went to scrounge another caramel from somebody in an adjacent bed. So much for family reunions!

All I could do after that was to continue round the ward as a general visitor, and work slowly towards letting drop who I was and where I was born. I heard myself sounding more and more middle-class, struggling to make meaningless small-talk, watchful, bored, only half-concentrated on those I was talking to, as if my main reason for being there was to find something humorous to take home to talk about over dinner.

I visited that ward four times in all. On my second visit I confided to an old dear who still seemed to have all her marbles that I was trying to find my mother whom I hadn't seen since I was a child, and on the third visit I used the two magic words 'Wood End'.

Whatever I expected my next visit to bring, it was certainly not what I got. I knew that a rush into my arms would have been out of character, that stony silence would be more probable, perhaps an avoidance of me or even an outright denial that she had ever set a bicycle wheel near Wood End. What actually happened was that I arrived with my arms full of flowers for the centre table and copies of Vogue and Harper's, only to be told that Mrs Sarah Davis had discharged herself two days earlier, wearing slippers and a nightdress and three cardigans belonging to other patients. The police had stopped her two miles down the road, but she had insisted on a change of hospital. She had no money, no other family, no support, nothing but what she stood up in, yet she was running away from me.

Later she claimed it was coincidence, that she had not been told who I was, and had just become bored with that hospital, and felt like a move. I assumed that decamping was her way of letting me know that she did not wish to be found, so I didn't rush to her new address, but wrote to her, promising that I wouldn't approach her until she was ready. I sent flowers, chocolates, money, even a new cardigan, which turned out to be the wrong size. Each time I wrote I sent a present, and always a stamped, addressed envelope for a reply. I remember writing, 'Please answer this letter, even if you feel you can't see me. There's no reason why we shouldn't correspond.'

Nothing came back, nothing for months. I'd promised I wouldn't approach her, but found it difficult to stay away. Several times I was on the verge of going, just to see if she were still there, just to peep through a door and watch her with the magazines and the caramels.

At last, when I'd given up hope, one of my self-addressed envelopes arrived. It contained a short note written by a nurse. I'd had no idea that my mother could neither read nor write. No wonder she needed so many magazines; she could only look at the pictures. 'No reason why we shouldn't correspond'! It had probably taken her three months to ask someone to read my letters to her.

All the note said was, 'Dear Jean, could you please send me money for some clothes, then I would be able to meet with you if that is what you want,' then the name printed in capitals, 'SARAH DAVIS', then in the nurse's hand again, within a bracket, 'Your mother'.

'Send me money for some clothes'! Even in my mother's old age, melodrama was never far away. It was shoes and a winter coat she wanted, because the season was autumn, and she didn't want to sit with me inside the ward, where everyone could watch and listen. As it turned out, there wasn't much for anyone to overhear. That's what my mother is like, one day wandering the roads in her nightgown, the next worrying what the patient in the next bed will think.

So we shared a bench in the grounds of the hospital, shivering, mostly in silence, for the best part of an afternoon, two strangers without much to say to each other. I wanted to tell her about my work, but found that I couldn't. Too many words were taboo – children, abuse, care, bonding, not that she'd have known what bonding meant. There we sat, facing front in our headscarves like two of those Russian dolls that fit inside each other, talking about the weather and what she'd had for lunch. She only asked three questions; was I married, did I live alone, and did I have a car? She perked up when I said I did, and suggested that if I visited her again we might drive out somewhere. 'If I visited her again'! I suppose neither of us knew how to behave towards the other. We still don't.

There wasn't much physically wrong with her. She was just destitute, and getting on in years; there are millions like her, She had been in various Council Homes, but, reading between the lines, had either played up and been moved on, or had grown bored with her surroundings and wandered away to find a friendly policeman. She preferred hospitals, because they were less permanent, less like a prison. She would put on an act to get herself admitted – pains in the chest (they have to keep you in for that), or she would pretend that she didn't know her own name or what day it was. She would sit there in Casualty, refusing to budge or pretending to faint; it would just be a character-part for her, 'The Old Cow Who's a Bit Doolally'. I could tell that she enjoyed it. Being my mother, and rather a bad actress, she would probably get the lines wrong, forget about her chest, and rabbit on about her feet.

She would have survived without any help from me. She is too old now to do runners when she gets bored. I can remember those varicose veins when they wore gravy-browning instead of stockings, and were often wrapped around a male torso, usually foreign. I wonder if she ever thinks of that now.

On my second visit, Sister took me aside, and asked me when I was taking my mother home. That took me by surprise. 'Home, Sister?' I said. 'What home?'

FIVE

For a whole week in the summer of 1953, Meryl and Jean had a holiday from real life. The sun shone, colours seemed more vivid, scents stronger and more pleasant, and there was bird-song everywhere. They would take a punt on the river, moor it to the tree-roots reaching from the bank into the water, unpack a picnic and sunbathe, just the two of them. It seemed to them that they never stopped giggling the entire week. Anything could set them off. It was as if they had inhaled laughing-gas.

They would set out early each morning, wearing their best summer dresses over bathing costumes, so that they could slip the dresses off and lie there by the river getting a tan, and when they grew too hot, they would sit under the willows, squinting up at the sun through the branches. They had discovered Rhyming Slang, and would play a game with it – 'strong light' – 'Snow White', 'sunburn' – 'Never learn': one had to guess at the meaning of the rhyme, and, so great was the rapport between them, that mostly each guessed right first time.

Every evening they would sit in the cinema, glowing from the sun. On the screen were technicolour pictures of romantic, exciting places and beautiful, intelligent, interesting people, and down in the darkened auditorium were Meryl and Jean, holding hands. Anything seemed possible during that wonderful week.

One afternoon, when they had been laughing easily for hours, Meryl suddenly became serious, and said, 'Whatever happens to us, I want you to know that I won't ever forget you. You're the best friend I ever had or ever will, the only person who understands me or really cares for me. I love you more than I'd love a sister. I'd be so happy, if only there could be just the two of us, and every day could be like this.'

The Monday of that week was a Bank Holiday, and the riverside was crowded. There were children running after ducks, teenagers in all shades of biscuit, wives walking arm in arm with husbands, their faces and shoulders pink from the sun. It was all dappled sunlight, gentle shade, ripples on water and jolly faces, like one of those Impressionist paintings of Edwardian people in summer clothes parading in the Park, where the children have hoops and straw hats, and time stands still.

Meryl and Jean were sunbathing by the river bank, when they saw Eric Morrison taking his family for a walk. When he saw Jean, the man who had been her Boarding Out Officer left his family, and came to say, 'Hello!' Then he asked whether he and his wife and their two small children might join the party.

He asked how Jean was, and told her that a sun-tan suited her, and that she was looking very pretty. He introduced his wife, and she seemed relaxed and at ease and not at all condescending. The children were toddlers, still in nappies under their dungarees. They laughed, and gurgled, and seemed to enjoy rubbing their noses against Jean's nose. They picked up twigs and bunches of grass, and presented them to her as if they were bunches of flowers. One of them sat on Jean's lap, and played with her fingers, and cuddled up to her, and did not want to leave when it was time to go. Even now, Jean Davis, the Social Worker, finds it difficult to express how protective she felt at that moment, how happy and how pleased with herself.

The Boarding Out Officer said that he was glad to have seen Jean, and glad that she was looking so well. He told Jean that she was going to make a fine woman. Those were his very words, 'You're going to be a fine woman, Jean, in spite of all you've been through. You've got it in you to help people and make them happy, I know. You'll always have some bad memories, but try to use them, and make them work for you. They'll help you to have insight into how other people feel, and you'll get pleasure, a lot of pleasure, from helping others. I have a lot of faith in you, Jean.'

Then he kissed Jean on the cheek, and gave her a phone-number to ring if she needed help, and she stood up, and hugged him very tight, and kissed the dandruff on his eye-lashes, and he smiled at her, such a loving smile. Meryl was weeping by the time the Morrison family left. She said Jean was lucky to have friends like that.

One of the reasons both girls were so moved is that the Morrisons had been so natural with them, a pair of rough and cheeky adolescents. There had been no pretence, no embar-rassment, just warmth and a real concern. Eric Morrison must have dealt with hundreds of young people; Jean and Meryl could have been nothing special to him. Yet, after they had moved a little away, both he and his wife turned to wave at the two girls, and Jean had the feeling that he too was crying.

Jean felt ten feet tall, almost as if she were floating, so happy to have seen him again, and that he had not just passed them by with a nod, or (worse still) pretended not to recognize her. While she was sitting with his baby on her lap, a toddler with shiny blue eyes like his, and lemon sherbet round its mouth, Eric had said, 'You seem to be very good with children, Jean. They like you. Perhaps that's what you should do, look after children.'

It's difficult to relate the 'me' now to the 'me' then, though I suppose that in some important ways I haven't changed all that much. My feelings for Meryl were very strong, more than a crush. We held hands in the cinema. I was allowed to stay the night at her house a few times, and we kissed and cuddled when we slept together. She was pretty, and seemed to be confident, and I was neither, but we did have other things in common. We both had a gaping chasm in our lives. When that's so, you either freeze up completely or you go around trying to get the world and its dog to hop into bed with you. Meryl skipped through life, suppressing an enormous rage, and I walked behind, picking up stray bits of affection she had dropped.

I was with her when she died, hadn't seen her for years before that, but we'd exchanged Christmas cards. She had married someone likeable and steady – you see, one can reform. She had given birth to two daugh-ters, and the family owned a detached house near St Albans.

When I saw her, she was in a private room, with the blind lowered. Her likeable and steady husband was sitting in the corner furthest away from the bed, crying his heart out. My first thought when I looked at her lying there, and then looked at him, was 'At last she's got the revenge she always wanted.' That's not very attractive I know, but I was angry – angry and shocked at her appearance as she lay there, more like someone in her sixties than her thirties: I was angry at what the disease and the hospital had done to her, a mere skeleton, drugged to the eyeballs. I had to keep telling myself, 'This is a shell, not the Meryl you knew, the Meryl who could make you feel needed.'

I'll never know if she was aware of who it was, sitting by the bed, gripping her hand, and talking nonsense about the Dame Alice Harper School for Girls, and the way the two of us would watch the sweet little things in their striped gingham dresses and silly hats troop through the school gates, before we ourselves turned on our heels and belted down the street to continue our educations elsewhere. I reminded her then of Eric Morrison and his wife by the river at Bedford, and how they had said we were special people and had a special future – maybe not a very tactful reminder, since her own special future had turned out to be death from cervical cancer in a private ward, but she wasn't in a condition to distinguish such niceties.

Afterwards her likeable and steady husband asked me if I'd found my mother. I told him I hadn't been searching for her, which I hadn't then. He said, 'I think you should, I really do. Meryl kept asking for hers, but no one seemed to know where to start looking.'

I thought it an odd remark to make to someone whom he was meeting for the first time, but I had written long messages on the backs of the Christmas cards, and I suppose he'd asked who I was, and Meryl had told him something about me.

I considered what he had said off and on for about a year. Then, as you know, I began looking.

PART THREE

Future Conditional

She negotiated Hyde Park Corner, and was heading north inside the Park towards the Edgware Road. She was not sure exactly where she was going, except that it would be north, but assumed that she would know when she had arrived. She did not expect that the police would follow her, or have the authority to send her back, but she would avoid the motorways, just in case. The A1 was said to be a good road, the Great North Road; that had a ring about it.

Michael's snoring had stopped. Twice at traffic lights she had glanced sideways, expecting to see his eyes wide open, knowing that when this happened she would have to pull into the side of the road and stop the car, before his panic caused an accident. It had not been easy getting him away, but it had been done. She had gone into his room, helped him finish the Giant Jigsaw, then taken him by the hand, led him into her room, closed the door, and lain down on the bed. Luckily he had been more puzzled than upset by her explanation that it could be Thursday whenever they decided to make it so.

'What about next week, Jean? How will I know then what day it is?'

'We'll sit down, and work it out together. We'll decide between us what day we want to be Thursday. How about that?'

So they had performed their Thursday ritual together, and afterwards he had obediently taken the tranquillizers she had given him, and meanwhile Joy had packed his suitcase. Everything was in his room. Michael never left his toiletries in the bathroom for Tony or anyone else to use. He would carry his sponge-bag around the house with him for days at a time, clutching it as if it were his wallet, and he a tourist visiting the souks of Tangier. His clean underwear was kept neatly folded in the bottom drawer of his dressing-table; Jean suspected that an inventory was taken of each item every night before Lights Out. Buying him new had been out of the question; the breaking in of new underpants or a new toothbrush took several days of hard labour, and a great many sedatives.

Maida Vale, Kilburn, Brondesbury, West Hampstead to the right of them, Willesden to the left. He had been dressed in his suit with shirt and tie – nothing unusual to alarm him – and led dopily downstairs into the dark street, bereft of both reporters and police, and placed in the passenger-seat, his seat-belt fastened, his suitcase with hers in the back. Jean and Joy had clung together for a moment on the pavement, then Jean, lightly bruised with hugs, had got into the car, and started the engine, and begun their journey, with Michael already snoring. Along Shoot-Up Hill, then into sleeping Cricklewood. This was the area in which she had started as a Social Worker. With no traffic on the roads, they had crossed from south into north London in less than half an hour, and Jean had moved back sixteen years.

Copperfield Road, Dollis Hill! Snow on the ground, 'Jingle Bells' from every transistor radio, and Jean Davis about to take her first child into Care. The name of the road had not been the only Dickensian aspect of that period of her life.

She had been a spanking-new, fully trained Generic Social Worker, 1971 model, equipped to deal with any human problem and many which might seem inhuman – the disabled, Divorce Laws, the law on juveniles, Legal Aid, Nursery School Provision, Drug and Sex Abuse, Absconding, Shoplifting, Rehousing, Intimidation by landlords, Neglect, Alcoholism, all of them headings in her notebooks. Smiling, they had said to her in the Department, 'If you're unsure, never act alone. We're always here to advise you.' She had not realized that this advice would only be available if she could outrun them, had long arms, a loud voice and a Gold Medal in lassoing Team Leaders.

They had said, 'There's no shallow water in this profession, Jean. It's everyone in at the deep end, and count the bodies floating on top.' They had explained that there were staff shortages, without adding that there had always been, and would always be staff shortages, and had given her a case-load of thirty clients on her first day, rising to a hundred and fourteen at the end of the first six months, and by the end of her first year she had begun to need pills to help her sleep, and other pills to keep her awake.

Copperfield Road, Christmas 1971. Jean's boots, lined with imitation fur, making patterns in the slush, and the words 'No reproach, no blame' going round and round in her head to the tune of 'Silent Night'. All the books agreed. Child-abusers have very low self-esteem. Never reproach, never blame.

Number Eighteen had been a corner house, and she had heard the child screaming from the other end of the road. They were the kind of screams that would have stopped a Jumbo Jet. They had also drowned out Jean's knocking, so she had gone to the side of the house, found the kitchen door, and entered uninvited. A black woman had been standing by the sink, six feet tall and as wide as a house, and oozing the self-esteem she was supposed to lack. Jean and the woman had stood looking at each other, as the screaming continued from an upstairs room. Then Jean, keeping her hand on the door-handle, had spoken her reproachless first words, 'Does your child cry a lot?' straight from the book. 'Sets your nerves on edge, I expect, when it screams like that.' The understanding smile intended to accompany the words was a little crooked, since one side of Jean's mouth seemed to have frozen. 'One of your neighbours heard it, and asked me to come and see if you were alright . . . if you needed help.'

The black woman had moved no more than a fraction to lean the weight of her buttocks against the sink. Between the non-judgemental sentences, and while the child above filled its lungs with air in order to scream again, both women heard the door-handle Jean was holding rattle. Jean released it, and wiped her sweaty hand on her coat; the kitchen was like an oven. 'I work with mothers and their babies all the time.' This was her first Home Visit, her first professional lie; there would be plenty more. The woman's right arm moved slowly until it was level with the draining-board. Six inches from her hand was an empty milk-bottle. The words straight from the book had not impressed this mother, whose huge fingers gripped the neck of the bottle, and began lifting it to take aim.

It had not been the United States Cavalry but the child itself who had saved Jean, choosing that moment to dash howling into the room and grab its mother round the shins. Naked and bruised, with new and raw strap-marks still bleeding on its bottom, it had cuddled its mother's legs for reassurance, had grabbed and kissed at the mother's left hand lowered towards it. Then, having kissed the hand better, the toddler had turned to inspect Jean, the visitor.

Until that moment Jean had thought that the child was holding part of a toy, but it was not a toy, and the child was not holding it. It was a leather bootlace, tied round the end of the child's penis, which had swollen to three times its normal size.

Jean had not been allowed to touch the child. The mother had explained that she was unable to untie the knot, because it had become too tight. She had said, 'No child of mine gets away with wetting its bed. That's not the way I was brought up.' And Jean had phoned for an ambulance, threatened the woman with the police if she interfered, and warned her that her little boy's foreskin might already be gangrenous. First Home Visit of a Generic Social Worker. Unto us a child is born, unto us a son is given.

On Christmas Eve, with madonnas and angels erupting all over the borough, she had visited another house, and found a child who had been dead four days.

The mother had been warned of her visit, and had taken the child out of its shit-marked, verminous clothes for Jean's inspection, removing some of its skin in the process. Having undressed it, the mother had then realized that she had nothing else for it to wear except its unused christening robe. Jean had been shown the child in its crib, a Christmas child which had died of malnutrition, hypothermia and general neglect, and, remembering the books, had spoken words of sympathy with the mother at her loss, while reading the washing instructions on the christening robe. The mother had looked straight at her, and asked her if she, as a professional, knew why there were so many cot-deaths these days.

'They don't have Christmases like that any more.' They do, of course.

Dawn! They were approaching Biggleswade in Bedfordshire

– would she ever escape Bedfordshire? There was a road-sign, indicating a lay-by half a mile ahead. With any luck it would have a toilet, or at least some tall bushes. Michael slept on.

By eleven o'clock they were stuck, sandwiched between a Volvo Estate and a baker's van, unable to move forwards or back. They were somewhere in either Leicestershire or Lincolnshire; Jean was no longer quite sure which. She had slept for a couple of hours in the lay-by, without waking Michael, and had then decided, since they were in no hurry, to meander, moving away from the A1 down any side-road where the names on the signposts looked interesting. In this way they would not only more closely resemble a couple on a motoring holiday with no particular destination in mind, but might hope to confuse any police cars which happened to be following. How could Jean have known that all traffic would suddenly come to a halt, and there would be police cars everywhere?

Even now one such was approaching her from the opposite direction very slowly, giving its driver time to note the number of her car, its description and that of Jean itself. Jean made a pretence of retrieving something from the floor of her car. If Michael were to wake now, it would be to discover himself surrounded by the vehicles of strangers, motionless in a strange town, with his friend and protector scrabbling by him on the floor as if in terror. Probably he would die immediately of the shock, and she would have the complication and expense of burying him. The police car had gone past; the driver had not even waved. It was leading a procession, clearing the road of Saturday morning shoppers. The driver of the Volvo Estate had switched his engine off, and the baker's man behind had left his van, and could now be seen through the windows of Bottoms Up Off-Licence purchasing his weekend's supply of canned beer.

The procession was led by a band. Behind it came a group of young girls, all dressed in bright orange, the two in front holding a banner on which had been painted the words 'Withlem Twirlettes'. Both the band and the girls were marching on the spot, moving only intermittently forwards, and the man carrying the big drum already looked as if he had had enough. Some of the Twirlettes were twirling, and others dropping, batons. Walking on either side of the younger Twirlettes were mothers, who wore their own uniform of black skirts and white nylon blouses, and who shouted oaths as they scampered to retrieve the dropped batons and return them to their off-spring.

Jean had blundered into the Annual Drum-Majorette Festival of the East Midlands. Fifteen teams were represented from three counties; they were sponsored by a brewery, two local Chambers of Commerce, an Insurance company, the makers of Distinguished Lincolnshire Pork Sausages and the East Midlands Arts Association, representing the Arts Council of Great Britain. The noise was confused; it was no wonder that so many batons were being dropped. Apart from the persistent beeping of stationary vehicles wishing to become mobile, each group of Drum-Majorettes had its own musical accompaniment, the Marching Band of the Withlem Twirlettes being followed by the van of J. Liphook, Greengrocer & Seedsman, on which two loudspeakers had been mounted so as to allow the Rayleigh Royals to twirl their own batons to a scratchy recording of the Beatles, singing 'When I'm Sixty-Four'. Add to this the raucous barracking of the lunchtime drinkers outside the Black Bull, the oaths of the mothers, and the whitter of complaint from the Drum-Majorettes themselves as they were bumped and kicked from behind by other Drum-Majorettes wishing to go faster. Add the hurdy-gurdy of the Blethnot Ambassadrices, the 'Seventy-Six Trombones' of the four trombones accompanying the Huntford Harlequines (who wore trousers of red satin and had brought an infant tambourinist for comic effect), add the bass drum, the snare drum and the two triangles of the Merrydown Marchionesses, add 'Viva España' on a wind-up gramophone in a baby's pram, add mothers and more mothers, the wails of lost children and damned souls, add bands and vans and more and more Drum-Majorettes, large and small, the large ones slapping their thighs as they twirled, the small sniffing and wiping runny noses on the backs of their batons, some in teams which seemed to be of hundreds, others merely of dozens, add judges, marking the Drum-Majorettes for poise and precision, flair, turn-out, athleticism and artistic impression, judges posted all along the route, hiding in telephone boxes, holding their clip-boards steady on the backs of their husbands, judges being ogled by mothers, male judges winking at the larger Drum-Majorettes, and middle-aged female judges misty-eyed at six-year-olds in shakos and short flared skirts, bringing back memories of Shirley Temple. Add and add, add beyond the height your imagination reaches, and know that there is yet more to add.

A perspiring hand is given a surreptitious wipe on a mauve skirt before sending a baton high in the air above Jean's car. Three unrehearsed sidesteps are quickly taken to catch it before it dents the bonnet. 'Back in line, Brenda!' Brenda is back in line, hat askew, sweat running down both sides of her face, giving a glaring smile in the direction of the clip-board on the steps of Spar Groceries.

'There's another judge, our Sharon. Don't look now, you great slag-heap! Give her an eyes right as you pass. And try to enjoy the bloody thing for Christ's sake. If I catch you sulking, I won't come out to support you again, and that's a promise. Beverley, Sharon's going to be doing triple-time right behind you, so lengthen your stride.'

'Does she have to? I've had blisters on these heels ever since the Multiple Sclerosis Benefit. If she takes the tops off them before tonight's Disco, I'll kill her.'

Jean counted two Drum-Majorettes with their arms in slings, and four with support-bandages on their knees or ankles. Many of the smaller girls gripped their upper lips with their lower teeth in a rictus of concentration, and several had bitten through so that blood ran down the sides of their chins like the Brides of Dracula. From a long way further down the line came barks and agitated screams and the noise of embattled mothers; an Alsatian dog had sunk its teeth into the calf of one of the Hillsden High-Steppers. Jean decided that she might as well take advantage of the delay by shopping for something to eat at a picnic later, and left the car. Shortly after she had done so, Michael awoke.

First there had been music of various kinds, all mixed together into a tangle of noise, and he had set himself the task of unpicking the mess of sounds piece by piece unknotting and separating them like differently coloured strands of wool. There had been scratchy records, relayed through amplifiers, a brass band coming close and then moving away, a pop song from a Ghetto Blaster going by on roller-skates, someone playing the spoons, triangle, comb-and-paper, a barrel organ, and now a dog howling and the scream of a woman. People shouting, someone swearing; the dog was His Master's Voice, going round and round in the middle of a record, while the band played 'Happy Days Are Here Again'. Petrol fumes. Car-horns, drowning out the brass band. High-pitched hysterical weeping between deep chesty barks, and other smaller dogs answering the barks, and car-horns answering the car-horns, until all the batteries were forever flat.

Sunlight reflected through glass on glittering braid. Knees going up and down, being lifted in slow motion and lowered again. Large sticks spinning in the air, and being waved threateningly. White thighs wobbling below ruby-coloured knickers. Everything through plate glass, which was how he always perceived the more interesting aspects of the world. Sometimes the glass was greasy and smeared. Swirling colours and glitter breaking through bars of sunlight, all reduced to particles of dust around a maker's name and a warranty to be shatter-proof.

The taut skin of a snare-drum being tickled, the loose skin of large thighs shaken. A tax disc partially obscures the face of a young girl with blood on her chin, standing next to a white blouse enclosing huge breasts. Faces, large and small faces, flushed and damp faces, faces into which blood rushed and from which blood drained away. Then another face, blocking out all the others, male, smiling above a new uniform, young face glistening, with gold bum-fluff below each ear.

'Do you have a driver, sir? Sorry to bother you; I can see you've been having a little sleep. But we thought we might clear some of this traffic. Is your driver about?'

Absolute necessity of holding himself together before the particles disintegrate, smearing the glass. His name is Michael. He wears a suit with a shirt and tie. He will address the face with politeness and reason before closing shutters. 'My name is Michael. I suffer from an excess of far-sighted ownsome-ness.'

'Oh, there you are, madam! I think you can back a little now, and get round. Sorry for the delay. Your passenger must have ear-plugs to be able to sleep through that lot. Mind how you go, now.'

So he was in a car, could now sense the movement of it, feel the cool air hitting his face. The pictures on the plate glass changed, bright colours giving place to trees, hedgerows and blue sky. His head ached, his neck would not move, and his limbs were rigid with cramp. Did he, however, wish to move? If he tried to move, he felt pain. He did not wish to move. He wished not to move.

'I'll stop soon, so that we can stretch our legs. You've had a very long sleep; I expect your head aches. I'll just get us a bit further away from the Filth and all those bloody stupid people, then we can sort you out.'

Sorting him out would not be easy, and he did not intend to make it easy.

The car had been parked in a small lay-by on a very minor country road. The door on the passenger side was open, and Jean sat on the grass close to it. She was peeling skin from salami with a pen-knife, and sipping from a can of Ruddles County Bitter. Laid out on a towel before her were tomatoes, two kinds of cheese, wholemeal rolls and celery. She had forgotten to buy salt.

'I thought nipping into that shop might be a good way to use the time. I hadn't reckoned with Mister Plod trying to chat you up.' She put a slice of salami in her mouth. 'This is very tasty, Mike. You should try some. You're going to have to force yourself to have a drink, at least. In this heat, you'll be ill if you don't.' She stood, leaning forward and placing the cool beer-can against his forehead. 'Let me just try to move you the tiniest little bit. The longer you stay hunched up in that position, the more painful it'll become.' She placed her free hand over his, and began rubbing his hand gently. 'We've got to get the circulation moving, Michael, or gangrene will set in. And you know what that means, don't you? All your more important bits will drop off.'

She was anxious, but must not show it. He was terrified of moving or being moved. Should she rush at him suddenly, and take him by surprise, risk his screams and what might follow? 'Try and waggle your fingers for me. If we start slowly, we can work up gradually.' His eyes watched her. 'There's just you and I here, no one else for miles. We've all the time in the world, and you can hold onto me if you need reassurance.' His eyes mocked her. She knew exactly what that expression meant. In the hospital they had told him that being manly meant being grown up, being taken notice of, going to work, being aggressive, punctual, winning the respect of others. Being childish, they had said, was playing the same record over and over again, sitting around eating sweets, dancing in a corner on one's own, and watching television in the afternoon. So he had decided to be childish.

Slowly she manipulated his fingers until they were spread wide, and he could close them into a fist and open again without her help. 'I'll bet if I told you today was a Thursday, you'd move soon enough.'

Then the words came. Quietly, almost in a whisper, but perfectly distinctly Michael said, 'If I believed everything you told me after this, I'd be insane, wouldn't you say?'

Eventually she was able to slide his legs round, so that he was sitting sideways with his feet on the grass. His head lolled, and he gripped the seat with both hands, but with a can of beer held to his lips, he was able to drink. With the drink, she gave him his medication, but withholding the tranquillizers. She was angry, guilty and felt sick. The only explanation she could think of for his long sleep was that Joy had given him extra tranquillizers behind her back before they left. It was dangerous and wrong. Jean alone was the person responsible for making sure Michael took his drugs. What had got into Joy, what could she have been thinking of? She herself had given him five milligrams extra. How many more must Joy have given him, for Christ's sake?

On the outskirts of Grantham, close to a canal, Jean stopped for petrol. Beside the Petrol Station was a Breakers' Yard, and beyond that a sign, reading, 'Eric and Bernard Ponsonby. Second-Hand Cars. Would you Dare Buy from Anyone Else?'

Jean asked what car the Ponsonby brothers could offer her in a straight exchange for her own, and was treated to a deal of tut-tutting and head-shaking, and a joke about how would she fancy a reconditioned bicycle. Eric and Bernard were not all that keen on straight exchanges; it took the interest out of the job. What they preferred was to sell at the prices marked on the windscreen, and buy as cheaply as possible. They had, after all, a business to run and nine infant Erics and Bernards to put through college. Who was the silent passenger who was hugging his stomach as if he had taken an overdose of beef vindaloo? He looked a right misery to Eric and Bernard. Why not dump him, and spend Saturday night with them, seeing the lights of Grantham? Mrs Eric and Mrs Bernard would not be put out in the least, since their own Saturday nights were invariably spent in Nottingham, where they went to see the wrestling. Eric and Bernard deserved the consolation, their wives being grapple-crazy.

Jean was flattered, and told them so. Eric and Bernard were large and round, with matching T-shirts and matching sweat-stains; they were the Tweedledum and Tweedledee of the Second-Hand Car Business. When they were enjoying them-selves, which clearly they were this afternoon, the bodies of both shook with mirth, and the mouths of both opened wide to exhibit the remains of yellowed teeth, quite untouched by dental instruments.

After Bernard had taken Jean's car for a run round the town to test its roadworthiness and 'to see what she sounds like' Jean was offered eleven hundred pounds for it, cash. If she fancied the five-year-old Metro with only forty-nine thou-sand miles on the clock, they were not going to screw her, since she was so obviously a lady; it was taxed until October, they'd throw in a tank full of petrol and a tyre-pressure gauge, and she could have it for seven hundred, which would leave her with four hundred pounds in her pocket and not a word to the tax-man. Alright, so it was getting on a bit, but it had been well looked after. They knew it was a goer because they had seen it used as a getaway car in a local bank-raid. Not that it was any of their business, she understood, but was she desperate for cash, or had her own car been used for naughties?

Jean drove away in the five-year-old Metro. It might well have been used exclusively for town driving, since for a considerable time it refused to move out of third gear. As for what it sounded like, Michael complained that its sounds were not as pleasant as those of the car Jean had sold. He particularly disliked a knocking sound which he located in the engine, and the whistle from an ill-fitting window set his teeth on edge. Also the Metro had insufficient leg-room.

Jean was glad to know that Michael had come out of shock, and was his usual self again.

Their hotel room was equipped with a shower-cubicle, WC and wash-hand-basin. The shower gave a choice of two temperatures, icy cold or hot enough to produce third-degree burns. Michael had spent fifteen minutes adjusting the two prints which hung on the wall opposite the two single beds, and had repositioned the electric kettle and breakfast tray (with tea-bags and separate sachets of instant coffee, powdered milk and sugar) four times, and the contents of the tray a dozen times. He had swivelled the colour-television set around so that it faced the wall, because the reflection on its screen of the room and himself moving around in it disturbed him, reminding him that once at a fairground he had wandered into a corridor of distorting mirrors, and had had to be taken from it, screaming, back to the hospital.

Jean stood by the window, looking down. Steven Gaines had once told her, 'They say we spend the first half of our lives recording, and the second half playing it back, like a cassette-tape.' She watched a young woman with heels far too high for her spindly legs stagger sideways from within the doorway in which she had stopped to light a cigarette. One hand held the cigarette a foot away from her mouth; the other clutched a shiny plastic handbag as far into her armpit as it would go. With elbows bent and lifted high, she looked like a crab about to do its shopping at the January sales. 'The accused was found guilty of being in charge of a cigarette on the public highway, while under the influence of heels.' They were in Doncaster, early on a Saturday night.

He had said, 'On Saturday nights, we always had a bath,

so as to be ready for Sunday. That was the day we used to go to this place, every Sunday in summer, and many in the winter too. That was when I was still small, and Mum was still alive. There was nothing much to see, just a bit posher than where we lived, one or two Antique shops, a pub with a garden at the back, a playing-field with a slide and some broken swings. It was the closest Mum ever came to living in the country; it was twenty minutes bus-ride from the centre of town. She went there to see the houses in the Estate Agent's window; she'd stand looking in that window for hours, licking her lips, and humming to herself. On the bus home she'd go on about how there was a bungalow with large garden for only £3,000, two minutes from the shops, a prime site just off the Bawtry Road. We never did get to look over any of the houses she found out about. The old man wouldn't hear of it.'

Down below, groups of young people cruised the High Street, pretending they were on a promenade somewhere on the Costa Brava. They wore shorts and brightly coloured beach-shirts, drank beer from the can, and threw the cans into the street when they were empty. They sang loudly, shouted from group to group, and openly tried the door-handles of parked cars. Unable to find room in the Car Park of the hotel, Jean had parked the five-year-old Metro under a street-lamp four streets away. This was Doncaster, early on a Saturday night.

She had located on a local map the place where the Gaines children had been taken by their mother to look at the windows of an Estate Agent, but it was not by the sea, not the place where he had shared a caravan with his father and two brothers. Nevertheless she would go there with Michael tomorrow, would look for the playing-field with the broken swings and the pub with the garden. Tonight what she wanted was an early night, and would have liked a long hot bath, or at least to have been able to take a shower. She had decided to change her own appearance as well as her car, and would begin with the colour of her hair; she had bought bleach while shopping for the picnic. The directions on the packet warned purchasers that, unless the preparation were to be rinsed out thoroughly after application, the manufacturers disclaimed accountability for any loss of hair. The wash-hand-basin in the room was too small to contain the whole of her head; a large pair of hands would have found themselves cramped for space. And nothing could be rinsed under the shower. Exposed to that scalding jet, Jean's hair-loss would be total.

Meanwhile Michael paced the room, shaking a sachet of Instant Coffee between thumb and forefinger to hear the noise the tinfoil made.

'Stop pacing, Michael.'

'It's alright to pace if I have a rational reason to be worried, or if I'm trying to work out a problem.'

'What problem are you trying to work out?'

'Why you and I are here? Why did we come here?'

'For a holiday.'

'It's not by the sea. Is it?'

'No, but we shall go to the seaside. Soon.'

Steven Gaines had said, 'My memory-tape keeps getting stuck, playing the same bits like a cracked record. You only have one life, and it's all gone wrong. I'm a perfectionist, did I tell you that? Maureen's had so much Valium over the years, she can remember almost nothing. I remember everything, some bits more than others, like the numbers of blisters and scars on my brothers' hands.' This man who remembered everything had remembered to stitch name-tags onto the collars of his sons' shirts. Did he now remember the nine-year-old boy, lying in mud, with his face pressed against convolvulus? Would he remember that for the rest of his life, as Jean would? 'I suppose I shouldn't have taken it so seriously. We were only children, after all. Children do muck about – you know, sexually; it's part of growing up, isn't it? But, you see, I knew it was all wrong, hated being so weak with them, hated needing them so much, and doing whatever they demanded. You always wish you could start afresh, don't you, wipe the tape clean, and wind it back to the beginning? I hope you'll remember that I loved my children.' Yes, she would remember that. 'Not like my old man, who had no time for his. Nothing is black or white, is it? You know I'm not a monster, don't you? I've told you things no one else must know.' Yes, she had known he was not a monster. 'I'm not sure why I talk to you, except that I want you to trust me, and know that I trust you. I'm not going to insist on access visits with Marianne until you think she's really settled in with these foster-people.' Had that been said before he had looked up the Register of Primary Schools in the Public Library, had sat down with a street-map, ticking them off? He must have made trip after trip, jogging and walking half across London to save fares, visiting every school, standing on the opposite side of the road to watch the children at playtime, until finally he had found the one he was looking for. And after he had seen his daughter, he had hidden himself, and followed her at the end of the school day to her foster-parents' home, planning for the day when he would kidnap her. It had taken months.

The directions on the packet of the Do-It-Yourself Hair Bleach stated that, in order to obtain a brighter, more-dazzling-than-summer look, the preparation must remain on the hair for twenty-five minutes before rinsing. Jean placed a towel round her shoulders, and worked the gooey substance into her hair. While they waited, Michael cleaned his shoes a second time.

At what stage had Adam Gaines attempted to take his sister's place in his father's affections? 'The boys play up more now Marianne's gone. They know I miss her. Seem to compete for my attention all the time. Adam's the worst; won't let me have a moment's peace. Insecure, I suppose. He's the most like me, always has been.' All the signs had been there, and she had done nothing. All she had noticed was a small boy mimicking a ballerina on the television, and it had not occurred to her that he was actually offering himself as a substitute for Marianne. 'It's all affection. It's only affection that goes wrong, Jean.' The same actions, the same movements, until Adam Gaines has been cast . . . until nine-year-old Adam has flirted his way into the part of nine-year-old Steven Gaines, but has played it too well, too believably, has allowed it to be seen, as Steven never allowed it to be seen, that he is enjoying what is being done to him, and so has ended his life counting the scars, not on his brother's hands, but on the hands of the father who bathed him, prepared his meals, and sewed name-tags onto his shirts.

'You're the only person who really knows me. Am I a monster?

147

If you told me I am, I'd have to believe you. That's how much I trust you.' Oh yes, there had been a great deal of that, a great deal of manipulation and moral blackmail, but that had been earlier when Steven Gaines' only crime had been incest with his infant daughter. And that was a common crime, seldom detected, almost as popular as Taking and Driving Away, an offence committed in Doncaster, as in many other towns, every Saturday night.

Jean began to rinse away the bleach. She had worked out that this could be done by filling the basin with water, and rinsing one side of her head, then emptying it and refilling it for the other side, then the same again for the back, which she could achieve by sitting in the room's one straight chair with its back to the basin, and allowing her head to loll backwards as if at the hairdresser's. Then she would finish off with a quick blast of iced water from the shower, then wait for the hair to dry. 'I'm going to look different, Mike. My hair's going to be blonde when it's dry, like Joy's.'

A Directory of Caravan Sites lay on the bed beside her. It was more informative than a Directory of Primary Schools; it listed the attractions offered by each. 'For Mums and Dads . . . For the kids . . . Fun, Freedom and Frolic for all the Family . . . All tastes, all ages catered for . . . Canteen facilities available . . . Self-catering only . . . Blue Dolphin . . . Primrose Valley . . . Wood Nook . . . Chestnut Farm . . . Fred Green & Sons, Skipton . . . Fun! Fun! Fun!'

Michael's expression told her clearly that he did not wish her hair or any part of her to be different in any way, not like Joy, not like anybody. She had hoped that she might be able to persuade him out of the suit and into lightweight summer clothes, a styled haircut, even an ear-ring, anything to make him look more like other people, but it was clear this would not happen. Michael said, 'Am I just part of the furniture in your life, Jean? Is that all I've become?'

'Furniture usually stays at home. I've brought you with me. It's not entirely convenient, considering your anxiety-states, because as well as having a holiday there's something else I have to do, which might involve travelling a lot. I want you to understand something. I'm not your keeper, your wife, mother, doctor or even your Social Worker.' She might have added, 'And I don't intend to put up with you for the rest of your life or mine,' but this would have thrown him into a panic, so she contented herself with, 'I'm just a friend, OK? I brought you with me because I thought you'd be unhappy, left behind with Tony while Joy was out at work. If you trust me, and help me, we could enjoy ourselves.'

'How? What do people do in hotels?'

'Just let me get this gook out of my hair, and dry it off, and we'll go downstairs and find out.'

She was not blonde, merely a lighter shade of mouse, and the village outside Doncaster was no longer a village; if Steven Gaines had driven what was left of his family in a blue van to hide there, it is unlikely that he would have recognized it. There were at least five pubs with gardens, and many more without. There were nine Antiques Shops and two Antiques Arcades, one of which seemed to sell mostly knick-knacks and junk circa 1935. Six Estate Agents plied their trade here now, and the photographs in their windows of desirable properties for sale revolved on circular racks, or were set with timing mechanisms to flick over, one on top of another like the pages of a book. The playing-field with its broken swings had long since become an estate of modern freehold housing-units, and those of the old village houses which remained had been gentrified, two or sometimes three cottages excitingly modified into one stripped-pine and polyurethaned open-planned home. The Village Green had become a shopping precinct, in the centre of which a plastic-marble fountain bubbled out coloured liquid; there was a lampshade emporium where once the village shop and post office used to be. All the large banks had branches here now, and queues had formed at the cash-dispensers. The battle for Sunday Trading had been won, and the victory must be celebrated. If Steven Gaines' mother had been allowed her bungalow off the Bawtry Road, it would certainly have proved a good investment.

Jean stood looking into the window of a shop selling modern pottery, with Michael beside her, holding the hem of her cardigan. She glanced at the queue at the nearest cash-dispenser, and wondered how many days a withdrawal made here would take to reach her own branch in South London, and whether there was already a young constable leaning over a computer and waiting for a red light to flash. She did not need money immediately, thanks to Eric and Bernard, and the hotel-bill could be settled by credit card. The hotel would probably send the slips to the credit card company weekly in bulk; that would give her a few days, by which time she would be somewhere else.

Michael watched a young man moving away from the front of the queue at the cash-dispenser, counting the money he had just withdrawn. The young man was wearing a beach-shirt with a pattern of parakeets. Michael remembered himself once standing in a queue to collect money, but it had not been summer then. He had spent Christmas listening to the sounds of the gas-fire in the room They had found for him. This fire ate coins which Michael had saved for it, and when it had eaten all the coins, it had become cold, and remained so until Michael could give it more coins. He had walked the streets for warmth. They had told him to do that. 'Keep moving,' They had said, 'you'll feel better. It'll give you an interest.' His landlady had spoken a foreign language, and had always kept a room's length away from him, so that he had been forced to shout at her. She had trained her cats to do their business in the bath, so that Michael had been reluctant to go to the toilet, which was next to the bath, and she had pretended not to understand his complaints.

Michael had queued. With a practised expression of normality on his face, he had stood in a line to be picked for Day Work. This act of normality dulled his wits, but it was casual undemanding work, frying onions to put with hamburgers, which were not made of ham at all, but soya beans and beef. He would toast sesame buns to catch the juices of the hamburgers, which had usually proved dry, and lacked juice.

Every day on the way to the hamburgers he had paused outside a shop selling caged birds, most of which had been smaller than those pictured on the young man's shirt, every colour you can think of, and a noise to set your teeth on edge. He had watched as the dead birds were brushed up from the floors of the cages. This was done every morning before the shop opened, just like hospital. Of the living birds, some were left to themselves, some had partners, others were in large groups. Some fought; some moped. Pointless to fight in such small cages, made things worse.

Colours you can only imagine, noise you can't bear. Bird-droppings and plucked feathers, cuttlefish and sunflower seeds, hemp seed and spilt linseed. Eyes too bright for their own good, claws clinging to the wire. Colours you have only dreamed of, noise that stays with you all day while you fry onions for the paper-thin hamburgers with no juice. Starlings flocking as you scrape burnt onions from the griddle, and hang up an apron to be used the next day by the person with the most normal expression. Queue again for a buff envelope containing a few pound-notes to change into coins for the noisy gas-fire to eat. Back again past the shop, now closed again, to count the bodies of dead birds lying among spilt seed. Unreal colours of dead birds, and only the noises of silence.

They had left the hotel in Doncaster, and, by using B-roads and country lanes, had crossed Hatfield Moors, passed through Epworth and Butterworth, skirted Scunthorpe, Yaddles-thorpe, Bottesford and Scawby, and stopped for lunch at Brigg. The Metro had developed another knock and a rattle in the exhaust.

At the entrance to the Dayjohn Caravan Park, twenty-four miniature Christmas trees in white plastic tubs lined the drive-way, all of them now rust-coloured, having died from lack of water. Suspended above the entrance between two poles twelve feet high was a string of light-bulbs, red, green and yellow, illuminated day and night to welcome visitors. Jean counted two blue vans in the Car Park. Would Steven Gaines have done as she had done, and exchanged his vehicle for another? It was unlikely that he would have had the opportunity to repaint it.

A cherry-red Renault Five had followed them for an hour during the morning. This afternoon, the same driver appeared to be using a metallic grey Ford Fiesta; the East Yorkshire Constabulary did not believe in pampering its employees. As Jean and Michael walked from their own Metro towards the caravans, Jean saw the Fiesta slow down as it overshot the entrance. She was not going to be allowed to get into any trouble.

The Dayjohn Caravan Park had been set out in three sections. Signs indicated that the area to their left was for 'Holiday Lets and Tourers', to their right for 'Long-Stay Residential', and straight ahead were 'Sales, Rents and Enquiries'. The caravans in this last area were empty, and had price-cards propped up in their windows. Among them was set a Portakabin Office-cum-General-Stores. There was a large poster in the window of the Office, setting out the items (plastic bucket and washing-up bowl, eighteen-piece tea-set, kettle and tin-opener) which would be provided entirely free of charge to the purchaser of any new or reconditioned caravan in the lot, and behind it could be seen the frog-like features of a man who watched Jean and Michael walking past.

The Long-Stay Residential Area was protected from the world outside by a high chain-link fence and a log gate with two padlocks. A line of privet had been planted along the fence, and where this had failed to root, or had been destroyed by children, the fast-growing cypress Leylandii had been used to patch it. Jean picked a place where the fast-growing Leylandii had not been fast enough, and gazed through. The residential caravans were by no means new, and if they had been reconditioned it was a long time ago. A mongrel puppy, tied by a long leash to the wheels of one caravan, ran whining back and forth in a semi-circle at the end of its tether. Two women stood on a pocket-handkerchief of grass, hanging out washing. A small girl squatted on her haunches to pass water, and fixed Jean and Michael with an unremitting stare.

What had Jean imagined she could do? Had she expected to look through a fence, and find the Gaines family taking tea al fresco? Even if she were to climb the log gate, with Michael complaining behind her, and ask from caravan to caravan, would she be told the truth? She returned to the office. Only the frog-faced man would have had some kind of contact with every one of his tenants. In any case, she could not expect to find the Gaines' at anywhere 'long-stay', where presumably most of the residents owned their own residence. She should have been looking at Holiday Lets.

She was mistaken, the frog-faced man informed her. Long-stay residents did not own their caravans, which were owned by the company, nor did many of them stay particularly long, since they were only granted short leases with positively no sub-letting. He would not go so far as to suggest that the long-stay residents were hand-picked, but the company did like to know what it was getting.

Were there any short leases available, provided that the applicant measured up to the required standard? The frog-faced man made a croaking noise at the back of his throat, and puffed out his chest. She was joking, surely? There was a Waiting List. If the company had room and planning permission, they could double the size of that site; there was a vogue for inexpensive country living these days. Why was Jean so interested? Well, he never knew; she might decide to set up in opposition.

Jean explained that she was looking for some friends. Unfortunately she'd forgotten their last name, but she'd met them on holiday two years ago. A family – husband, wife, boy of . . . must be twelve now, girl aged six or seven; the husband was a body-builder, most distinctive. They'd said they were coming up here this year, and hoped to meet her, but she'd lost the letter, and her head was like a sieve. They had a blue van. She thought they might be looking for a permanent site.

Michael had remained behind her. She couldn't see his face, and for all she knew he might be mouthing, 'Lies! Lies!' at the frog-faced man; Michael disapproved of all lies except his own. The phone rang. As the frog-faced man lifted the receiver, his head moved from side to side, and his lower lip jutted out petulantly. It was a lady-friend. Would Jean excuse him? Jean remained where she was, and endured a conversation which seemed to be conducted entirely to impress her. The frog-faced man's eyes shone with self-esteem and anticipation. Had his lady-friend really enjoyed the evening? Even the last part? That was a bit naughty of her, wasn't it? Jean moved away, and began to study the Tariff of Weekly Lets. She was relieved to see that Michael was reading the instructions on a cylinder of Calor Gas. In June, July and August, the High Season, the minimum weekly rental of a caravan was a hundred and twenty pounds. How could Steven Gaines find such a sum? Licensed Bar, Social Club, Laundry with Automatics. No, the frog-faced man had nothing against a repeat performance, just provided it didn't lead his telephone caller and himself into anti-climax. Jean pushed a note in front of him, on which she had written, 'The man I am looking for rapes and murders small children. So would your girl-friend mind if you rang her back?'

No, Jean did not have a photograph of the person she sought. She did know his name, but that was of no use, since it had been in all the newspapers, and therefore he would not be using it. He had used a blue van, his wife was severely depressed and looked it, and the two children were as she had described them. Had the man not read any of this in his newspaper or seen the Photofit on television?'

The frog-faced man, now he put his mind to it, did vaguely remember something. Child-abuse, wasn't it? There was so much of that sort of thing about these days; it was getting to be like Northern Ireland, and just as sick; you couldn't do anything about it, so you might as well switch it off.

A map of the coast from Skegness to Scarborough was spread out on the desk. Red stars marked the positions of Caravan Sites. There were thirty-seven. Jean asked the man to place a tick beside those Sites which he knew to have been operating twenty years ago. The man shook his head; he had only been in Mobile Homes for eighteen months, and only then because a family grocery business in Halifax had collapsed under him.

Who would know? To whom could Jean talk? The man thought, rose from his desk, paced the floor of the Portakabin, asked Jean to give him time. The only Site he knew for sure to be old was Freelands, because there were jokes about its having been inspected by the Health Authorities in 1959, when two prisoners of war had been found under the floorboards of the Social Club. But that was inland. How did Jean know that the people for whom she was searching would be on the coast? The man flicked through his Address Book, looking at the names, and shaking his head. When he had reached the letter S, he sighed heavily, turned back to B, and reached for the phone.

* * *

Mr Braithwaite was a character. Everyone said so, and Mr Braithwaite believed them. He was seventy years old, and arrived at the Lounge Bar of the up-market pub in which Jean had been instructed to wait for him, wearing a bright red neckerchief held by a Boy Scout's Woggle, a light blue blazer with brass buttons, off-white trousers, green canvas shoes, no socks, no shirt, and over all a stained fawn raincoat.

'I don't know who you are, do I?'

'Is that why you wouldn't talk on the phone?'

'Absolutely.'

'Why is it necessary to be so cautious?'

'Computers for one thing. Freedom of Information Act for another. You're official, aren't you?'

'I'm only asking about Caravan Sites, not about how much you've got in the bank.'

'Just as well, young woman. You might get a surprise. There isn't any area of endeavour, is there, in which people don't cut corners?'

'Meaning?'

'Some of these so-called Sites might not be strictly legal. I know mine have all their paperwork up to date, but if I was to go around shopping my competitors, how would that look? I'll tell you. Not well.'

'I have tried to explain that I'm not interested in blocked drains and dangerous play-areas. I just need to know which Sites were operating as such twenty years ago. It's vitally important.'

'Must be.'

'Why do you say that?'

'Well, I don't expect that fella at the bar, watching us, is doing it because he fancies you. No offence. I think I recognize Mr Plod when I see him.'

'Yes, that's a Detective Sergeant. So now you realize how urgently I need the information.'

'And why could the Force not approach me directly? You're not a policewoman. I watched you arrive; you crossed on an amber light. And your friend beside you, why is he tearing up beer-mats? That's hardly constabularial behaviour.'

'I'm helping the police with their inquiries. I know the man they're desperate to find. That's why I'm asking the questions.'

Mr Braithwaite looked towards the bar at the Detective Sergeant, sitting on a high stool. The detective nodded to Mr Braithwaite, who returned his attention to Jean. 'Public service, public service, and not a penny off the rates! Show me that map again. There's ten Sites in the Scarborough area alone. Five at Filey. Whitby's beyond me. How far north do you want to go?' Jean pointed at an area of the map. 'Too much is made out of this abuse, to my mind. Tell people something's wrong, and they get ill thinking about it.' His forefinger wavered over the coastline. 'In the old days you grew out of it naturally. "Give me a sixpence, and you can play with my willy." What was wrong with that?' The forefinger came to rest. 'That's an old 'un. Opened nineteen fifty-two, with the Lord Mayor and some pop singer with acne cutting the tape in a Force Nine gale. There's another; that's three miles inland. And there! – terrible Site, can't get rid of the sewage. This one here's old, same as the buggers that live there – Residential for Retireds – got their own Neighbourhood Watch, and a fortnightly visit from the chiropodist.'

In all there were seven. Jean said, 'Which of these is close to a pier?'

Mr Braithwaite looked at her. 'You don't want much for your pint of John Smith's do you? Shall I take you up to the man's front door, and knock on it for you?' He thought for a moment, and then said. 'We lost one pier in nineteen sixty-two. That used to be here.' He indicated, and Jean made a note. 'There's something like a jetty there, but I wouldn't dignify it with the name of pier. None of them are that close.' Again he paused to think. 'How old was this man of yours when he was last there?'

'Nine or ten.'

'Why didn't you say? Distances are different to the young; someone like you should know that. Three or four miles is nothing to a good strong lad. I'd say that's the pier you want. So it could be any one of those three sites.'

James Gaines

James Gaines, wearing pink plimsolls and a pink sun-dress made for him by his father, tapped the palm of his hand against the rail of the pier as he walked. His blond hair had been curled, also by his father. At the end of the pier, boys of his own age were fishing.

On the evening they had left London, James had returned home to find only his mother there, packing a tea-chest in the lower room. He had gone up to the bedroom he shared with Adam, and found the place in a mess, pillows thrown about, and bedding pulled from the mattresses. He had begun tidying the room, remaking the beds and cursing Adam under his breath, but his mother had come into the room and, without speaking, had taken the blankets and sheets from him, had carried them down to the lower room, and had placed them in the tea-chest.

He had asked for Adam. Three times. But she had moved to the window with her back towards him, hiding her face from his. All she had said was that he was not to go out again, but must wait in the room above until his father returned.

His first thought was that there had been an accident. Adam was always rushing into the road to cross ahead of people, dancing backwards in front of them, pulling faces and acting the goat. His second thought was that Adam, like Marianne, had been taken into Care. The last time he had seen Adam had been that morning, on their way to school, when Adam had hung back, hiding in the doorways of shops, saying he didn't want to go, threatening to make them both late. Adam had said that everyone would ask him about the bruise on his face, and he didn't know how to explain it.

James had witnessed the blow which had caused that bruise, Adam had been acting silly as usual, running from the upper to the lower room wearing only underpants, trampolining on the beds in front of their father, pretending to be a muscle-man one moment and a ballerina the next. Later in the lower room he had wriggled and giggled like a girl, trying to slide himself onto their father's knee, and had been warned to stop being silly and not to get over-excited, and had not stopped, but had gone on, trying to embrace and kiss their father, and had suddenly received a violent slap across the face which had knocked him to the floor. James had pulled Adam up from the floor, and pushed him upstairs to their room, but not before noticing the expression on their father's face, and that both face and neck were red with anger.

Their father had never hit any of his children in that way before. They had all three suffered light taps and warnings of more severe punishment, but the blow to Adam's face had made a bruise from his eye to his jaw.

Later, when both boys were in bed, their father had come into the room, and knelt by the side of Adam's bed. He had apologized, and Adam had said that he was also sorry. They had kissed, and their father had cried a little, staying by the bed holding Adam until Adam had fallen asleep.

Not until two days after they had arrived at the seaside had James discovered what had happened to his brother. He had been told that the reason why they had left London, and the reason why he must pretend to be a girl, was that they must hide from the police and the Social Services, who wanted to remove him from the family, and place him in a Children's Home. The police would have a copy of his school photograph, and would be looking for a family with one son and one daughter; they had taken Adam already. If James disguised himself, they would not be found. The arrangement was temporary. James would not be asked to attend school as Janie Jackson.

Two days after their arrival, and three days after becoming Janie Jackson, James had been standing on the pier, watching a group of boys fishing. One of the boys had got down from his perch on the pier-rail, and rummaged in his bag for bait, producing from it a screwed-up piece of newspaper containing a carton of maggots and worms. The boy had knelt down, flattening the newspaper against the slats of the pier, had tipped the bait onto the paper so as to choose the maggot most fit for his purpose, and James had seen his brother's photograph printed in the newspaper under the headline, 'Father Sought for Sex-Attack and Murder of Son'.

James had asked the boy if he might have that page of the newspaper, and the boy had grinned, and asked what he would be given in return. Thus reminded of who and what he was supposed to be, James had placed a hand on the boy's thigh, and asked him what he would like. This had caused so much amusement among the boy's friends, and embarrassed the boy himself to such an extent, that he had returned quickly to the safety of the rail, leaving the bait and paper where they were, and indicating with a wave of the hand that James could take what she wanted.

He had bent down, using the side of his hand to slide the maggots and worms away from his brother's face, and heard one of the boys on the rail say, 'She's not afraid of worms, then. Make someone a good wife, her will. Next time you get an offer like that, Pinky, tell her to put her hand on what I've got here. Ain't half got a nice tight little arse on her, an' all. Look at that!'

'Don't tell me where you are. I've always had my suspicions that this phone is tapped . . . Oh, they do, do they? Well, at least you can't get into trouble if the boys in blue are right behind you . . . How the hell should I know how you can shake them off? Change the car, dye your hair, pour Michael into Bermuda shorts. The most distinctive thing about you two has to be that bloody suit of his . . . Look, I've got to go. There's a Case Conference any minute . . . Well, if you get tired of being followed by the Filth, why not just come home? Turn the car round, bring the Filth back with you, make them look wallies . . . Alright then, risk what's left of your career for the sake of one child who may be dead already . . . No, I know I shouldn't say that. I'm sorry . . . Daniel? He's fine. Standing here with me now. It's his Case Conference I'm going to be late for if you don't get off the line. I've got to get the room ready. You know what they're like here . . . I need some company, Jean. I thought it was going to be fun, being on my own, but it isn't . . . Only one. Down to his jockey shorts, then brewer's droop set in. The house is like a Chapel of Rest . . . Of course you're just on a bloody holiday; did I say different? Just don't take so long about it. Hugs and kisses. Going now. And don't let that schizoid bugger wear you down. 'Bye.'

Joy turned from the phone, and spoke to Daniel. 'And never let me hear *you* use language like that, young man. I'm going to that bloody room to check that it's alright for our visitors. You stay here. Do some deep-breathing exercises to keep you nice and calm. Remember what we've rehearsed, and hang loose, OK?' The boy nodded. 'Good lad!'

* * *

'The main question we have to address is whether Daniel is still a danger to other children. The psychiatrist's report isn't very encouraging on that score, is it?'

Heads were being shaken. The room smelled of warm vinyl and cigarette smoke. She should have opened a window, but had used what little time she had to rearrange the chairs, which had been left in rows, all the easy chairs facing the one hard-backed chair in which the subject of the Case Conference would be expected to sit. God! had they learned nothing?

She had spent hours with Daniel, rehearsing for this meeting, had told him the sort of things the other people would have to say, and had warned him not to build up his hopes and expect to be allowed home. Going home, she had explained, must be their long-term project. He must have patience, she had said, and not only have it, but be seen to have it. 'Very adult, that, Danny Boy, if you can manage it. What's important is to make a good show. An impression. Most of these buggers see dozens of young 'uns like you every week. We've got to make sure that they remember how nice you were. Sweet reason, Danny. That's what we've got to be, as sweet as pie and as reasonable as we can manage without actually getting down and licking their arses.' Daniel had grinned at her.

Now they sat in a circle, everyone having rejected the hard-backed chair, except Daniel, who had entered last, and now sat with head lowered, studying his hands.

'Daniel was most disruptive when he was at home. He had to be watched twenty-four hours a day. Not very fair on his brothers and sisters!'

'We've had one or two nasty incidents at school, haven't we, Daniel?'

There were six other people present, a Fostering Officer, the family's Social Worker, the Head of Education for the Children's Home, Daniel's Form Teacher, a student Social Worker, there to observe, and Daniel's father.

'He's still resisting boundaries, isn't he? Doesn't like boundary-setting. Complains of rules, then just goes ahead and breaks them.'

'Would foster-parents be able to give him twenty-four-hour supervision?'

'I think we have to face the unpleasant fact that he couldn't be fostered in a home where there were other children. Younger children would be at risk, and older children – well, we could be said to have acted as *agents provocateurs* if anything were to go wrong.'

Heads were being nodded. The family's Social Worker plucked strands of greasy hair from the side of his face, released the rest of his hair from an elastic band at the nape of his neck, shook the entire mane, and proceeded to re-form it into a pony-tail. Over the upper rim of his National Health spectacles, he surveyed the other people in the room before speaking. 'Statistics show that many children regress at the commencement of fostering. Given Daniel's particular problem, plus his temper and aggression, the bottom line is that a fostering placement would be difficult, probably impossible, to find, don't you agree?' The Fostering Officer did agree. 'I also think that, if we're to be a hundred per cent honest, we have to say that even if Daniel had shown us signs of improvement, which he hasn't, the home situation would still not be feasible. His mother, as you know, had a nervous breakdown, and is in and out of hospital. She couldn't possibly cope. I'm sure Daniel's father will bear me out.'

Daniel's father made no verbal response. Although he sat in a chair next to his son, so far he had not spoken to him, touched him, or acknowledged his son's presence in any way.

Nobody rushed to fill the silence which followed. Daniel's father turned his face and torso further away from his son, and looked towards the window, moving the muscles in his jaw, clenching and unclenching his teeth, but his mouth remained closed.

Finally it was Joy who spoke. 'With all due respect to the psychiatrist and the school, who may not have noticed much improvement in Daniel's behaviour, I should like to say that all of us here, where Daniel lives, have done so. He spends a large part of each and every day here with us, and we're very pleased with him. He's clean, tidy, caring for others. If he has a problem, he brings it to me, and we discuss it together. His attitude is mature and thoughtful. In fact, if everyone in this house was as adult as Daniel, we could send them all home tomorrow.' She waited a moment for those who were shifting uncomfortably in their seats or flicking over their notes to get settled. When she had regained their attention, she said, 'Now, Danny, what about you? This is your Case Conference. What would you like to see happen?'

The family's Social Worker lifted his flat briefcase from his knees, and dropped it to the floor in front of him. 'I'm going to be a wet rag on this, I'm afraid. Can we please not hear from Daniel at this point? Later perhaps, when we've got the logistics of one or two, or even ninety-four, other things sorted out. That way we might avoid allowing ourselves to get side-tracked into emotional –'

Joy interrupted. Remembering what she had told Daniel, she attempted to smile in a friendly manner, but it was clear to everyone that this smile, which became increasingly shark-like, was in direct contradiction to her real feelings. 'Sorry, but I disagree. If we're going to talk about Danny as if he weren't here, why have we put him through the emotional upset and aggravation of attending? He wants to be here, and we want him to be here. That was arranged some time ago; let's not forget it. Any Court Order restricting his movements has to be reviewed regularly, and he's old enough and intelligent enough to have preferences about where he lives. I think you should hear them.'

'This is just divisive. I'm sorry I can't –'

'Tough titty, mate!' Goodbye sweet reason!

'Can we all remember that there is a child in the room?'

'More than one, it seems.'

'Perhaps Daniel would excuse us for a moment.'

'Daniel, you stay where you are.' Joy rose to her feet, moved across the circle to stand in front of the family's Social Worker, crouched down so that their faces were level, and spoke quietly, but in a tone which everyone could hear. 'Listen to me, and listen carefully, Sunshine. You're on my territory. Try to do my job for me, or instruct my client once more, and you'll leave by that window, head first.' The window through which she had threatened to throw him was reflected in the Social Worker's spectacles, behind which his eyes were wide with fear. Joy sniffed with satisfaction at the aroma given out by the Social Worker; it was the sweat of a frightened man. She had certainly made an impression. She moved back to her seat, and began speaking again in a controlled and businesslike manner. 'Daniel has discussed with me – as his Key Social Worker – what he would like from this conference. He knows what he wants to say to you all. Now let's hear him speak, shall we?'

Daniel remained with his eyes lowered, looking at the sore which covered the knuckle of his thumb. His legs dangled from the seat of the chair, with his spotlessly clean trainers suspended four inches above the grubby haircord carpet.

The people in the room waited. After several moments of silence, Daniel's father moved to the window, where he stood watching an elderly dog roll about in a sandpit, after which it got to its feet a little unsteadily, shook itself, and urinated into the sand which young children would later use to build castles.

The family's Social Worker looked at his wristwatch. Then the Head of Education cleared his throat, and began to speak. 'Quite frankly, I think Daniel is too young to attend this conference, and too young to take part in the discussion about where he should be placed.'

He looked to Daniel's Form Teacher for support, and she gave it. 'I agree. I also think that, at this moment in time, he has, by his actions, forfeited his right to be part of a discussion concerning his future. After all, what is the point of raising a child's hopes, only to see them run into a brick wall when we announce the decision we already know we have to make? It's not as though we have that many alternatives.'

Joy counted three heads nodding, and then said, 'Danny is not unfamiliar with having his hopes raised, only to see them lowered again.' She had an uneasy feeling that this might be a mixed metaphor, but when she considered the strangled Socialspeak everyone else was using, a mixed metaphor or so might be excused, as coming from a full heart. 'Aren't you trying to have it both ways? Forfeiting his rights suggests a degree of choice, an awareness of the consequences of his actions. Being too young to be present while strangers decide your future implies a lack of awareness.'

'Hardly strangers,' the Form Teacher said, and all the heads nodded again, except the one head which was still staring out of the window.

'Well, I'm in a position to tell you that Danny is not too young, because he is aware. Nor has he forfeited his right to be heard. Even a condemned man is allowed to make a statement. And, like the condemned man, Danny knows better than to expect to get what he wants just by asking for it. He feels, as I do, that he'll be all the more ready to make whatever is decided here work if he's present to witness how that decision is arrived at, and is allowed to put his point of view. He has no more wish than you have, ladies and gentlemen' – the family's Social Worker flinched at this disgusting epithet – 'to come back to this room time and time again. Have you, Danny?'

The room had become very hot. She should have opened a window, but it would be a mistake to do so now, since that would distract them all, giving them yet another excuse to ignore Danny. The trainee Social Worker yawned, and began wafting her notebook in front of her face. Joy noticed that Daniel's cheeks had turned bright red. That would not be caused by the heat of the room. She had misread the signs, had thought that the stillness and the lowered head had meant that he was remembering her instructions to be modest and shy. She had said, 'Don't show off, Danny. Hide your intelligence just a little bit. They'll like that. Do it for me.' She had said, 'Give them that "Sorry for causing trouble" look, the one you give me when you think I'm getting heavy with you.' He had spent an hour ironing his clothes to have them right for this interview, and what Joy now recognized as she looked at him was not the 'Sorry for causing trouble' look, but a volcano of rage building up inside him.

'Are you alright, Danny?' She must get him out of the room. Anything could happen. Danny placed both his hands on the sides of the hard-backed chair, and slowly, and with seeming difficulty, edged his buttocks to the front of the seat. Christ! had he stuck something up his bottom while her back was turned? 'Would you like a drink of water, Danny?' He was standing now, his head still lowered, had placed his trainers on the carpet as though about to walk on hot coals, and now stood in front of his chair. Joy was at the door. She opened it, and moved quickly to the window, leaned past the boy's father, and slid the sash-window upwards. Anything for distraction now, but nobody had been distracted. None of them except the boy's father looked anywhere but at the boy, all aware that something was wrong, watching the bright red of the boy's face, listening to his jerky and erratic breathing. Danny was holding his breath and then releasing it in an attempt to hold himself together.

Slowly, as though struggling against gravity, he lifted his hands, and placed his thumbs inside the waistband of his neatly pressed shorts. Cool air now moved through the room from window to door, yet Joy felt a cold sweat breaking out between her shoulderblades and at the backs of her knees. He was going to expose himself. To show the buggers. At any moment he would rip off those shorts, slide the spotless underpants down, and produce from his bottom like a rabbit from a hat a bouquet of trick flowers, which he would then hold under their noses for their approval.

She moved quickly back to the open door, and called the boy's name. There was no response, He was mumbling now, standing in the centre of the circle, his lips forming hardly audible incoherent words, saliva running down his chin, his body rocking to and fro, the fingers of each hand sliding backwards and forwards along the waistband of his shorts.

They waited, mesmerized, leaning forward in their seats, straining to hear what the boy was saying. Only the words 'like' and 'would' had been clear so far, and these two words were repeated over and over again, each time a little louder with the rocking of the boy's body. With each failure to force more words out, and to communicate with the listeners, Daniel's fingers came forwards, and felt for the button at the top of his fly.

'Would . . . like . . . would . . . like . . .' The rocking grew more violent, the colour of Daniel's face more vivid, the veins of his neck and forehead more prominent, the sweat-stains on his carefully chosen shirt larger.

'Danny!' She was pushing, squirming, forcing her way between two chairs to get to the centre of the circle, kicking a briefcase, almost treading on spectacles. Daniel meanwhile ceased rocking, raised his head, and did what she had instructed him to do, which was to pick somebody out and look them straight in the eye, so that Daniel's father turned from the window to find Daniel staring straight at him.

Silence. Then the dam broke. Tears flooded from Daniel's eyes. Among angry sobs and gulps for air came words which were now clearly audible and almost coherent. 'Daddy . . . please . . . Home, please . . . Promise, Daddy . . . Be a good boy.'

As Daniel's father turned his back on the room and on his son in order to continue his observation through the open window, the family's Social Worker rose to his feet, moved his chair back to break the circle, and turned to mutter something to the Fostering Officer beside him, whereupon Daniel, with flailing punches, with kicks and head-butts, forced the family Social Worker into a foetal position on the grubby haircord carpet, where Daniel joined him, grabbing at the family Social Worker's clothes and hair, knocking off his National Health spectacles, and securing a grip through the check trousers bought at the Oxfam Shop on the family Social Worker's testicles, which Daniel twisted and wrenched until he barked with agony. Joy was strongly tempted to leave the room and go straight home, but instead she joined the others in dragging Daniel off the family's Social Worker, whose whimpering and reproaches served only a little to dull the edge of her despair.

Michael was leaning against a wall. He knew it was there, and he was there; his back could feel the bricks of the wall. It was the wall of a Ladies' Toilet, and he was waiting outside it for Jean. She had made him take off his jacket and tie, had said he would look odd and draw attention to himself by wearing them in such heat. He had rolled his tie, and placed it in a trouser-pocket. She had wished him to leave his jacket in the car, but he had preferred to carry it, in case they entered any place where the wearing of a jacket would be appropriate.

They had visited many seaside resorts, all of them crowded with noisy people, pushing and jostling. Jean had asked questions at two Caravan Sites, with Michael standing a little behind her and to one side; he had been forbidden to hold either hand or cardigan. They had driven and driven, and had discovered that, in heavy traffic, the Metro overheated. The Car Parks everywhere had been full, just as this one was full; they had driven round it five times before finding a space.

The bricks of the wall were behind him, and before him were row upon row of the bonnets of cars, all shimmering in the sun. As a small boy, he had once fainted in a crowded Department Store. He had been waiting then, waiting by the large glass doors for his parents. Later they had explained to him that he had placed too much weight on his heels, and that Guardsmen on parade in hot weather often had the same problem. They had loosened his tie, and taken off his jacket, and told him what a good little Guardsman he was to stand there on sentry duty.

Now, as he stood with his back against the wall, he adjusted the distribution of his weight by rising on his toes, counting ten, then lowering his heels again. Since he liked the feel of the wall behind him, and the knowledge that Jean was on the other side of it, he slid his back upwards against the bricks as he rose on his toes. The noise of the cars, as they moved slowly over what looked like cinders in search of places to park, was like a steamroller flattening out breakfast cereal. Two cars had begun hooting at each other, as both drivers tried to manoeuvre into the same parking-space. The first hoot was long and loud, and gave him a shock, so that he lowered his heels to the ground quickly, scraping his back against brick harder than he had intended. He felt a twang of elastic against his shoulder, and suddenly his trousers seemed much looser.

Michael looked down at his feet. Two buttons he knew to be his lay among the crushed cinders. They were the buttons to which he attached his braces. He felt at the front of his trousers. Those buttons were still in place. He reached his hand behind him, and knew at once that his braces totally lacked attachment at the back.

One hand holding his jacket, and the other the front of his trousers, he bent down to pick up the two buttons. They were a little away from the wall, and he had to stretch. As he rose again, he pressed his buttocks against the wall to prevent the trousers slipping down further. Although he was sweating, it seemed to him that his lower half was now cooler. He felt odd, undressed, and quickly lowered his head to check the zip-fastening of his fly. In hospital, tokens had been given, sweets, trips to the pictures as rewards for keeping one's fly buttoned. They had evaluated one's behaviour there under four categories –

communicating and relationships, self-care (which included the fastening of flies), work and recreation, and expanding personality. There was a woman watching him.

She had stepped out of one of the hooting cars, approached the Ladies' Toilet, and now stood with a hand lifted to shield her eyes from the sun. The woman had tight rolls of curls, a white powdered face and a pencil-thin line for a mouth. It seemed to Michael that this woman was the landlady whose cat had done its business in the bath, and she proved it by opening her mouth wide, and making a miaowing sound. He must shout at her, and tell her that he was waiting to use the bathroom, and would she please clean the bath out.

Two more women and a young girl had come from inside the Ladies' Toilet, and joined the miaowing woman. Michael struggled with his trousers, trying to get the tie from his pocket to tie around his waist, so that he could go to the door of the toilet, and shout for Jean. One of the women was talking to him, calling him names and asking him questions. The shimmering heat-haze from the car bonnets was everywhere, making him feel faint; he must put his head between his legs, and take deep breaths, must explain to the landlady that he was waiting for Jean. She was backing away from him, holding up a bread-knife to protect her face. Someone asked him what he thought he was doing there. He must explain that he had to be here, had to wait outside the glass door or he might get lost. The young girl was screaming to her mother to come away. Arms were being waved. A handbag at the end of one of the arms was being swung. Michael began to shout, breathless, explanations tumbling out of him. He had to wait where he was by the glass door until his mummy came; he was never to go on the escalators in case he fell through the joins; he only did as he was told like a good boy, and it was not his fault that the hamburgers were dry and the birds were dead. He began to put on his jacket in order to make a good appearance, and his trousers fell to his ankles, tripping him as he tried to escape, so that he lay among crushed cinders as the women shouted and kicked. Michael lay there, the prey of angry women, trying to explain, gabbling too quickly to be understood, saying that he remained unconfirmed, that no one had ever confirmed him, that all his predictions had proved wrong, that he had given up on people, and consequently his thoughts remained invalidated and unconfirmed.

'Well, this is fun, isn't it?' Joy sat slumped in an armchair which had seen better days, and seen them long ago. The television screen flickered in front of her, presenting a double image. 'This is supposed to be the Men's Singles, but I can see four blokes and at least two balls.' Daniel leaned against the out-of-tune piano, picking at one note with a bruised finger. Above his right eye was another bruise, caused by the buckle of the family's Social Worker's belt. 'Just you and me, eh, Titch? Confined to barracks on a day like this!' She waved at the contents of the room. 'Just look at this dump. A pool-table with tipless cues and torn felt. A pot of dead flowers. A knackered Hoover. A vandalized Barry McGuigan poster. A Team Leader's dog with fleas, and a fart to take the gloss off paint. Two Swedes on the box, who can't decide how many balls to play with. And it's still only Tuesday.' She watched him. 'We can always stick our arms out of the window, and get those sun-tanned.' He remained as he was, pressing and releasing the one yellowed ivory. Joy switched off the television. 'Well, which would you rather do, help me wash and set my hair, or do some ironing?' He shrugged his shoulders. 'Not still worried about that stupid Case Conference, are you?' He shrugged again. 'There'll be plenty more. And I'll be there, rooting for you, shan't I?' He lifted his head, and looked at her. She waited for him to smile, but he did not smile. 'All that rehearsal, and we still forgot our lines. I thought that fiddling with your trousers was a bit over the top. Had me worried, that did. Thought you were going to give them a floor-show or something.'

'What kind of floor-show?'

'I don't know, do I?'

He thought for a moment, and then said, 'Yes, you do. You must know.'

'I only know from the notes. What other people have said. I think it's time I heard from the horse's mouth.'

He walked slowly round the Lounge of the Children's Home, picking up objects and replacing them. At the pool-table, he smoothed the worn felt with his fingers. When he had reached the furthest corner of the room away from Joy, he stood facing the wall with his back, and said, 'You won't like me.'

'Do I like you now?'

'I think so.'

'And you also think I know what your problems are. So why are you scared of talking about them, and getting things straight between us?'

Silence. Then, 'Ask me.'

'Ask you what?'

'If it's true that . . . You know. That kind of thing.'

'If that's the only way you can do it. But I'd rather not put words into your mouth, Danny. I'd rather if you could tell me what happened.'

'No. Not that way. Ask questions. Then I'll tell you.'

'Can you answer with me holding you, if I come over there?' No answer. 'I'm nervous too, Danny. I need to be liked as well, you know.' Finally he nodded.

They stood in the corner of the room, holding each other. She had turned him towards her, and allowed him to hide his face against her chest. Pressed together like this, she rocked him.

Among the questions to which Joy already knew the answers, there were others to which she had no answers.

'What age were you then? Six or younger?'

'Younger.'

'What was it that was put inside you, something like a crayon?' No answer. 'Or part of someone?'

'Part of someone.'

'Fingers?'

'Yes.'

'Any other part?'

'Yes.'

'Did you know the person?'

The boy nodded.

'How well, Danny?'

He explained that, if he had not known the person well, he would not have allowed it to happen.

'Was the person in that room with us this morning?'

Danny did not answer this question, nor Joy's next, which was whether the person had spoken to him during the Case Conference. Or to anyone.

'This is most embarrassing.'

'Yes, I know; I'm sorry. I shouldn't have gone for the woman like that. It's just that I heard this noise, came out of the Ladies, and saw her kicking Michael while he lay on the ground. I blacked out for a second or two.'

'Is the gentleman alright now?' Michael sat in a corner of the room at the Police Station, curled up into a ball.

'He will be. It's a setback. It wasn't his fault. What happened was that a man who has spent most of his life in various hospitals, and who is attempting to adjust to the outside world, was confronted by a woman whose hold on reality seems to be no more secure than his own. Also, for reasons I don't quite understand, his braces snapped. Michael would no more expose himself than he'd take up public speaking. You realize that if she'd pressed charges, I'd have had to counter-charge her.'

'I've told you: charges will not be pressed.'

'She started the violence. Your young officer acted over-zealously in insisting we come here.'

'You had punched the woman in the mouth, Miss Davies, and pushed her to the ground, and your friend was rolling about with his trousers round his ankles. Certainly my life would have been easier if he had not brought you in. We've been instructed to leave you alone.'

'Instructed?'

'Advised. Requested.'

'By whom?'

'If we did encounter you, we were asked to give you a message from a friend. Detective Inspector Lang begs you not to approach Steven Gaines on your own. Well, now we have encountered you, and you have the message.'

'Begs?'

'That was my word.'

'But I have no idea where Steven Gaines is. I told you; we're on holiday. My Department has given me indefinite leave, and suggested sea air.'

'Did they also suggest you should change your car and the colour of your hair?'

'That's what holidays are for, aren't they? It's so long since I took one, I've quite forgotten.'

'Have you also forgotten that you're wanted in London for questioning?'

'Wanted? Are you suggesting I've broken house-arrest?' He looked away. 'Your people have been following us for days. Why haven't you bundled us into a car, and driven us back to London?' Even as she asked the question, Jean realized that she secretly wished that the police would do just that. What real hope did she have of finding Steven Gaines, and persuading him to hand over Marianne? – and James; she mustn't forget James, who must now also be considered at risk. And even if she could find him, how could she persuade him, Steven Gaines who talked only to her, Steven Gaines who trusted only her, with Michael tugging at her cardigan or going into catatonic states outside every Ladies' loo?

With this realization came another. As long as there was any hope at all, real or unreal, the Inspector did not want her back, nor, wherever she went, from Caravan Site to Caravan Site, would she lose Mr Plod in his pitifully unconvincing Renault or Fiat.

'The Inspector believes that you have unfinished business with Gaines. That you want to talk to him before we do.'

'The Inspector is wrong. I have nothing to say to Steven Gaines.'

'Or his daughter? If she's still alive?' Jean did not reply. 'You seem to have formed an attachment to Caravan Sites, Miss Davis. Why is that?'

'Social Studies. I may decide to write a paper about the conditions I find there.' It was a game, both players knowing that, whatever she said, he was not going to interrupt her search, and would always be close behind.

'Do you have friends or relatives in this area? It seems an odd place for someone like yourself to choose for a touring holiday.'

She realized that he had dealt her a winning card, but she must be careful not to overplay it. 'I like odd places. If your people continue to follow me, you may find yourself in a lot more. However . . .' Careful now! Keep the touch light if you hope to convince. 'I do have friends not too far away whom I may visit.'

'May?'

'Probably will.' Sarah Stoner – Sarah Petherton as used to be – now out of Social Work, married, and living with her husband, Bob, on a smallholding in the East Riding. He had a job – accountant . . . atomic physicist . . . ICI executive . . . something – and she ran the farm.

'Probably?'

'They're not expecting me. But I probably shall go.' She remembered that there was a damp ball-and-chain in the corner of the room. 'I mean, we'll both go.'

'And your friends are?'

'Mr and Mrs Robert Stoner, Fenwick House Farm, Lower Tilsbury. It's an organic smallholding near Maltby. Mrs Stoner and I trained together. We're old friends.' Surely the only point of games was that one enjoyed playing them. All she had to do was to go and stay with Sarah and Bob until the police were convinced; they would not waste manpower by keeping someone permanently hanging about the farm. Then Jean must find some means to slip away without being noticed. Perhaps she could equip Michael with hooves and an udder, and pretend to be driving him to market.

'Would your friends know Steven Gaines?'

'I'm quite sure they wouldn't.' Game, set and match to Miss Davis.

Marianne Gaines

Wherever she looked, the rim of the sun-hat made a line along the top of her picture. She could make two more boundaries, one on each side, by placing the palms of her hands against her cheeks with the fingers stretched upwards. Her picture now had a top and two sides; she hadn't enough hands to make a bottom. She made a list in her head of what she could see without moving her eyes. Two fields, an old barn, a hedge, four trees at the edge of the wood, the sky, part of a cloud. She could hear the new puppy, sniffing and scratching at the roots of the hedge below her picture, but to see it she must move her eyes, so it didn't count.

Something she could neither hear nor see, but knew to be lying on the grass under the steps where she sat, was the sheet of writing paper on which her father had printed her new name. She had copied her father's writing, over and over on both sides of the paper, so as to be sure of remembering it, a C and an L and an A and an I and an R, Clair Jackson, Clair Jackson, over and over. I am Clair Jackson. I am not Marianne Gaines.

The steps on which she sat led up to the door of the tin house, which only had one room, in which she, James, her mother and her father all slept. Her father couldn't touch her.

At night there were different noises here, very different from the noises in the house in which she had last slept, which had many rooms, both upstairs and down. In the tin house with its one room, at night Marianne could hear her father breathing, James sobbing, her mother talking, speaking words from a dream which nobody could understand. She could also hear the noises of outside the house, an owl hooting, an animal barking or howling in the wood, and close to the tin wall against which she slept the noise of another animal, which scraped out holes all round the house. Each night she waited, listening for the animal's snorting and sniffing down below the side of the tin wall, and for its cough, which was like that of an old man, waited for the scratching against the wall close to her face like fingernails on a kitchen surface, with the new puppy whining and shivering, close to her under the bedclothes, waited afraid, but did not cry, or call out, or go to her father's bed, because her father shouldn't touch her.

She had been a motorcar, had lain on a high bed in a hospital, being a broken motorcar with its bonnet up, while a man who hummed to himself tried to mend her, half of the man hidden under the tent-like sheet which had covered her legs. They had given her a fluffy rabbit to hold, and had told her that she could keep it, but the man had stopped humming, and had appeared from under the bonnet, sighing and shaking as he removed the sheet, and she had known that she was no longer to be a motorcar, and had not been mended.

A cloth parrot on a perch swung from the ceiling of a room where a fat man sat on the floor, surrounded by toys, lots of toys, too many for her to make a list in her mind. Toy people, a house with far too many rooms, toy furniture – a table, a bed, a TV set – a toy toilet that wouldn't flush. Had she remembered to flush the toilet she had used after the man had tried to mend her? Yes, she had watched the red water turning to pink, and frothing.

There was a cardboard face which could only smile or frown. The fat man had held it up to show her. 'Look! Smile! Frown! Smile again!' The fat man's arm became a rag crocodile with rubber teeth. On the fingers of his other hand were more dolls, or just the heads of dolls, nodding. 'Hello! Hellooo! Hello!' Nod, smile, frown. All toys, too many for a list. Crayons, paints and Plasticine. The man made a noise every time he moved to get himself more comfortable. There was a button missing from his shirt, and his stomach fell in rolls, one roll on top of another.

She had stood with her back touching the door, looking up at the brightly coloured cloth parrot, while the man said, 'Hullo, Marianne. Come and sit down here. Do you see anything you'd like to play with?' He had opened a box with other boxes inside it, and the smaller boxes had boxes inside them. 'What sort of toys do you have at home?'

Outside the window, birds singing, and the man sighing as he had struggled to his feet. The sound of a plastic fire-engine being crushed under his shoe. The turning of pages, as the man sat behind a desk, pretending to read, but watching her, while she lay on the floor where he had sat, counting all the toys she could see without moving her eyes.

After that she had been taken to a house with too many rooms, all smelling of furniture polish, and had been given a bedroom of her own. She had been given dolls, many dolls, to share her room, and stop her being lonely, they had said. These were not dolls she had chosen, but dolls they had wished her to have, and she had decided to be a doll herself, a doll which could open and close its eyes but never moved them sideways, a doll who never said 'Mummy' and 'Daddy', a doll which never spoke at all, even when it was asked to speak. And she had formed a list somewhere in her mind of the things this doll, Marianne, could and could not do.

The doll had eaten the food placed before it, and had slept on the bed made and turned down for it. It had listened to stories read to it, or the ones They made up in their heads, specially for it. But the stories had not been real. Nobody in these stories ever really got hurt, and nobody ever grew up and married their father.

At all times, even sitting in the bath, she had been a doll with the name of Marianne. At these bath-times she had watched, without moving her eyes, the woman who played pretend-games of not watching her. This woman had a smiling face with sad eyes. She would stand at the basin, washing a face she had already washed half an hour ago. She would clean teeth which were already clean, while watching Marianne in the mirror. She would comb her hair, pluck eyebrows, wash her hands again, all while Doll Marianne lay back in warm water, squinting through bubbles at rainbow lights. The pretend-game would end with the woman's taking a large towel from a heated rail, and holding it out for Doll Marianne, to be wrapped in it and hugged, while the woman talked quietly about how much she loved the doll, Marianne, and how she wanted it to be happy and feel safe. In this part of the pretend-game, the woman told the doll, Marianne, how pretty it was, kept saying it until her voice got lower and deeper and sadder, seeming to come from inside her chest, and she would beg the doll, Marianne, to say something to her. Doll Marianne's part in the game was to go limp, to hold her eyes very still and stop them from blinking, pretending not to see the woman, but noticing whether the woman cried or not, for that was also part of the game, the part which determined who had won and who had lost. Mostly the doll won.

Now, no longer a doll, Marianne sat on the steps of a tin house, while the new puppy scratched an ear, showing its pink stomach and the long hair out of which it peed. *'Daddy will meet you by the bus-shelter in your road at five o'clock. Don't tell anyone. It's a secret.'* Standing by the wall of the new school, the older girl reading those words from a piece of paper, and holding up a fifty-pence piece before dancing away.

Music from the radio downstairs in the kitchen, then talk, and the woman singing to herself over the talk. More music, loud music, as the doll, Marianne, stood on a chair to reach the locks on the front door, then carefully put the chair back against the wall of the polished hallway.

Cold rain soaking into her dress. Warmth inside the van which was taking them to a holiday by the sea. Steam on the windows. The back of her father's head. His eyes in the mirror, looking behind him. Waiting for his eyes to look at her. His eyes looking. He had not touched her, but she was no longer a doll.

Her father leaving the van, and her mother now driving. Her mother telling James to sing to her, to talk and keep her awake so that there wouldn't be an accident. Darkness and swerving, dazzling lights. James singing Christmas carols when it was still summer, and the windscreen wipers scratching against the glass. James putting his arms around her, and giving her a towel when she wet herself.

Then the tin house they called the caravan, tin on the outside, painted and rusty, and wood stuff inside. Waiting for her father to bring food and money. Feeling hungry. Then the noise and smell of a motorbike, with the new puppy sitting in the saddle-bag.

She had seen the sea, but only once, and not for long. She had been woken early, and taken on the cross-bar of a bicycle. There had been no one else there, and they had walked along the beach, throwing sticks for the new puppy he had bought her. Sand had got inside the shoes the foster-people had chosen for the doll, Marianne, to wear. They were red sandals, not real shoes, and sand had got inside, and she had kicked it out again through the holes while her father had talked to her.

He had kept saying that they would be safe here, and asking her to tell him that she understood. She would be safe with him now, did she understand? She had kicked sand, and looked at the sea and the pier, and had thrown sticks. He wasn't going to let anyone take her away again. He loved her and worshipped her, and wasn't going to touch her again, did she understand? She had kicked sand, and nodded her head, but had not understood.

She had not understood why Adam had gone away, why James pretended to be a girl, and why she could not be Marianne any more, but had to have a new name. Or why her father wasn't going to touch her.

* * *

Jean had been warned when she phoned that Sarah and the children would be out in the fields, making hay while the sun shone, and they were.

'We used to make hay very prettily by stacking it against tripods; they were called "haycocks", I think, something phallic and primitive. It was more work, but they did look so nice.' At the other end of the field a baling-machine chugged and spluttered as it hoovered up dry grass, to be excreted into neat bales at ten-yard intervals along the row. 'When Bob and I first came here, I'd be ringing round, trying to book someone to come and cut the hay for me, and they'd always say, "Tell your man to give us a ring when he gets home from work, missus." I used to get quite cross, though it would have been counter-productive to show it. When one remembers all the women over the years who've kept the farms going, and around here they still think you're a second-class citizen if you sit down to piss!' Sarah's children in bathing trunks ran about the field, throwing the hay at each other, and performing little dances when it touched their bare skin. 'Do take your jacket off, Michael, or you'll faint in this heat.'

On the way back to the house to make tea for the men operating the baler, Sarah showed off the sheds she had constructed, and introduced her visitors to some of the farm animals. A pig stood on its hind legs to sniff at their hands, and, amazingly, Michael did not back away. 'I'll never win the Duke of Edinburgh's Award for carpentry, but I do like knocking things together. We call this one Colditz; the pig is Glenda Grubnose – not my choice of name. The worst job around here is patching hedges when animals have escaped. Make do and mend; that's Organic Farming. What I like best is lambing time, and herding the geese home on summer evenings. We'll be doing that later on; you can help. I can get quite moist-eyed sometimes.'

'Sounds idyllic.'

'Sometimes. I got moist-eyed for quite a different reason two years ago, when we lost two cows, fifty per cent of our beef. One got bloated, and the other tried to jump over the moon, and ripped her stomach right open. That was twelve hundred pounds down the drain. In the same month, we had to have the clutch on the tractor repaired – two hundred and fifty pounds before they'd even look at it. You can't insure individual animals on a place this size, unless of course you're into angora goats.'

In the huge farmhouse kitchen they stood beside a scrubbed wooden table, and awaited instructions. Sarah brought five home-baked loaves to the table. 'I'll carve, Michael can butter, and Jean do the fillings.' Michael looked upwards at the objects suspended from the ceiling, three pairs of ladies' tights, each containing a large ham. 'It's alright, Michael; they're not the bodies of my husband's girl-friends, just what remains of Pinkie and Perky. Glenda, whom you've met, has to wait until there's an R in the month before she gets to try on my tights. We're not strictly legal, of course. I take the animals to the slaughterhouse, watch them being cut up, then bring all the bits back here to package them. The room in which that's done should be inspected and passed by some official with a briefcase every year, and it hasn't been. Then I make sausages right here in the kitchen, terribly naughty that. The way round all the regulations is to sell the animals on the hoof, but there's less profit.'

Thank God for Social Workers' training. Sarah was at ease with Michael, so Michael was at ease with her. At ease and matter-of-fact. Just the same, she was talking a great deal. Jean realized that on most days, while her husband was at work, Sarah would have nobody but the younger children to talk to at all, certainly nobody who spoke her language.

'We never intended to make a full-time business of it. At first I just grew what we needed for ourselves, then Bob started taking orders at work for free-range eggs. We put an advert in the window of one of the Whole Food Shops, and now we have five shops taking all the veg and fruit we can supply, and regular customers for the meat. A lot of smallholders can't eat the meat they rear; they get too fond of the animals. But I won't pay shop-prices for meat, so if my lot want roast pork, it's Glenda or nothing, and the same goes for Bertie the Bullock or Larry the Lamb.'

Michael said, 'Is that Bertie the Bullock Jean is slicing now?'

'Him or a cousin. Do you mind?'

'Not greatly. But I would rather do the buttering.'

'You're doing it very well. You have a nice judgement of quantities.'

'Thank you.'

Sarah said to Jean, 'It's the older farmers who are more sympathetic, oddly enough. What we try to do isn't all that far from what they were doing before the dreaded pesticides, nitrates and mountains of surplus food. The local Godfather has taken me under his wing. Lovely old fella, likes a bit of physical contact while he's telling you what you're doing wrong with your brassicas, and thinks that calling them "brassières" is the height of rural wit. "Them slugs bin taking great bites out of your brassières again, missus woman." I'm talking too much, aren't I? Why don't you stop me? Shut me up. Tell me to calm down and take myself in hand. You were always very good at that. I'm nervous, I suppose. And also very very glad to see you. The two seem to go together, for some reason.' Jean lifted an index-finger, and wagged it. 'That's it. Thank you, Very calming. One thing I don't get a lot of here is conversation on equal terms, except with Bob, and that's different. I just can't believe you're still doing it.'

'Wagging my finger at you?'

'Social Work. I couldn't wait to get out of it, Hell! woman, you must be a masochist. You'll never believe this, but I took Emmie and Frazer into town one day without washing them first. I was in a panic about something or other, and Emmie screamed all round the Shopping Precinct, so I walloped her right in the middle of Mothercare. Three days later, the Cruelty people made inquiries about me in the local pub. No kidding! Did the landlord know me? Was I a frequent visitor? Were the kids alright? So Liz, the landlord's wife, decided to wind them up a bit, put on the face she saves for funerals, and told this Cruelty woman that I'd once put the two older kids between the shafts, and used them to pull the plough, and that's how they came to have stripe-marks across their backs.' She stopped slicing bread, put her hand over Jean's while Michael looked away, and said, 'It's really good to see you, love. You mustn't mind if I seem to gloat, but you've reminded me how lucky I am. I've missed it – of course I have, or I wouldn't have gone into it in the first place – missed some of the clients even, but there were over a hundred, and I wasn't sleeping, and Bob said, "Bugger this for a lark! I'm taking you out of it before you drive us both mad," and the relief, love, the sheer relief, of not having to carry everyone else's garbage around, and having time to concentrate on my own. Now you say something.'

'I'm envious.'

'What of, the mucking out or the kids?'

'All of it, except the trips to the slaughterhouse. I'd have to pay a woman to come in and do that.'

'You wouldn't be short of applicants, believe me. I met most of them in my previous employment.'

Outside, across a wide courtyard surrounded by traditional buildings of stone and pantiles, the tiny figures of Emmie and Frazer could be seen approaching at speed. A moment later they were filling the kitchen with their presence, standing on an upturned bucket to take gulps of water straight from the tap, and splashing the water over each other. Jean said, 'How old are the other two work-horses?'

'Harry's fourteen and Cora's twelve. After her I had a nice long rest until Frazer five and a half years ago, swiftly followed by dearest ragamuffin, Emmie. She almost dropped out while I was spring planting. Another ten minutes, and she'd have taken root in a neat line of lettuce.'

A pile of sandwiches sufficient to feed an Army Corps had been made, but the two women talked on, and Michael sat listening and intermittently watching Frazer and Emmie, who were playing tag all over the house, hiding in cupboards and scuttling under tables. While Frazer stood at the top of the stairs, covering his eyes, Emmie, flushed and excited, ran back into the kitchen, grabbed both Michael's hands, pressed them against the sides of her bright red face, then replaced them on his lap, and slid giggling to hide beneath his chair.

'You've made a conquest, Michael.'

'Shush, mummy!'

'We'd better take these sandwiches to the horde outside.'

Jean helped Sarah with the herding of the geese, and Michael played Snap in the kitchen with Frazer and Emmie. At dinner he ate everything put in front of him, and was seen to enjoy it.

He was seated next to Emmie, who both demanded attention and generously gave it, behaving towards him rather in the manner of Queen Elizabeth the First with a favourite; one felt that at any moment she would reward him with a Monopoly on Salt. Michael looked at Jean with a smile as wide as a barn door. What Jean had failed to achieve after months of endeavour, Emmie had managed in only a few hours. He had taken off his tie, and looked almost handsome in the candlelight. He drank three glasses of wine, the same ration as the two older children, Harry and Cora, and when, at ten thirty they went sleepily off to bed, announced that he was feeling sleepy also, and went off to his own bed without demanding that Jean should accompany him.

'Amazing!'

'He certainly seems to have taken to the kids.'

Jean said, 'And they to him. I wonder if it'll last.'

Bob said, 'You need help. Am I right?'

'Some. I'm not sure yet what or how much.' Jean explained that, if they could put up with her and with Michael, she needed to stay at least for long enough to persuade the police that she was actually visiting friends, so that they would drop the surveillance, and she might be able to slip away unnoticed.

'And Michael?'

'That's one of the problems.'

'You want us to look after him for a while?'

'Oh God! Would you? A week would do. Less than a week.'

'Is he safe with small children?'

'I think so. But then I wouldn't have believed . . . I'd never have believed that Steven Gaines would have murdered his son . . . murdered and . . . I can't give a written guarantee, but there's nothing in Michael's history to indicate . . .'

Bob said, 'We'll have a fair idea before you leave, anyway. I can look after his medication while you're away.'

Jean was surprised. Sarah said, 'It's alright. Bob may look like an absent-minded computer-boffin to you, but he does have hidden depths. He knows more about medication for the brain and all its mysteries than I do.'

'I had a brother a lot worse off than Michael, but with a similar illness. And I'll be here; I'll make a point of it. I was going to take a week off to help with the hay and look after the kids, so it's no problem. But it really can be only a week from the day you leave, so you'll have to get your skates on. Where have you looked so far?'

Jean explained about the Directory of Caravan Sites, as modified by Mr Braithwaite.

'Those will just be the approved Sites, won't they, with Bars and Clubs and tumble-driers? If your man was going to this Site twenty years ago, it could be off the list, if it still exists. There are some really run-down places about. Everything broken, kids running wild, cardboard and corrugated iron keeping the weather out, all-year-round places guarded by Alsatian dogs; the Social Services stay well clear. You'd think you've stepped back to the nineteen thirties.' He turned to Sarah. 'Do you remember that place we drove up to by mistake, when we were looking for those goats you wanted to buy? They as good as set the dogs on us, and we were only asking the way. It was somewhere on the edge of the Dales, run by an old woman; caravans plonked every which way in the middle of fields. Everyone there looked as if they were on the run from the police.'

Sarah said, 'He'll need some kind of casual work, unless he's got a source of money.' The Inspector had said that Steven Gaines would need some kind of casual work, and had suggested that defrauding old ladies out of their pension books might be the softest option. 'He's got his family with him, so it couldn't be a circus or a travelling fairground, or anything that moves about. Of course the Fun Fairs at the seaside up here are semi-permanent, all season anyway, but it's still casual work. If you could combine a Fun Fair with that pier you told me about . . .'

Jean said, 'You're right. You always were right.'

'It's only a tiny chance. You've got to accept that you probably won't find him.'

'You were right about that essay of mine on Durkheim and delinquency seventeen years ago; it was crap. And you're right now. Put the pier, availability of casual work and caravans together, the third being least important, and there's a small chance.'

'You're not really going to tackle him alone, are you?'

'I know him. I'm not in any danger.'

'That has a familiar ring to it. We both know how many Social Workers every year are beaten up by clients they know well. He killed his son – right?'

'I think I may know why. I think I should have known why much earlier. We took – *I* took, literally picked her up, and took – the daughter away, and the younger son began ... began ... flirtatiously began ... Oh, shit! And I even saw him, Sarah, saw him and didn't realize what he was trying to do. I'm in no danger from Steven Gaines if I can find him. The children are in danger, and I'm about the only person he might ... willingly ... without doing anything stupid ...'

'And the little girl's seven years old? I remember an idealistic Jean, drunk as a lord, sitting on the floor of a bed-sit with her essay papers torn up and strewn in shreds about the room. She was weeping, very unusual for this young woman, and she was telling me about a shed in a wood somewhere, and a father who crept up the stairs to do mischief. I'm worried about your motives, Jean.'

'Hard-headed ... rational ... cool ... clear-thinking! I hate you.' Jean grinned and squeezed Sarah's hand, while Bob poured more wine. 'It's not that. There have been lots of seven-year-old girls over the years. If this case has become too personal, it's because I've made too many mistakes.'

Bob said, 'I've been thinking about the car.'

'You're worried it's going to pack up on me? So am I.'

'You changed your car, but the police know all about the new one. If you leave it here – conspicuously – and Mr Plod's still keeping half an eye on the place, he'll think you're still here. Meanwhile you've left in my car, early in the morning before Mr Plod is up.'

'Doesn't that make you an accessory?'

'To what? You haven't committed any crime. Anyway, if you choose to borrow my car without telling me, I can't be blamed. I might do a bit of work on yours while you're away.'

Jean found that her eyes were wet, and something emotional seemed to be happening in her chest and throat. 'You two!' she said. 'You two!'

Sarah said, 'Your hair looks lovely; the sun's brought out the highlights. If you were to cut an inch off all round the sides, it'd look rather like mine. I've got one of those big floppy straw hats, with daisies all round the rim. I could lend it to you. Then if you're driving Bob's car, and wearing that hat, anyone who did see you leaving would think it was me.'

'You think of bloody everything, don't you?'

'We farmers get a lot of practice in criminality.'

Bob said, 'If your man has read the papers, he'll know you've disappeared. Will he guess that it was in order to come looking for him?'

'Oh, yes. I think he'll be expecting me.'

The watch had been a twenty-first birthday present to herself. She had chosen it alone, bought gift-wrapping so that she should have something to unwrap on her birthday, and when the silver string had been unfastened, and the fancy pink paper neatly folded, she had hated what she saw, nineteen pounds, seventeen and sixpence worth of smugness glowing back at her, and she had said to herself, 'I'll have to lose it, dip it in hot water at the first opportunity, step on it accidentally.' Now, nearly twenty-six years later, in the blackness of a cheap hotel-room, its florin-sized luminous dial a self-contained button of light, the watch glowed at her, informing her that there were still five minutes left before two am, that it had kept perfect time since she had bought it, and would continue to keep perfect time for the next six hours until breakfast.

It was not going to be an easy six hours. Her mind was racing. Thoughts interrupted other thoughts. Questions she had to ask herself came and went without answers. Usually she lacked time for introspection, would welcome an hour or so of soul-searching, but not like this, not this way, not lying in a narrow single bed in a tatty bed-and-breakfast hotel, with Disco music thumping away in the distance, water moving reluctantly through sclerotic pipes, and the floorboards in the corridor outside in intermittent but perpetual grumbling argument.

The curtains at the window were so thin that they might as well have been made of Cellophane. Moonlight flooded the room. She had never been able to sleep in the light, had required thick curtaining to recreate the tomb (or womb). She closed her eyes, and after-images exploded behind the lids, miniature meteors, shooting stars in embryo, wriggling tad-poles of thoughts which would never become frogs, far less handsome princes. And faces, the faces of strangers, the faces of children, mouldering and falling away into darkness, to be replaced by other faces. *Now you see me, now you don't.* And the face leaning over her in the bus, its features slipping away like ash from the corner of its mouth – '*Whose little girl are you, then? You look like Daddy's little girl to me.*'

Once in the middle of winter, when snowflakes fell like feath-ers from the sky, a queen sat sewing at an open window which had a frame of black ebony (*with flies and bluebottles spinning on their backs*). The queen pricked her finger, and three drops of blood fell onto the snow. The red looked so beautiful against the white that the queen thought, 'I wish I had a daughter as white as snow, with cheeks as red as the blood, and hair as black as the window-frame.' Soon afterwards, just such a little girl was born to her, and the queen called her 'Snow White'. But a year later, the queen died, and when another year had passed the king took to himself a new wife . . .

If a girl can't form a positive identification with her mother, not only does she get stuck in Oedipal conflicts, but regression sets in. It's all there in Snow White – weak father, nasty step-mother, obligatory hunter taking the dratted infant off into the woods, and leaving her there to the mercy of the wild beasts because he hasn't the guts to kill her himself, plonking some poor possum's lungs and liver down on the table for the wicked step-mum to fry up for breakfast, talking to her own self-image in a mirror that talks back. Meanwhile, back at the shack in the woods, seven helpful dwarves – 'little men' with phallic hats, delving and penetrating into dark holes to mine for gold – get it? 'We're going for gold lads. Pull your hats well down.' And you can forget about your Dopey, Sneezy, Grumpy, etc. That might have been Walt Disney's idea of the way Pre-Oedipal little boys view their willies, but it ain't mine, and after a few more of these lectures, it had better not be yours . . .

And all seven dwarves had said, 'Lock the door, and don't let anyone in but us.'

If only she had borrowed some of Michael's Valium! She couldn't take five and a half more hours of some moth-eaten lecturer misrepresenting Bettelheim. Why was she here? Why had she left London without even a second thought, dragging Michael with her? Why had she visited Caravan Site after Caravan Site, behaving like some bloody private detective, which she was not, and never would be? Why did bits of what he had said to her about his life of twenty years ago keep popping back into her mind? (*My memory-tape keeps getting stuck, playing the same bits over and over like a cracked record.*) The white-painted stone supports at each corner of the caravans, the wooden steps covered with rotting carpet, the brightly painted bricks, lattice fences, smelly toilets, were these what he had told her or what she had seen? Prestige, Status, Brookwood, Rio Vista, were they the names of makes of caravan or the names of caravans themselves, chosen names, 'Rose Cott', 'Noreenly', 'Mayfrank', 'Willow Bank'? What name would Steven Gaines have chosen for his new home?

He had not spoken of uninhabited caravans, derelict tin shells with broken windows and ripped polythene flapping in the breeze, of caravans tipped onto their sides or left suspended on three piles of white-painted stones. He had not mentioned the spray-painted graffiti, 'Pauline is a shit. G.D.' Was that where the Gaines family lived now, as squatters crouching below the level of shattered windows, hiding behind the legend of Pauline the Shit?

He had said, 'My memory tape keeps getting stuck, playing the same message over and over like a cracked record. They were all basic colours, not pastels like today. If you'd been allotted a yellow caravan, you knew it would look like the yolk of an egg. The tyres would have been painted black, all looking as if they were flat, because no one had scraped away the earth to paint the bottom of the tyre. Metal parts were painted with that silver paint like the sort you see on old cars; it's grey more than silver, and looks as if it's got lumps in it, very unnatural.'

No humour, no irony from the man who had sat beside her on a park bench, speaking of unnatural matters. He had re-membered everything, and so much in that unpleasant time had pleased him – the slipway for the lifeboat, the pier of course, the benches facing out to sea, even the names of the houses on the sea-front, 'Sea Crest', 'Ocean View', 'Fair View',

'Sandy Cove', remembering and chanting these unremarkable names as if they were a charm to reassure him. I remember, therefore I am. 'Sea Cot', 'Neptune's Lodge', 'Marianne Villa'. The pier of course. Look for the pier, and find a source of casual employment not far away; the Caravan Site itself is the least important of the three elements. The entrance to the pier had four towers, painted white, Turkish-style, with pointed roofs rising to a spike like Prussian helmets – maybe Turkish helmets also; a spike on one's hat could lend a lethal quality to the merest 'How do you do?' The hut at the end of the pier had always been locked, and there was a poster on the wall inside, only part of which could be seen when he was lifted up to look through the window, a poster with pictures of every kind of sea-fish, and underneath each one, the fish's name in print too small for him to read.

And she had said, 'If one's going to take refuge in memories, Steven, one should concentrate on the best times,' forgetting that, if one could ignore the little matter of his brothers' abusing him, these may well have been the best times.

He had aged before her eyes, sliding his forefinger and thumb along the creases in his trousers, brushing away imaginary crumbs from his lap, and reminding her of someone else, as he said, 'There was a kind of safety, I suppose. Once you could remember the names of things, then you'd always know where you were. Whole streets would go there. People who lived next door to each other the whole year round would insist on having the caravans next to their own neighbours, as though living for a week beside people they didn't already know would change their personalities. Affairs would go on, just as they did the rest of the year. Mr B and Mrs C meeting up in the bushes, and being careful to leave the bushes separately afterwards, but everyone knew. The whole shop-floor of the Works walking one way along the promenade every evening at a certain time, with the foremen and the bosses walking the other way from their boarding-houses and hotels. Caps touched, and hellos shouted. Every evening the same stroll at the same time, like a roll-call. "Where's Jim? He's late." "Be here in a minute. Just tying the dog up." If it rained, you played cards, or sat by the window, watching the woman in the caravan opposite putting her curlers in. Would she manage to cram sixteen in today, or would it be the usual fourteen, with the same bits of loose hair left dangling at the back? Apron, cardigan, bedroom slippers, just like at home. For cold days, the paraffin stove, with its little window always blackened up so that you couldn't see if it had stayed alight or not, and had to open a window now and then to let the fumes out. I looked at a brochure recently in a newsagent's – "Super Holiday Complex. Mobile Homes with Showers and Own Toilets, Colour TV, Fridges, Washing-Machines. Safe Children's Play Area and Assault Course."' Then he had smiled at her, not reminding her of anyone else but himself, and said, 'Children's Assault Course, Jean! What will they think of next?'

The smile had come in stages, first hesitant, trying it out with the eyes still dead, then the relief that she wasn't angry at his joke in bad taste. And she had sat next to him, smiling back, Miss No-Reproof of 1986.

What time did Discos stop? The luminous hand of her twenty-first birthday present seemed to have stuck at twenty to three. The Detective Inspector picked his way delicately through the thin curtains, and came to sit on her bed. The moonlight shone through the dark blue barathea which covered his chest, and glittered on the silver trimmings, and he spoke exclusively in elegant italics.

'*What on earth do you think you're doing?*'

'Trying out this mattress for size, Inspector. There's a hollow in the middle.'

'*Suppose you find him, what then?*'

'I'll know.'

'*And if you don't?*'

What she'd do, that wasn't the question. And finding him wasn't the question. Too many questions, too many thoughts, too many memories. When she knew which of the questions was the real question, she'd know the answers to all the questions.

'*Didn't they teach you miracle-workers anything at Training College? Didn't they warn you never to go into any situation unprepared? "Think! Consult! Act! Report!"*'

Oh yes, dear; always report. Neat handwriting, if you please. And whatever you may personally think, try to make your reports a little more objective if you can. They look so much more professional that way.

The Ration Book mentality. Snip, tidy, cut around the per-
forated edge. Do not fold here. That's the part you hand in
for your hysterectomy, dear, and don't forget to keep your
Nervous Breakdown coupons safe and sound. Who knows
when you might need one?

This Social Worker has undertaken work beyond her competence. What competence?

'*Thirty-seven Public Inquiries since 1974! What a growth industry
for the lawyers! Something like seventy-seven children on the Abuse
Register in Haringey alone, and not one of them with a Social Worker.
The figures for Humberside up eighty per cent in a year, and if the kids
there see one of your lot in a fortnight, they can think themselves lucky.
The world needs Social Workers, Miss Davis, or thinks it does. I am
right, aren't I? It is still "Miss", isn't it?*'

'It's nice to know you're needed, Inspector.'

'*You are, you are. Look what a help you've been to me! Social
Workers are user-friendly; everybody should adopt one. I wouldn't be
surprised if there aren't people sleeping in this flea-bitten hotel right
now who could put you to some use or other. Everyone needs an Aunt
Sally to cuddle up to, am I not right, Miss Davis? Surely that was the
only reason that someone like you, someone with your background, was
allowed into the charmed circle – the need outweighed your
inadequacies?*'

In one of the many pep-talks at College, they had said,
'You have the opportunity and ability to contribute to Man's
awakening, to help awaken the sleeping Christ in Man.' And
just remember what happened to Christ! 'You are the food,
the shelter, clothing, love, the recognition, the sense of personal
worth, the belief in some real purpose to life.' But just remember that helping someone to come alive is playing with
fire, for they often wake with a sword in their hands.

'Gardens are not made by crying, "Oh, how beautiful" and
sitting in the shade, are they, Cynthia?'

'Sorry. What was that?'

'Kipling, Cynthia.'

'Oh, right. Of course. Sorry. Kipling. Didn't he do something on multi-racial adolescents?'

Of the nineteen would-be alarm clocks, waiting to awaken
Man, who had sat with notebooks at the ready on that first
day of Training, two had breakdowns during the course

('Mainspring over-wound. Fly-wheel all to cock.'), Cynthia had been asked to leave ('Lacks the vitamins of Mental Health'), three had been dropped at the end of their first year ('Attempting to use Social Work as the quickest way out of Manchester'), and of the unlucky thirteen who had finished the course, only seven had remained in Social Work longer than two years. 'You lot are supposed to be the embodiment of the Social Conscience, operating at the storm centre of conflict, employed at the very spots where public sensibilities are at their most tender, and you sit there before me, nursing hangovers, and have the gall to admit that you haven't a clue what a mother of three in two rented rooms is allowed for her heat and light.'

'A mother of two now, Miss Davis. If we're lucky. In a one-room caravan, most like. Will they still be there, huddled over a paraffin stove, when winter comes? What are you going to say to your friend when you see him? Surely something in those books you were supposed to read might help you. You had three tea-chests full, blue paperbacks mostly, ever so dense.'

'I read them. Most of them. Something of most of them. The majority were concerned with children. I'd hide a book on child-development inside one on socio-economics. Even then I was looking for something. The books I read were concerned with children who never grew up, stunted innocents who spent seven days a week mining for precious metals in the mountains, deformed, misshapen little beings, who'd sit before you humming as their tiny fingers worked away, modelling over-sized Plasticine penises with razor-sharp fins.' (At what stage is the child now? One is good, five is bad. How good is the child's emotional resilience? Has it experienced good bonding? What does the child feel? What is his/her understanding of what has happened? Is the child aggressive, passive, withdrawn? (Tick box.) Does it make eye contact? physical contact? Is the child provocative? One is strong, five is weak.)

'The amount of sensuality even a very small child carries around with it, Inspector, is amazing. Those three tea-chests and two short academic years had to contain Freud, Jung, Piaget, Klein, Bowlby, Winnicott, Anna Freud, Erikson, Fromm, old Uncle Tom Watson and all. They had to contain twelve pieces of written work a year, a final thesis of twenty-five thousand words, placements, in-course training, tutorials, counselling, role-play. I always played the victim; I did it so convincingly – mother of six, ten weeks behind with the rent, live-in lover a drunk and she suspects he's sleeping with the oldest daughter, but he does bring in some money, and hasn't given up sleeping with her yet, so she's not all that keen to lose him – Ladies and gentlemen, I give you Miss Jean Davis in another award-winning role. (It was, and still is "Miss", Inspector.) Two years of group work, of being observed, broken down, taken apart and putting myself together again! Two years of interpreting jargon in which nothing was ever what it seemed, and everything had a hidden meaning, even the jokes about penis-envy from a tutor with urine-stains on his trousers! A great deal was said about finding oneself, and coming to terms with what one found, so whenever I could, I bounced up and down on someone's shoulders, squealing and laughing under tall trees through which the sunlight filtered, and imagining that I was chasing the sun. I imagined wild flowers in jam-jars dying for lack of water, and flies on a window-ledge spinning round with their legs in the air, crying, "Give us a fuck, mister. Give us sixpence." I imagined fat dinner-ladies, glistening with sweat as they rattled aluminium pans, and threw back their heads, their mouths wide open, laughing, laughing like the toy policemen in Amusement Arcades. Two years, Inspector! And the only thing worth re-membering was when somebody said, "No one is ever fully qualified. Continued learning is needed throughout your pro-fessional life."'

And Steven had said, 'I'm not frightening, am I? Do you think I'm frightening?' She had not thought he was frightening. 'Have you noticed how we always give the names of animals to the people we fear? Fox, panther, wolf-man. Some-times we just say "animal", "must have been an animal", "that animal".'

'*Infants abandoned on dung-hills are not to be tolerated as one of the normal sights of life, Miss Davis. Thomas Coram, late eighteenth century. I went to College too, you know. We haven't progressed much, have we? Even your dwarves laid Snow White in a glass coffin to discourage the worms and thieving magpies. No prince is going to bring you back to life if you're lying under some bushes with your knickers round your ankles.*'

There had not been knickers round Adam Gaines's ankles, but darned grey socks with a red trim, and it had been the police who had loosened the short trousers and white underpants, looking for the stains of semen. A healthy clear-skinned face, pressed against the spikes of hawthorn and the spotless white trumpet of convolvulus. Blond eyelashes at which she had stared, expecting them to move.

'The older boy must be an interesting age by now, wouldn't you say, probably as randy as all get out? You know, at the pace you've been going, you'll be stumbling over two little graves in the grass with two wooden crosses. "Here lies Poor Fido, a man's Best Friend." Or would it be more like, "Oh, could you keep me, mother dear, from Him who ever loved me so? I do not wish to linger here. Mother, dear mother, let me go"?'

'I shall find him.'

Arms frantically turning, legs pumping at the foot-pedals, spinning round and round on their backs, thrashing and kicking, 'Come in, Number Seven. Your time is up.' Her fist banging at the door below, her voice screaming up at the window to be let in out of the rain, pleading, crying, promising good behaviour, while the palm of his hand made circles on my stomach, touching me properly and improperly for the first time, I feeling his warm testicles in my hand, there in my hand, feeling the size of him, the hair and the sweat on him, the stubble of his beard against my face, the smells of wood-smoke and tobacco, and then the pain.

'You don't think much of the mother, do you?'

'Not a lot. I suppose you've tried the foster-parents in Bournemouth? I don't know whether her real mother is still alive, Maureen Gaines was never very talkative, not to me anyway.'

'And you say that later you saw the two of them together in the Market, that whore on a bike, your mother, and the man who may or may not have been your father? He was buying her a pair of nylons, was he? Pale, cinnamon-coloured stockings with a spider's-web design up the heel, were they? And while he held them up to the light to look for ladders, the whore on a bike turned and looked straight through you, did she, and smiled as if she were showing you something? What was she showing you, Miss Davis? I am right, aren't I? It is still "Miss"?'

'She was showing me. Yes.'

'*Showing you what?*'

'Who it was forced her to put on red shoes, and dance until she died.'

'*Dead, is she, your mother?*'

'In a sense.'

Steven had said, 'It's like links in a chain. Something happens to you like that, and you think it's horrible, so bad you can't ever talk about it, can't ever see the lower half of yourself in a mirror without feeling dirty, and remembering what was done to you against your will. But later you realize you're not as innocent as you thought, because now you're just as capable as anyone else of losing control and behaving badly. You think that perhaps it wasn't all their fault. At first it may have been. Maybe. But then later, when you know it's the only way to get their attention, you provoke them, see if you can get them excited, since that seems to be the only power you have. It's conditioning, I suppose. Loneliness is so destructive.'

'*Alright, let's be sensible about this. Suppose that tomorrow you come face to face with this man who buggers and strangles his children?*'

'Child. One child.'

'*One strangled, two buggered, and the third we're not sure about, because you became obsessed with the little girl, and didn't take as much notice as you should of the boys. Alright. You're face to face, he's looking straight at you, and you say to him . . . what?*'

'Shut up! Just shut up! Just for once in your life, button that fucking interrogative lip.'

'*You still haven't got it clear in your mind what you're doing here, have you? I think you're beginning to wish you'd stayed back in London being courted by the press, and left it all to us. It's not too late, you know. Right up to the very moment you see him, you can always pull out.*'

'No.'

'*Why not?*'

'I'm his Social Worker. The family's Social Worker.'

'*But more his then theirs, wouldn't you say?*'

'I would not.'

'*You'd get a chance to talk with him, you know. Probably. After we'd got him under lock and key. Not that I could promise what state he'd be in by then.*'

'Exactly!'

'*Exactly what? Look, all we require from your lot are the kind of miracles which will make our lives easier, and we're fully aware by now that miracles sometimes backfire. But what you keep demanding is that we should all change, whereas it's the delinquents you should be concentrating on, the social deviants. They're the ones who need to be altered, to be made less delinquent, less promiscuous, less poor, less ignorant, less of a bloody nuisance.*'

'Not very far-sighted, Inspector.'

'*My sight stretches as far as the body of a nine-year-old boy in a muddy field. You identified him for us. How long ago was that?*'

'Backwards is the wrong direction. Try looking in a different way, damn you! Find new dimensions in a social illness. Look at psychological disorder, and see a different kind of sense. Not acceptable, not socially acceptable the way society is now, but a sense none the less. A conditioning, Inspector, a chain of events that even a body-builder can't break out of, not on his own.'

She was talking aloud, had raised her voice, and was almost shouting. Someone was banging on the wall of the next room. She looked again at her watch, and discovered that the luminous hands had been moving faster; it was almost four o'clock. The Disco had shut down, and she hadn't noticed.

'*What you're saying, Miss Davis, is that buggering one's offspring has a kind of logic to it, if one has been buggered oneself in childhood. Sins of the fathers visited on the children, and then on the children's children, until none of us is safe, bending in the street to pick up a coin. I can't believe they let you out of College thinking like that. We knew you were left of centre, but that kind of thinking gives liberalism a bad name. Oh yes, we had to do a little checking up on you, of course.*'

Whose little girl are you, then? And the ash falling.

'*We'd no idea you had such an interesting youth, Miss Davis. Bit of a late developer, one could say. You must have wowed them in College with your reminiscences of the Remand Home.*'

'You'll be alright, Jean. You have experience of life.' They had meant that she was a mature student from a poor background, deprived and even, for a while, depraved, and that they felt all the better for having her on their team. They had said, 'Social failures, Jean, are simply those people who have failed as yet to persuade society to help them enough.' She, Jean, had achieved upward mobility by persuading society to help her enough.

They had stood before her, giving her advice which was often contradictory, but could always be justified theoretically. Those who can't, teach, and those who can – pay social visits to black women who tie up their children's willies in leather thongs. Jean had burned the midnight oil, catching up on an education which had been deficient in theory, however strong in practice. She had huffed, and puffed, and blown down some of their theoretical houses with her reports from the field. Had the course lasted any longer than two academic years, and had she not rationed her frank and honest reports from the grass roots, her maturity and experience of life would have begun to embarrass them, her reminiscences of the Bus Station and the Remand Home begun to pall.

'In the Remand Home, girls who wet their beds were forced to drink the urine of those who did not.' Comment on this practice in terms of (a) sympathetic magic in primitive societies; (b) the Victorian concept of making the punishment fit the crime.

'One toilet bag and flannel, one hold-all, one comb and hairbrush, six handkerchiefs, one toothbrush, five pairs of socks (white), three bras, six briefs, two nylon slips, two skirts (grey), two cardigans (grey), four blouses (white), one coat (for best wear), one swimming costume (one-piece). All articles should be clearly marked with laundry-resistant label showing owner's name.' From the Remand Home, Jean had been moved back to one Children's Home, then to another, until finally she had been considered a young adult, and had been transferred to a Hostel for Young Adults.

There had been jobs, dead-end jobs of various sorts, none of them gaining her enthusiasm, and there had been unemployment, but she had not been one to sleep away her days in parks and squares, and she had returned to the Children's Home, and applied for a job as a cleaner. 'You seem to be very good with children, Jean. They like you. Perhaps that's what you should do, look after children.' From cleaner she had been promoted to General Assistant, had learned to drive, had ferried children and Young People to and from the Juvenile Court, and had assisted a qualified member of staff to take the children on Outdoor Weekends, rock-climbing, sailing, abseiling, trekking.

Jean had not been qualified, but had determined to be, not only because she had believed that being qualified would bring her closer to children, but because the children who sat behind her in the mini-bus with faulty brakes needed a role-model, adept at more than using the hand-brake to pause at traffic lights. She had begun studying for O Levels, and thereafter for A levels. There was no side about it; no one hid the fact that she herself had been in Care. She was just Jean, neither qualified staff nor inmate, Jean without prospects of having children of her own; she did what many had done before, and concentrated on work. When she was in her late twenties, it was suggested that she should apply for a place at Training College as a mature student. And she, thinking all the time that she was becoming closer to children, to being part of their lives, began the process which would take her further away.

Are all patterns repeated? Is that their nature? Reading them stories late into the night. Listening to secrets. Overweight Linda, stunted and undernourished Christopher from Belfast, anxious Andrew, Molly and Peter. 'Hugs and kisses to my best friend, Jean.' 'I love you, Jean,' scribbled on the inside of a torn cigarette-packet and slipped into her hand. Questions to be answered: 'How do you multiply?', 'What's the longest river in Germany?', 'Who discovered penicillin?' Studying to catch up, learning so as to stay one question ahead. Not that they ever minded if she didn't know; they would find out together.

Summers sunbathing on the grass, applying cream to Christopher's fin-like shoulderblades. 'You must have a favourite, Jean. Tell us.' 'Who do you like best? Go on, be honest; it's me, isn't it?' 'You're our favourite.' 'Don't tell her that. She'll get big-headed.' 'You're not going to leave us, are you?' On the contrary; they would grow, and leave her. Five noses all about to peel. 'Does a sun-tan make you look thinner?' Christopher's head turning towards her, lips pressed tightly together, left eyelid winking up at her, his back moving with suppressed laughter. Evening walks in autumn. Five hands all wanting to be held at the same time. 'You should've been an octopus, Jean.' Five pairs of eyes, squinting into hedgerows and up into trees, looking for abandoned nests. 'Why do we always have to turn round, and go back there? Why can't you be our mother, Jean? We could live in a proper house then. Yeah, we'd behave for you. I'm sure we would.' Molly, hastily wiping her blackberry-stained mouth.

Winter and Christmas. Faces in candle-light. Eyes too bright, reflecting tinsel and wonder. 'If I die from this flu, Jean, will you be there to see they bury me properly? I don't want no hymns, just the Sergeant Pepper album.' Whispering in corners, sheepish grins. Christopher breaking into a public phone-box to buy Christmas presents. Wrapping-paper and silver string hidden under beds. 'To Jean with love from Peter. To make you smell even nicer.' Bath-salts. Bedroom slippers from Andrew, chocolates from Linda, a scarf from Molly. And Christopher's smile because she has saved his parcel until last, a pair of three-inch *diamanté* ear-rings and a gold charm-brace-let. 'Be our mother, Jean.' At twenty-one, she had given herself a birthday present.

Spring, and more walks, looking for snowdrops. Five hands to hold in equal turns. No favourites. Six people sitting on top of a hill to form a magic circle. 'Why magic?' Because we're all friends, and nobody can separate us, that's why, fart-face.' Family differences forgotten. 'You could adopt us, Jean.' 'Naaa! She'd have to have a husband, and then she'd go off us. We don't want any of that, thank you very much.' Five small faces look up from their Nature Study collection of gras-ses and leaves, ten eyebrows forming question marks, until Peter, the spokesman, asks the question, and is answered by a shake of the head.

'You don't want a husband, Jean, do you, not when you've got us?'

'*You were a good amateur, Miss Davis. Highly recommended. Now you're a pro, who's been sent off the field for misconduct. A transfer to a lower league might be the answer. Old People's Home, perhaps.*'

Did she really want to go to the toilet? Could she bear to get out of bed, and tramp down the corridor, banging the fire-doors behind her? Men always did it in the wash-basins of hotel rooms. The man who may have been her father had stood, leaning against the open window, and peeing down onto the patch of garden she had tried to cultivate.

'All that's important now is how fast we can get to him.'

'*We could be quite close. Do you suppose he's lying awake like this, wondering where we are, if we're breathing down his neck? Is he listening for noises outside, a twig breaking or the creak of a gate in that lattice-fencing they like to stick around their tin boxes? If he needs to piss in the middle of the night, does he tramp to the stinking communal toilets, disturbing the undernourished Alsatians who scratch out their beds in the earth under the caravans? Is he a risk-taker, Miss Davis? Does he have balls? Answer on one side of the paper only. Is he sitting on a park-bench right now, looking up at the stars, wondering if the weather tomorrow is going to be suitable for child-molesting? You had a rapport with him –*' pronouncing the 't' again – '*You were friends. You're the only person who really knows him, the only one he's talked to at any length. Yet all you seem to know is where everyone slept.*'

'I know more than that, a lot more.'

'*Why are you looking for him?*'

'I want him to tell me why he did it, and why he didn't come to me. It's a personal thing, Inspector, most un-professional. I want him to explain to me what I did wrong. A selfish thing, but I need it. I need to know.'

'*Better. Not the whole truth, but better.*'

Had the man who peed out of the window been her real father, or had that part been taken by someone else, a Pole or a Czech, some early refugee wearing cast-offs from a village Jumble Sale? Had she been the result of a one-off coupling in the bushes?

'*Why didn't you ask him? You had the chance.*'

'I never went back there, not for a long time, not until much later.'

'*But you did go back. And before that, you waited for him to come to you, waited in Bedford, watching the buses arrive at the Bus Station, with their lights reflected in the puddles, remember? You watched from the steamed-up windows of the Waiting Room, all those buses and all the hours in between, waiting in case one of the people getting off might be he, in case he came to look for you, to take you away with him. Cambridge! Hunstanton! St Neots! London! Watching the names roll round at the front of the buses! Any destination would have done, wouldn't it, just as long as it was you and he? And at other times standing by the hair-slides and hair-ribbons in Woolworth's, or roaming the market-place, hoping you might bump into him, waiting by the Children's Boating Lake, haunting everywhere you'd been together! You*' *must have loved him. There was no one else, was there, never has been?* *You're still looking for him, Jean. It is "Jean", isn't it? You still have* *unfinished business with him, even though he must be past seventy by* *now, if he's still alive. And you did go back, Jean. You had your* *chance to finish the unfinished business. Why didn't you take it?'*

'It was too late. I'm not even sure why I went.'

'Think about it. You'd just started at College; you wanted to show *what you'd achieved. Your teachers had told you that you should "find* *yourself", hadn't they, told you that nobody can avoid the pain of life,* *but you should examine your problems, take them out, look at them,* *name them, and accept them as yours and no one else's? And so, filled* *with the confidence and strength of self-analysis, you went back to* *Wood End. To look for what?'*

'I told you; I don't know. Me, I suppose, to look for me, the six-year-old me, the eleven-year-old me, the scared frightened me who'd allowed it all to happen, the barren twenty-eight-year-old who'd been told to find herself.'

'And when you got there?'

'The first thing I noticed was the new roof. It wasn't sheets of corrugated iron any longer; it had been tiled. The stonework of the walls had been recently painted, and there were steel window-frames where the old rotted ones had been. There was a small neat garden, with polythene cloches protecting lettuces and things from the rabbits. I walked round the house, keeping my distance from it. Someone new might have been living there. All the improvements suggested new people, and I was pleased, glad I wouldn't get to look inside. It was as if the old house hardly existed, except in my own mind, and that was a relief. At the rear of the house there was a small shrubbery, set around a septic tank; they actually had inside plumbing. Then I noticed that someone was working in the kitchen. The window had steamed up, but I could see that it was a man. He was washing up; I could see him placing the dishes in a rack to dry themselves. Then he saw me, wiped some of the steam from the window with his hand, and we both stood, just watching each other. After a few minutes, he opened the back door, so I had to go towards him. He had no idea who I was, and at first I didn't recognize him. I said, "I'm looking for Mr and Mrs Davis," and he said, "I'm Mr Davis. What can I do for you?" He must have been in his mid-fifties then, but he looked more like seventy. I said, "You don't know me, do you?" and he thought for a while, and then shook his head. I said, "Jean," and waited. Nothing, so I said again, "I'm Jean," and still he didn't understand. I had to spell it out for him, and tell him that I was Jean, his daughter. And he just stood there with his hand on the door, ready to close it. Nothing, no reaction, not a word, as if he were thinking, "So what? What does she expect me to do about it?" We just stood there, the two of us, like strangers without speaking, until I asked if I might go inside, and he turned, and shuffled ahead of me. "I'm afraid your mother left here nearly six years ago." That was the way he put it, "left here" not "left me". He was shuffling about, moving things, as if he were trying to remember what one did on such occasions, what one said when a long-lost daughter returned after eighteen years. No eye contact. He never once looked straight at me. He was offering tea, apologizing that there weren't any biscuits, saying he didn't keep much food in the house for himself; it went off too quickly, and anyway he ate his main meal at the farm. Yes, he still worked at the same farm, had to because this was a tied cottage. The intermittent limp had become a shamble. He kept wandering about, tidying things, taking tiny steps in bedroom slippers with their backs worn down. He'd bump into things, and say, "Well, now! Well, now!" The upright cock-sure body had shrunk into a question-mark, with his chin jutting forwards, his neck muscles tense from the strain of supporting his head and preventing his face curling downwards into his chest. There was no beard, no stubble, just a very old and tired face, much too old and tired for a man still in his fifties. He had short neatly cut hair and a Bedfordshire accent. That was something I hadn't remembered. All those times over all those years when I'd heard his voice inside my head, he had never spoken with an accent, never pronounced "rain" as if it were the name of a German river. I don't think he accepted that I was who I said I was. He wouldn't have behaved like that, would he? I wasn't Jean to the man I met that day, any more than he was the man who had terrified me at one moment, and bought me presents the next. He even called me "Miss". "That chair's a bit unsafe, Miss. Try the other."'

And Snow White tried all the seven beds in turn.

'We drank our tea, with him standing looking out of the window, and he apologized again for the lack of biscuits, and said it was a pity I'd missed my mother, as though she'd only left an hour earlier. I asked him why she had left, and he didn't give me an answer, didn't even bother to change the subject. There were silences, long silences which neither of us filled, while he waited for me to go, to disappear as I'd done eighteen years earlier. I wanted him to ask me why I'd come back, but he didn't – didn't even ask if I was married, where I lived, or what I was doing. I'd intruded into his little world, and he was waiting for me to leave. I kept biting back the questions I wanted to ask. Did he remember what he'd done to me, what we'd done together? I knew that he would re-member, but of course he'd have had to say he didn't. And when I asked if I could see upstairs, he must have sensed something, because he said it wasn't convenient, wasn't tidy. "I'd be shamed," he said. Yes, that was the way he put it. And anyway, he said, there was nothing to see, only the one bedroom. I said, "Yes, father, I remember it," and then I left.'

Back pressed against the horsehair mattress, eyes on the watch in the shoe beside her bed.

'You're lovely, Jeannie, and you're all mine. Who do you belong to?'

'You, daddy.'

'Who do you love now?'

'You, daddy.'

'Say, "I love you, daddy."'

'I love you, daddy.'

'Tell me I make you feel good inside. Tell me you like what I do to you. You do like it, don't you? Here's some more, then. And more . . . and more. I'm filling you up inside, so you'll never feel empty. Are you sore there, my precious, sore all the way up? Bite me. Bite me here. Bite me where it will show. Bite hard until the blood comes. Let her see what we've been doing. Let her see how much you like me making you sore. Let's show her.'

'*It's clear now, isn't it? It's come clear, hasn't it, Jean?*'

Yes, it was clear to Jean that the man who had offered her

202

tea, and apologized for the absence of biscuits, the man who was not able to show her the bedroom upstairs because he would be shamed, that man was not her father. Jean's father was hiding in a caravan by the seaside with a depressed wife and two small children.

'*Right!*' said the Inspector, the moonlight glittering on the silver trimmings of his uniform. '*Getting there, aren't we?*'

She walked among side-shows, smelling the diesel fumes and the different coloured paints from the children's roundabouts and miniature Big Wheels, pear-drops for the cherubs, sherbet for the mermaids and Neptunes, peppermint for the satyrs and icecream soda for Tom Mix and other heroes of the Wild West.

She watched coy toddlers lifted up and placed in miniature fire-engines, watched a father wrap his child's fingers round the rope of the bell, then shake the fingers to cause the bell to ring. 'Fire!' the man shouted. 'Fire, Timmy! You'd better get to it quick,' and the child hid its face, embarrassed for him.

Tractor, double-decker bus, aeroplane, sports car, an ostrich which was bigger than the bus. She watched the small bright clear-skinned faces as they were carried past her, faces that were conscious of being watched, faces attempting to act the part of driver, pilot or ostrich-owner, faces longing for anonymity and wishing that they had never allowed themselves to be persuaded onto this revolving stage.

The roundabouts, the Big Wheel, so much in the fair-ground moved in circles. Even the bumper-cars sometimes spun on their own axes until the attendant limped from his position next to the hut in which the operating machinery was housed and from which the taped music was played, to jump onto the side of the spinning car, help the rotating driver to turn the steering-wheel, then jump off again to give the car a shove. The limp reminded her of her father's limp; it seemed put on.

The attendant wore dark glasses, denim jeans and a denim shirt open to the waist. He had shoulder-length hair, which was probably a Hippie wig. A well-built man, who took care of his body. She knew at once that he was Steven Gaines.

Then he saw her, and came towards her. He took her by

the arm, and they walked together through the Fun Fair. 'I knew you'd come looking for Marianne. I'm glad you got here before the police.' They walked along the promenade, past benches painted Local Council green, now filled with holiday-makers facing out to sea. No one looked twice at the child-murderer and his assistant as they passed. Cafés, Snack Bars, Amusement Arcades, Gift Shops! On past the Yacht Club with its balconies, where the rich sat sunning themselves while Jean Davis and Steven Gaines walked beneath them in silence.

They sat side by side on a bench, as they had so often done before, not in a park beneath trees this time, but in a glass-fronted shelter on the headland, looking out over the cliffs and the sea below.

'No one comes up here when the weather's fine. James spends a lot of his time on the pier, just as I used to do.'

'How did you get here?'

'We travelled separately a lot of the way. And I adapted something of Maureen's for James to wear, so that they'd be a mother and two daughters.'

'And you?'

'Motorbike.'

'Stolen?'

He shook his head. 'I didn't lie to you, Jean, when I said I didn't know where my brothers were. Until a few weeks ago, I had no idea. Then I saw Alex's photograph on the Sports Page of a newspaper in the Public Library. He was handing over a cheque to a young footballer, and underneath was the name of the Club he seemed to be involved with; the paper said he'd raised a lot of money for them, and was in line for a seat on the Board. That's where I drove when we left London. Told them at the Club that I was Alex's brother, and they telephoned him for me.' He paused for a moment, smiling to himself. 'He named a pub where we could meet. No question of me going to the house or meeting his family, no question of eldest brother welcoming kid brother home – and this was before there'd been anything about me in the newspapers. The moment he saw me, he broke out in a cold sweat, and couldn't stop shaking. All I said was that I needed help because I was on the run from the police. It could have been for anything, something quite minor even, but he never asked, didn't want or need me to tell him; he knew it wouldn't be for anything minor. Even after all these years, it was like he could still read my thoughts, just by looking at me. Odd, isn't it, how power changes hands? Seeing him like that, unable to hold himself still, his eyes darting this way and that, it had a calming effect on me, as if now it was his turn to do the whimpering and struggling. "Please, Stevie! Don't! Don't do it to me, Stevie. It hurts." He's the one with all the money, the one with the beer belly and the gin-and-tonic complexion, the one with the gold cigarette-lighter and the private dentist, and suddenly I'm the one who can spoil it all for him. Have spoiled it. Not a good example to set young people, having a brother who's done what I did. Then there's always the chance that what he and I had done as children would come out at the trial. He's probably abroad by now, sold up and gone – Costa Brava or somewhere. He certainly arrived at that pub prepared. His pockets were bulging with fifty- and twenty-pound notes. Couldn't wait to see the back of me.'

'What happens now? What are you going to do?'

'I expect the police are following close behind you, aren't they?'

'They were. I got rid of them for a while, but I don't know for how long.'

'I shouldn't think they'd be far away. It's only a matter of time.'

'No, they won't be very far away.' She looked away from him at the entrance to the shelter, and above it to the pane of shattered glass on which the words 'Piggy is bent' had been written in spray-paint. 'I'm still your Social Worker. I'm supposed to help you.'

'I need your help.'

'I can't hide you. You know that. I couldn't anyway, because I wouldn't know how. And the children are at risk.'

A spurt of anger. 'Not from me!'

'No. Sorry! What I mean is, officially, legally, they're at risk.'

'I won't stand trial. I won't go to prison. It'd be a life sentence, and the judge'd say, "Life means life" – something like that. Bestial crime, mustn't be released, risk to the public, something like that. And then . . . in prison . . . I've thought about this a lot, Jean; I've lain awake thinking. In prison . . . If I'm lucky, they lock me up separately. If I'm unlucky . . .'

'It's not a question of luck. They have to confine you separately with other . . .'

'Child-molesters? Perverts? I'm not like that; you know I'm not. With Marianne . . . it was out of love. I know what I've got to do, but I need your help.'

They sat side by side in silence, as they had often done. Then Jean said, 'And Adam? Was that out of love?'

'You want to know what happened. Well, I knew you would. You want to know why I didn't phone you, and say, "Please, miss, I've done something dreadful." You want to know why the man you said wasn't a monster proved you wrong. That hurts, I expect.'

Jean said, 'Let's talk about the shoes I helped you choose for him, the blue pullover for school, and the shirt with his brother's name-tag. Then you can tell me about the bruises on his neck and the fractured arm.'

'It wasn't like that either.'

'Nothing seems to have been like that. You'd better tell me what it was like, Steven.'

'I couldn't bury him, didn't have a spade. Then I realized I didn't want to, didn't want him to be hidden for too long. Don't you see, it was natural to run away, to get Marianne away? That was natural; anyone would. But I knew I couldn't hide for ever; I was bound to be caught. Don't you understand, it's instinct? You try to get away to somewhere safe, you try to make it last as long as possible, but all the time you know it's got to end; you want it to end. But I couldn't stand . . . ordinary prison maybe, but what it would be for . . . them not understanding, you see, and you couldn't make them understand . . . that's no life for a man like me; it's worse than death.'

It would be no life for a man like him; no doubt of that. What is a child-molester? What is a pervert? Little Miss No-Reproach of 1987! She remembered the Inspector, '*Not much of a contest, was it? – Mr Universe and Tiny Tim! All this, and just for a bit of how's-your-father! How do you feel about men who bugger small children, Miss Davis? What, in your professional opinion, makes a father drag his nine-year-old son around the bedroom, fracture his arm, split his lip, then throw him face-down on the floor to fuck the tiny arse off him? It is "Miss", isn't it?'* She said, 'What happened, Steven?'

'He came home, hadn't been to school. Normally I would have taken him back to school myself, but he looked so unhappy, kept following me around, and holding onto me. I'd hit him the day before for being silly . . . flirting, and embarrassing everyone. I'd hit him harder than I meant to, and felt sorry because I know how lonely you feel when someone you love gets angry. He said he didn't want the other boys at school to see the bruise, didn't want to tell them how he'd got it. He was worried I wouldn't like him any more. He was sorry for what he'd done, because he wanted me to be happy. How many nine-year-old boys can say that to their fathers, Jean?'

She did not reply, and he began again. 'I told him that I loved him, and said again that I was sorry I'd hit him. He could stay off school if he'd help me. I was going to clean both rooms, wash down all the floors and ceilings. And it was alright to begin with, while we were downstairs, though he never left my side, kept touching me, holding onto me, hugging me. I felt so sad for him, I couldn't meet his eyes, and that must have made it worse for him. When we got upstairs, he wanted to wrestle, wanted me to carry him on my back or to let him sit on my shoulders while we bounced about' (*through sunlight filtered through trees, chasing the sun*) 'as though he was a toddler again. I wasn't angry, didn't want to hit him or hurt him again, so I played along with him. We had a pillow-fight and a bit of wrestling, and I lifted him onto my shoulders, and gave him a cloth to wipe the ceiling. There was no fight, Jean, no struggle except in play, but the play-wrestling wasn't enough for him. It was as if he had to prove that what I'd said about loving him was true. He wanted me to make love to him, didn't say it, but held me, hugged me, stroked me, undressed himself, and lay there, looking at me.'

Again, a silence. Jean held in imagination a picture of a naked small boy, looking upwards, with behind his head the spikes of hawthorn and white trumpet of convolvulus. And a mattress, over which the muddy boots of a young policeman had walked. Steven Gaines said, 'Don't believe all I tell you. I knew early on what was going to happen. I want to try and be fair. After all, it's only what I remember, and it makes no difference now to anyone but you.' For a long time he remained inside his head, remembering, and then said, 'I looked down, and saw him smiling at me, heard him making that noise he sometimes made, sucking in air between clenched teeth and moving his tongue over his lips with his eyes half-closed, saw the smallness of his body as he rolled onto his side, all the time looking back at me, and smiling. It wasn't him, wasn't Adam I was looking down at. I was looking in a mirror. He was so insecure, you see. All that affection didn't satisfy him, didn't prove I could love him without doing that to him. He wouldn't believe me, wouldn't take my word for it. I've tried to remember different, tried to convince myself that I must have blacked out, but there was no black-out, and I can still smell the cleaner we'd used on the walls, still smell it on my hands and on his hands, feel his fingers moving over my lips, still feel his small teeth biting my shoulder, still hear him saying, "Love me, daddy. Please love me." I've tried to remember different, but I was looking in a mirror.'

Steven Gaines removed the dark glasses from his eyes, held them in front of him, and studied them. 'What I saw in the mirror was an eight-year-old me lying naked on a bed, writhing and wriggling and making noises of contentment, because some-one had liked me enough to take that much interest. Then I was the grown-up me, shouting "No! Stop it! Stop it!" over and over again, as I held his neck and shoulders, shaking him and trying to remove the smile and stop the noises. Then I was dressing him, putting him back into his school clothes, saying to myself, "I'll take him to school, so he won't miss a full day," patting his cheek and telling him to stop playing games, all the time putting clothes onto a limp body as if I was dressing a doll, telling him he could go to school because I'd proved how much I loved him. "It's History after lunch, Adam. You've done well at History."'

It was history; he had done well at history.

Steven said, 'I know what I've got to do. I've only got one option. But I need your help to make sure I do it properly, that it's finished and done with before the police find me. I'm not very brave.'

He tried to smile at her, and she tried to return his smile. Jean said, 'I'm not very brave either but I'll do my best.'

She was sitting in yet another Waiting Room, looking through yet another sheet of plate glass at the buses and coaches outside. This was a larger room than the one in which she had sat for hours many years ago. There was no steam on this window, no puddles of rain on the tarmac, and none of these buses and coaches were bound for Cambridge or Hunstanton. Nevertheless she was waiting now as she had waited then.

She watched the wheels of the buses making slow circles in the shimmering heat-haze rising from the tarmac, watched excited holidaymakers shielding their eyes to scan the skies as they alighted from buses, saw others sniff the air and turn to their companions to announce, in all that stench of diesel, that they could smell the sea, watched them as they stood, impatient for their luggage, trying desperately to decide whether they ought or ought not to tip the driver, watched them watching others to see whether they tipped or no.

She watched departing passengers, more sun-tanned but less excited, handing over their baggage to be squeezed into the boots of coaches. Among these stood the four whom she had driven to the Bus Station, two adults and two children, a small family group with no more luggage than two plastic carrier-bags. The bag carried by Maureen Gaines contained her pills, a box of tissues, some magazines which she was unlikely to read, sandwiches she was unlikely to eat, a cardigan for extra warmth and a purse containing what was left of the money given to her husband by his brother plus what he had earned since their arrival, enough to keep a family of three in London for perhaps three weeks.

When she had seen the coach depart, Jean would telephone Joy, and arrange that Maureen Gaines and her children be met in London, and found somewhere to live. Sufficient coins for that telephone call were already in her pocket, together with a slip of paper on which was written the number of the coach and the time it was due to arrive. That was what Jean did, had done for many years, tidy people's lives, and watch (sometimes, as now, from a distance and sometimes close) to make sure that the lives remained tidy. Order and planning she had been taught, could surmount most obstacles, though one must always allow for human nature.

James Gaines, still dressed as a girl, stood close to his father, holding the other carrier-bag, which was fuller and heavier than his mother's containing comics and magazines for himself and his sister, cans of cool drink, sweets and potato-crisps, and a pair of trousers and a shirt with a name-tab stitched inside, into which he would change in the toilet of the coach somewhere between here and London. Marianne Gaines, who had looked at Jean without seeming to recognize her, held the new puppy higher in her arms so that it could lick her face.

In the Waiting Room, a baby began crying, and was joggled up and down by its mother. Small children with sticky faces and peeling noses shared toffees, and played tag between the pieces of luggage, and a woman with a bright red face, sitting next to Jean, offered from her handbag a choice of three pills against travel-sickness. Jean explained that she was not travelling, but waiting for someone, and turned again to look out of the window. The last thing she needed was the distraction of a lonely woman's medical history, recalled at length. She must watch, notice everything, be ready to act. He had been silent in the car. He might weaken now, break down, try to go with them. They might refuse to leave him.

The person for whom Jean was waiting put an arm around his wife's waist, and kissed his wife's forehead, while his wife gripped his shoulder, and leaned her weight against him for the last time. Watched closely by his wife, this person spoke to his two remaining children, stroking their faces and touching the tops of their heads as he did so, all in dumb-show, and his lips were too far away for Jean to be able to read; she discovered, humiliatingly, that she would very much like to be able to read those lips, to share this moment. He was smiling, telling them a joke probably; that was what fathers did when saying goodbye to their children.

Now the driver of the London coach was climbing into his seat, looking towards the four people still standing by the entrance. He started the engine. Steven Gaines leaned to kiss his wife for the last time, as James took his mother's hand, and attempted to lead her into the coach. Steven Gaines lifted his daughter into his arms, kissing her again and again, while her free hand explored the false hair on her father's head. Steven Gaines' wig was removed from his head by his daughter, Marianne, and his son, James, took the wig, and placed it in his white carrier-bag, and so they mounted the steps of the coach, James, Marianne and their mother.

Faces at the window of the London coach, as it backed away in a circular movement from its station. Hands waving. A well-built man standing alone in the Coach Station, waving goodbye to his family. A well-built man, turning and walking with a slight limp towards the Waiting Room. Now she had him to herself at last.

'Do you mind if I close the curtains? The sunlight gets too strong in here at this time of day.' She agreed, and the threadbare curtains were drawn, leaving slits, gaps through which Jean could still see the fields and the sky outside, but preventing anyone outside from looking in.

What daylight entered the room now was amber, an unreal light. There were objects in the caravan which had been left behind, small evidences of family life. A child's book, *The ABC of Animals*. A larger book, *Great Twentieth Century Wonders of the World*. A box of watercolour paints; the colours had been mixed, and almost used up. A child's purse. Coloured pencils. A comb and two pink hair-slides. A scrap of paper with the name 'Clair Jackson' printed on it many times. Pinned to a cupboard door was a child's painting of trees, many trees, large and dark trees forming a forest, with just one very small patch of bright colour at the very edge of the picture, a small girl with her back turned towards the painter. Steven said, 'I know everything there is to know about caravan-dwelling, except how to keep it tidy. I bet you can't smell carbolic, though, can you?'

Jean shook her head. He had poured water from a jug into a kettle, had lighted the Calor Gas ring, and was boiling the water for tea. It was now the middle of the afternoon, just an ordinary afternoon on which the family's Social Worker had called for tea and a friendly chat. Nothing was going to spoil it. Time was not pressing. Steven appeared calm, even peaceful. Everything had been decided. They had driven from the Coach Station in silence, enjoying the green of field and hedgerow, and were now waiting for the kettle to boil.

Steven wiped two cups with a tea-towel. Jean was sitting on the edge of the double-bed. Pinned to the side of the upper of the two bunk-beds opposite were a couple of cards from a Happy Families pack; she could not make out which. She said, 'Talk to me. Tell me about the times you were most happy. See how many good things you can remember.'

He poured tea into the cups. 'Do you know St Ives? Ilfracombe? Carbis Bay?' She shook her head. 'Falmouth? Bude? Penzance? St Austell?' She shook her head. 'Never been down there? It's wonderful.' He brought the tea, handed her a cup, and sat on the lower bed opposite. 'I spent two summers down there, nineteen seventy and seventy-one; I was seventeen, then eighteen. Fun Fairs, cafés, deck-chair attendant. I was even a Life-Guard once – more like a Relief Life-Guard while the real one had his appendix out; I was an unreal Life-Guard.' She smiled. 'There! I've got you to smile. Don't be frightened.'

'I'm not frightened. Tell me about when you were a Life-Guard.'

'Nothing to tell. Everybody seemed to be able to swim. I walked up and down the beach, flexing my muscles to give them their money's worth, and got a rash from lying in the sand for too long, but it was a really good time. I'd intended to spend just a month in each resort, working my way around the whole coast of Britain eventually, but it was so good down there, I went back the second year. I had lots of friends there. Seventeen years old, and not a care in the world. My mother was dead, my brothers had grown up and found girl-friends, I'd left home. I discovered I didn't have to be any good at making friends; on that coast at that time everybody was easy with each other; *they* made friends. The friendships weren't for ever, but that was alright; that was the kind of friendships they were. I had a good opinion of myself then, too good probably. Anything was possible. I'd started the body-building so as to make something of myself, and people found me attractive, even liked my accent, and seemed to like me. They do when you're happy, have you noticed?' Yes, she had noticed.

'Nothing depressed me; nothing got me down. Late September, I'd make my way back to London; work wasn't hard to come by then. In May, I'd give in my notice, and be off again. I'd nobody to account to.'

'Your mother was dead, you said?'

'In 1965, when I was twelve. Laid out in the front room, just as she'd wanted. We'd only been allowed in that room at Christmas; she'd kept it for her laying-out. She'd even joke about it. "Don't crack those walnuts in here, our Alex. I don't want folks wading knee-deep in nut-shells when they come to view me." And I'd pipe up, "It'll be a walnut coffin, mum. It's all we can afford." "Best oak, young man, or I'm not going. Look at the state of the knuckles on that hand. They've not worked all these years, to be fobbed off with walnut veneer. I want something as lasts." Alice Mary Etherington, eldest child of a family of thirteen. "You're my third and last, Steven. You'd have suited me better if you'd been a girl, but at least you're healthy, and a lot less trouble than the other two." There was a longish gap between us. Bill had been at school for some time when I was born; Alex would have been seven. We were a bit better off by then, so I got things they'd had to go without. The old man never stopped complaining about how much my pram had cost him, "Price of that would have kept a family of six for three months in my day." I've no idea what the pram must have looked like, but she'd clearly been determined to make a show. She'd have been nearly forty when she had me; I must have surprised her. For the first five years, I don't think I was ever out of her sight. Even after I'd started school, she'd sit with me for hours of an evening. The boys would be out playing, and he'd be at the pub. Reading! – she was always reading; she liked that; she'd read aloud to me. By the time I was seven, Greek legends had taken over from fairy tales – Jason and the Golden Fleece, Theseus and the Minotaur, Perseus and the Gorgon, that little boy who tried to fly with wings of wax, and the sun melted them, and he fell into the sea; she'd ambitions for me, I think. She'd say, "If you make a mess of this life, Steven, there's only one person you can blame, and that's yourself. Always own up, and start again with a blank page." The caravan holidays we had before she died were some of the best times. She'd hang a blanket up around her bed, and then pretend to be a nineteen twenties flapper, all girlish and giggly, peeping round the blanket, batting her eyelids and putting on a show. If it was bad weather, she'd organize us, so that every evening we'd have to take turns, and entertain the others. A song – a poem even. Bill could play the mouth-organ, and we'd sing together. The old man never entered into the spirit of things, but even he never got off scot-free. He always had to recite "The Green Eye of the Little Yellow God" night after night, always prompted by Mum, and always in the same places, and when he'd finish we'd all recite a prayer aloud that the weather would change. Would you like another cup of tea?'

He refilled her cup, and brought it to her. 'When she was in hospital, I visited her every day. I'd be the only one there usually, the only visitor in the ward. The roles were reversed then, Mum sitting up in bed in her blue crocheted bed-jacket with satin ribbons, her body getting smaller and smaller, and me in school uniform reading to her. She reminded me of something I'd forgotten, something she'd said to me when I was eight or nine. She'd said that she and I were more alike than the rest of the family, and that if anything dreadful ever happened to me, I had to tell her, no matter what it was or how difficult to put into words; if I couldn't bring myself to say it, I'd to write it down. I hadn't understood what she meant when she said it; then, when she was dying, it was too late. We were alike, but not as much as she thought. I wasn't as clever, not by a long way. I missed going to see her one day close to the end. No real reason, a bit of rebellion at being tied to someone who's about to leave you, and a lot of sadness. I hated the smell of the ward she was in, and the other patients watching as I sat there reading to her. Then of course I dreaded going the next day, kept rehearsing my list for excuses. It turned out she hadn't noticed I'd missed a day, or else she pretended she hadn't. All she said was, "There's a blood-thirsty bit coming up on the next page –" it was about the Trojan War I was reading. "Better skip it; the woman in the next bed's having her first operation tomorrow." She was lovely, so lovely and so sane. How could a person like that have given birth to . . .?'

The cup dropped from his hands. He was sobbing. Jean picked up his cup, and took it and her own to the sink at the other end of the caravan. He said, 'Don't be frightened, Jean. This was bound to happen.'

He had begun to unlace his shoes, now wet with spilled tea. Tears clung to his lower eyelashes, before dropping onto the backs of his hands, which still held the shoe-lace.

She was standing beside him, the fingers of one hand touching his hair. Sunlight from the window behind them, an unreal amber light, was filtered through the threadbare curtain. She was speaking in a tone as unreal as the light, whispering as though in church, telling him that it would be alright. They were Henry Moore figures of Mother and Child, turning from stone into rounded globular shapes of amber oil, suspended in water, and all contained in this one small lozenge of a room surrounded by fields.

Then she had brought him over, obedient as a child, to the double bed on which she had been sitting, holding him close to her and speaking again, this time more naturally, less detached, reassuring him that she was going to stay, was going to help him; she would be with him, and everything would be alright. There was plenty of time. They would do nothing until the daylight had gone, nothing except rest.

Slowly he took hold of her hand, and lifted it to the side of his face moving it gently against the stubble. Then he was gripping the hand tightly, pressing it against his cheek and against his lips, speaking very quietly, almost inaudibly but with urgency, saying that he knew she would make sure his wife and children were cared for. He was thanking her for all she'd done, telling her again not to be frightened, asking her not to hate or despise him when he broke down, because that was bound to happen. He was begging her not to let him weaken. It would be just like drifting into sleep, he told her, would last no more than a few minutes, and then be over.

Beads of sweat had formed at his neck and throat. She touched them with her fingertips, brushing them away. The sweat was cold to her touch. More beads formed, then ran from his throat through the hair at the centre of his chest. One by one she undid the buttons of his shirt. He lifted each of his arms in turn like a child having to be helped out of its clothes. He watched as she knelt to remove his shoes, watched her looking up at him, and lifted each foot for her to remove his socks.

From his trouser-pocket he produced the Army button she had given to his daughter, holding it out in the palm of his hand to show her. She said, 'Did you know my phone-number was inside?'

'Yes. She showed me.'

'I wanted you to use it.'

'I thought it was meant just for Marianne.'

'For her and for you. I knew she'd give a button like that to you.'

Still kneeling, she placed her lips against his shoulder, and after a moment he leaned his head against hers. Outside the window, a shadow crept across the fields, a cloud moving across the sun, darkening the room and causing him to shiver.

She kissed his eyelids and eyelashes, and moved her fingers through the hair at the nape of his neck, then down along his spine, feeling the coolness of his back, and holding him closer to her. The large cloud moved away, trailing smaller clouds behind it, dappling the amber light in the room, and in this dappled light Jean cradled him, held him tightly to her, this child, this baby she could never bear. She lowered him gently to a lying position on the double bed under the tiny window, and lay over him, so that her warmth would stop him shivering. They talked together in lowered voices. She asked him why he was limping, and he explained that he had landed badly, jumping from one of the bumper-cars, and had twisted his ankle. They smiled together, and talked about the Fun Fairs in which he had worked, and of the oddities of those who patronized them, of the parents who sat in the cars beside their small children, and returned to childhood, while the real children relegated to being passengers, became bored or embarrassed by their parents' behaviour. Lying side by side, they talked of many things.

Then Jean rose, and removed her own clothes in the amber light, but warmer now with the promise of evening. She lay down again beside him, and stroked his face, shoulders, chest and arms; she removed his trousers; smiling, she moved her hand over the white hips and sun-tanned thighs. Smiling, she stroked him, circling his belly with one hand, while taking his penis and testicles in the other until he was erect. In exciting him she had excited herself; this was not at all, she discovered, like the dutiful Thursday night couplings with Michael. She kneeled astride him, and placed him easily inside her.

Lying beneath her, and smiling back up at her, he reached out an arm to touch her breast, lifting his body to meet her, his mouth on her breast, tongue searching, licking, sucking curling round the nipple, teeth biting on the nipple, at first gently, then with force.

Liquid light. Moving together, and falling apart. Descending into whirlpool after whirlpool. Rolling over and through long amber grasses, with his breath now above her. Swimming ahead, then waiting. Quivering on the edge, and stepping back. Floating weightless, spreading herself to meet and take in more of him. Two shapes moving in slow motion, globules of amber oil clinging together. Soft flesh, hard muscle, twisting, turning, stretching, stroking, crashing, falling, negotiating to become one, to form one single different shape.

One final ascent back up through the whirlpool, through warm, bubbling, tingling water, through mist, through cloud, upwards and higher until finally there is no more light.

All the unreal amber light had gone. From where she lay, she could see the gap between the curtains, and what it revealed was blackness.

He had removed his weight from her, lain at her side, kissed her face, lips, shoulders, breasts many times. Many times. He had rested the side of his face on her stomach. Later she had felt the stubble of his beard on her thighs, had felt his hand slide between her thighs, and the fingers moving, trying to part them again, while she had watched the blackness beyond the curtains and willed it to change, first to grey, then purple, then pink, and at last be daylight, but it had remained black. He had moved his tongue in upwards strokes along the inside of her thighs, had opened her gently with his fingers, and placed his tongue inside her. And she had shivered, and continued to shiver, as he had done, shivering with continued intensity into climax, after which they had again lain side by side, and had kissed, and sighed, and the sighs had become a kind of laughter, a strange laughter of relief and apprehension.

Now he was standing naked at the other end of the single room, in his hand a box of matches, and before him on the table a small paraffin lamp. She heard him shake the match-box, heard the match being struck, saw the flame of the match being held to the lamp, smelled the paraffin, saw a larger yellow flame appear; then he lowered the flame, and it turned to blue. His expression was calm, peaceful, concentrated. Jean saw the small blue flame now reflected in eyes that were no longer frightened, no longer sad.

He moved towards her, carrying the lamp. He placed the lamp on a shelf, then knelt at her feet. He touched the soles of her feet, and began to count the toes, and she drew them away. He caught hold of her feet, and kissed them, and she laughed, and told him that he might think twice about doing that if he knew where they'd been. Jokes were safe now. He noticed something lying on the floor under the bunk-bed opposite, and reached to pick it up.

He smiled at her, and palmed the object like a magician, then placed his hands behind his back for a moment, before holding two clenched fists out for her to choose. She tapped the right fist, and he turned it over slowly, spreading the fingers to form an open palm. Resting in the palm there was a pink hair-slide, which he took between his fingers, and attempted to fix in her hair.

Jean threw up her arms to protect her head, and prevent the slide's being placed there. Steven said, 'Don't be afraid. I'd never hurt you.' She cried out, screamed, kicked, struggled, wept, snatched the hair-slide from him and threw it across the room, while he watched her, astonished, not attempting to defend himself against the flailing hands which struck his face and chest. Then she closed her eyes, and fell back on the bed, listening to the sound of an animal scratching its claws against the tin wall of the caravan.

He waited for her to open her eyes and look at him again. Then he said, 'How old were you during all that?' She shrugged. He said, 'About eight?'

'Yes, that would be it. Perhaps a little younger. Sorry.' He lowered himself to lie beside her. She said, 'I can't leave you like this.'

'No. Not yet. Don't leave me just yet.'

For another hour, they remained as they were, he sometimes kissing her face, she touching his chest and shoulders with her fingertips. Finally he eased her back against the mattress, placed himself on top of her, and entered her again.

'Who do you love, Jean? Say it.'

'You, Steven. I love you.'

'Never be frightened of love. It should please you. It should make you feel more alive and happy.'

They were sitting side by side, as they had often done before. Her right arm supported his head; her left arm was holding his left hand. One of his fingernails had been crushed, and was now dead and blackened. The hand was dry, blistered, engrained with oil from the bumper-cars. It was a large hand with long straight fingers, spread wide now because her own short stubby fingers were intertwined with them.

'I'm thirty-four, Jean. That's no age at all.'

She had held many hands, had reached out and taken them into her own or had been offered them to hold. Depressed and depersonalized adolescent girls had held out hands to show her the scars; these were girls whose anxiety and lack of self-esteem had led them to pick at their wrists with razorblades. She had taken the hands, had studied the system of veins the tendon and the pulse, as she had listened to the tired, flat, monotonous voice and watched the insistent pulse trying to break through the almost transparent skin. They had described the release and relief they felt as the blood appeared, the sight of it a proof of their own existence. 'Even when it hurts, I still feel as though I'm not here. I don't exist until I see the blood. Then I seem to relax.'

The hands of the girls had been limp, cool, damp, almost lifeless. The hand she was holding now was strong, dry, warm and full of life, and it gripped her own hand, moving the fingers.

He said, 'I don't seem able to let go of you.'

'I don't want you to let go. Stay like this.'

Her face touching the side of his face, his eyes looking down, concentrated on their two hands, waiting.

'I can't remember what I've told you. I keep thinking that

there must be more, and if I don't say it soon it'll be too late. But there is nothing more though, is there?' She kissed the side of his face. Slowly he turned to face her, and to look into her eyes. He touched her own lips gently with his own. 'The most important thing to remember, Jean, is that I'm not a monster.'

He tried to remove his hand from hers, but she held onto it, gripping it hard, kissing him on the mouth over and over as he tried to release himself, and he was saying – or trying to say, as she tried to stop his mouth, 'I do love you, but there's no other way. You know me better than anyone else; you know I'm not brave. Just hold me, and talk to me. Let my hand go. I promise I'll be alright. Please! Please, help me. Just this once. You said you would. You promised. I do love you, Jean.'

She looked down at their two hands. She watched her own fingers unloosen themselves from his. Tears streamed down her face. Steven said, 'Come on, cry-baby! You're the one who's got to be strong. Don't cry now. Just keep saying, "I'm here, Steven. I'm still with you. You're not on your own. I'm with you." That's best, my love, best for both of us. I couldn't do it without you. If I start shaking, hold me. Don't cry, and don't allow me to mess it up. Promise?' He wiped her tears away with his fingertips. 'I can trust you, can't I?' He turned her face towards him, holding it between his palms. After a moment, she nodded. He said, 'Say it. I know you can be strong when you need to be. That's why I love you.'

Jean said, 'Yes, I can be tough. You can trust me, because I love you.'

Slowly he unwrapped the small rectangle of waxed paper, and held the shiny razorblade between his thumb and forefinger. He bent the fingers of his left hand backwards, and stretched them wide to study the pulse at the base of his thumb. 'Tell me about your childhood, Jean. Talk to me about your work.'

She watched him, remembering her promise but not wanting to see. Deliberately he felt for the pulse, found the artery with the tip of his finger, placed the edge of the blade on top of it, held it there for a moment, then took a deep breath through his mouth, closed his eyes and pressed hard, moving the blade from left to right, then back again, several times.

Jean had imagined that the blood would creep out, that it would be like a spreading pool. Instead it spurted.

She must not faint. She said, 'I'm with you. I love you. You're not alone.'

The pulse continued to spurt crimson arterial blood into the air above Steven's wrist like a fountain with a faulty pump. Blood hiccuping from his wrist.

'I'm here, Steven. Here beside you.'

He had planned it, tried to imagine what it would be like, but had not expected surprise, had never allowed for the shock he would feel, the nausea in his stomach, the tightness in his chest and throat. It was not in the least like drifting into sleep. The sudden force of the blood had caused him to drop the razorblade. He must pick it up quickly, or it would be difficult to hold.

'Don't stop. Keep talking to me.' Colour had drained from his face, and beads of sweat stood out on his forehead.

'There's a river in Bedford.' She could hear the tremble in her voice. The fingers of both his hands were now covered in blood as he attempted with his right hand to place the blade between the fingers of his left. His face was ashen. His throat had formed a seal, and he kept swallowing to release it.

He said, 'Hold my arm, please. Keep it from shaking.' He clenched his teeth, veins standing out in his neck, his eyes looking sideways at her like a small sickly child approaching the school gate. She placed her hand on his forearm, steadying it against his thigh, and he placed his right wrist on top of the blade, and pressed down on it. He said, 'Go on. There's a river in Bedford.'

'It's called the Ouse. I'm here with you, Steven. You're not alone.'

The razorblade dropped from his fingers. It had made little more than a scratch on his right wrist. The thing would take longer than he had planned, and would not be like drifting into sleep. He said, 'I would've liked to have done it properly.'

She took her face between his hands, and kissed him. She said, 'You have. I love you. You're not alone.'

She watched the crimson blood rising in miniature fountains from one wrist. From the other it did trickle; she had not been so far wrong. Blood trickling down his thighs and hers, his legs and hers, seeping into the mattress beneath them. He was not alone. She said, 'There are walkways on either side of the river under horse-chestnut trees.'

His right hand was groping towards the wound, gripping the left wrist as though trying to close the wound up. Blood trickled between his fingers. The right hand jerked as though the pump in the wound were shaking him apart, jerking him to pieces.

His lips were moving, but without sound, an old man's lips. What was he trying to say to her? His eyes pleading. Sadness in the eyes such as she had never experienced before. '*I'm thirty-four, Jean. That's no age at all.*' A frightened old man, trembling and mouthing words she could not hear. An old man sitting in a pool of his own blood, the blood caught between his thighs, covering his limp penis, matted in his pubic hair. His shoulders hung forwards, elbows digging into his sides while his body seemed to shrink in front of her. Her own fingers with blood on them, moving, making circles in his hair. This was the man she loved, and she had told him so, an old man and a small child, her own child and lover, chosen by her but kept for so short a time.

'Brave, Steven, no one braver, my love. I'm still with you, still here holding you. Go to sleep now.'

She had expected to be with him, to share it with him, but she hadn't. She was beside him, touching him and holding him, but not with him, not now at the last. He was alone, and she was alone. A child knows its own mother; Steven was not really her child, and they both knew it. In the end, you just go on pretending until there's no longer a need.

Meanwhile the need remained if only for a few more minutes. What may begin as pretence can generate its own reality. No reality is finite. We are all actors, after all.

She kissed him, and said, 'Go to sleep now, Steven. Go to sleep, my love. I'll tell you a story.' His eyes were already closed, but he was breathing, and the blood continued to flow. So Jean began:

'*There's a river at Bedford, the Ouse, with walkways on either side under horse-chestnut trees, and a Boating Lake for children near it, with paddle-boats, all of different colours like shrunken Mississippi* steamboats. *Swans and ducks would waddle up for bread. I used to think it was perpetual summer . . .'*

The river runs in a circle; it never reaches the sea.

Arena

☐ The Gooseboy	A L Barker	£3.99
☐ The History Man	Malcolm Bradbury	£3.50
☐ Rates of Exchange	Malcolm Bradbury	£3.50
☐ Albert's Memorial	David Cook	£3.99
☐ Another Little Drink	Jane Ellison	£3.99
☐ Mother's Girl	Elaine Feinstein	£3.99
☐ Roots	Alex Haley	£5.95
☐ The March of the Long Shadows	Norman Lewis	£3.99
☐ After a Fashion	Stanley Middleton	£3.50
☐ Kiss of the Spiderwoman	Manuel Puig	£2.95
☐ Second Sight	Anne Redmon	£3.99
☐ Season of Anomy	Wole Soyinka	£3.99
☐ Nairn in Darkness and Light	David Thomson	£3.99
☐ The Clock Winder	Anne Tyler	£2.95
☐ The Rules of Life	Fay Weldon	£2.50

Prices and other details are liable to change

ARROW BOOKS, BOOKSERVICE BY POST, PO BOX 29, DOUGLAS, ISLE OF MAN, BRITISH ISLES

NAME..

ADDRESS...

....

....

Please enclose a cheque or postal order made out to Arrow Books Ltd. for the amount due and allow the following for postage and packing.

U.K. CUSTOMERS: Please allow 22p per book to a maximum of £3.00.

B.F.P.O. & EIRE: Please allow 22p per book to a maximum of £3.00.

OVERSEAS CUSTOMERS: Please allow 22p per book.

Whilst every effort is made to keep prices low it is sometimes necessary to increase cover prices at short notice. Arrow Books reserve the right to show new retail prices on covers which may differ from those previously advertised in the text or elsewhere.